A FRENCH DECEPTION THRILLER

A Forgery in Lyon

BOOK TWO IN A SERIES

JANICE NAGOURNEY

CASTLE BRIDGE MEDIA
DENVER, COLORADO, USA

CASTLE BRIDGE MEDIA
Denver, Colorado

FRENCH DECEPTION: A FORGERY IN LYON

ISBN: 979-8-9872083-8-0

Prologue

January 2010

HE HEARD VOICES—NOT WORDS, only muted sounds. He felt his heels dragging through the gravel, heard that sound too. He tried to open his mouth, tried to scream, to tell them to stop, to put him down, but his face, like his body, was frozen, immobile. Then he felt the cold water holding his body in its icy grasp. He spun down into a dark vortex, pulled along by the current until his body rose to the surface, and he gasped for air. On his back now, he opened his eyes, looking up at the starlit sky.

He floated downstream until his head struck some reeds at the river's edge. The water was shallow there, and he managed to crawl up the muddy riverbank. He was shivering; the chattering of his teeth reverberated in his head. He squeezed his eyes closed, and when he opened them again, he saw a stone cottage. On all fours, he slithered through the mud up to the cottage door. He did not recall seeing the cottage before. Yet, weak and exhausted, he moved his hand over the base of the building, found a chink in the mortar, and extracted a key. He shook violently, but after much effort, he was able to insert the key in the padlock that held the door shut.

He collapsed on the floor and removed his wet clothing with trembling fingers. There were tools and gardening implements laid out against one of the cottage walls. In the center was an old wooden table with two chairs. An armoire stood against the wall behind the table, its doors open. Some old clothing hung from metal hangers, and on the armoire's floor was a pair of worn boots. On the other side of the armoire, there were three glasses, two mugs, some flatware, a few chipped plates, and a small gas camping stove. A bed was pushed up against the third wall; on it was a sleeping bag, covered by a moth-eaten woolen blanket. Naked and shaking with the cold, he crawled into the sleeping bag and fell asleep.

It was dark when he awoke. In the moonlight that filtered in through the dirty windows, he saw a small kerosene heater. He wrapped himself in the blanket and fished around in the armoire until he found a box of matches. He then adjusted the wick, lit the heater, and got back into the sleeping bag. He fell asleep again.

The next morning, the room was warmer, but the garments he had worn were still damp. He picked them up and draped them over one of the chairs to dry. Next, he turned his attention to the clothing hanging in the armoire, pulled a shirt and jeans off the hangers, and tried them on. They fit. He found the old pair of work boots at the back of the armoire—they were his size as well. He continued to look through the armoire and found two bottles of water and some food—instant soup and instant noodles. Using the small gas camping stove, he made himself a meal.

He stepped outside the cottage. To his left, some distance away stood a large house, but it was as unfamiliar to him as the cottage. His stomach grumbled; still hungry, he went back inside, made the remaining container of instant noodles, and finished drinking the bottle of water. There was an open bottle of red wine on the kitchen table. He removed the cork and poured a small glass, but the odor of the wine made him nauseous as he brought the glass to his mouth, and he stepped outside to empty it. Looking towards the big house, he thought he saw a woman standing in a doorway, but she meant nothing to him.

It was too cold to remain outdoors for very long. He went back into the cottage, slipped into the sleeping bag, and again fell asleep. Previously his sleep had been dreamless, but this time there were vivid images.

He was walking along a river until he turned to cross a long bridge. He saw two rivers converging and looked up at the pastel facades lining the rivers' quays. He strolled down an endless road filled with fruit and vegetables of every type and color. Yellow and white cheeses shone their lights on him. He collided with bloody sides of beef and heard the crackle of chickens roasting on a spit. Then he was falling down a funnel into darkness.

He awoke with a shudder.

The clothes on the chair were now dry. He changed back into them and put on an old coat that was hanging in the armoire. He put the remaining bottle of water in his coat pocket, turned off the heater, and locked the cottage door, returning the key to its hiding place. He turned to the right, walking away from the big house and following the riverbank until he came to a small road that led to the highway.

Although he had been living rough for the past days, he still found a trucker willing to pick him up and take him as far as the train station in Mâcon. He scavenged food from restaurant bins in the train station and hopped on a TGV to Lyon. It was a short ride, and no one came to check his ticket. As always, Gare de Part-Dieu was packed with commuters and long-distance travelers. In the crush of moving bodies, he managed to lift a wallet from a woman's open backpack. He went to the men's room, locked himself in a stall, pocketed 350 euros, and threw the wallet into a trashcan.

Place des Terreaux . . . Place des Terreaux. The words looped through his mind. He got into a taxi at the front of the station. "Place des Terreaux," he told the driver, although he didn't know what that meant. But when the driver dropped him off, he recognized the Hôtel de Ville de Lyon on the east side of the square. He sat on a bench, searching for another familiar feeling. When it came, he stood up, walked to the north side of the square, wended his way to Montée de la Grande-Côte, and started to climb the steep hill.

Midway, he stopped to catch his breath, looking down the street at the panoramic view of Old Lyon and the Fourvière Basilica bathed in the gentle light of the evening sun. Turning to plod on, he stopped in front of number 102, climbed to the third floor, and rang the bell. He heard footsteps, and then a woman opened the door. "Bruno!" she exclaimed. "Is that really you?" She wrapped her arms around him. "Come in, come in." He stood in the entryway, searching for her face in his memory.

"Bruno," he said. "Is my name Bruno?"

Chapter One

June 2010
Trubenne, south of France

FRANÇOIS TRAN STOOD ATOP A ladder, a veil of white dust covering his chest and arms as he sanded down the wall. *Allez Ola Olé* was playing, and he hummed along, while his two sons worked in an adjacent room.

The three men were shirtless in the summer heat, their sun-tanned skin a deep golden brown. Alex Thornhill had repressed a smile the first time she saw François at work. The tattoo on his chest— a sun, tiny birds and a palm tree—looked like a child's drawing. She liked François and his sons and didn't want to risk hurting his feelings by asking how he came to choose that particular body art.

Three generations of the Vesla de Trubenne family—Richard, his cousin Charlotte and his niece Alexia—had been hooked on Richard's project to revamp the château and upgrade the surrounding vineyards. Employing the Tran family was a step in their ambitious plan.

Alex had been peeling away layers of wallpaper in one of the bedrooms. There was something satisfying about exposing the bare walls, preparing the room to make a clean sweep into the twenty-first century. Satisfaction mixed with gratitude that she had realized her dream of discovering her roots here at Trubenne. It felt good to be away from her job as a fashion stylist; at least for this summer, she had traded her branded clothing and accessories for stretched out t-shirts and cut-off jeans.

But for Alex, realizing the dream was not the end of the story. *Is this all that there is?* The thought nibbled at the edge of her happiness. A touch of *ennui,* the feeling that despite being where she wanted to be, doing what she wanted to do, something was missing.

Uncle Richard had left a copy of yesterday's *Figaro* open on the kitchen table. Alex glanced at it as she poured herself another cup of coffee. Summer sales—*les soldes*—would be starting in a few days, running from the end of June to the beginning of August. She was enjoying her time at Trubenne, and for the time being she'd shut the door on trendy clothes. But she felt an urge to go up to Paris and see what was on offer. She might not even buy anything—just go to look.

"I'm thinking of going to Paris for *les soldes,*" she said at dinner that evening. "Is it okay for me to stay in your apartment?" she asked Richard.

"Of course. I'll tell Maria to be expecting you."

She turned to Charlotte, "want to come with me?"

Charlotte smiled, "If you don't mind, I think I'll pass. I'm long past the time when I relished fighting my way through a crowd of shoppers."

Chapter Two

Croix-Rousse, Lyon

THE *CLICK-CLACK* FROM MADAME de Prie-Louvois' stiletto heels echoed as she walked through the apartment's empty rooms. She waved her arm in a wide arc. "This is what we call 'factory architecture,' *chère Madame*." The flat had been a silk factory in the nineteenth century. It had four-meter-high ceilings; the exposed beams had been used to steady the vibrations from the Jacquard looms. The worn floor tiles glowed in the sunlight that streamed through the windows.

The client, a slender woman, her face framed by a cloud of dark red hair, nodded. "Yes, I know. I've read about the *canuts* and their struggles."

"Ah yes, *les canuts*. Well, times have certainly changed; this is now a quite exclusive neighborhood."

Marie-Agnès Duvalois knew that was just so much commercial puffery. If she had wanted to live somewhere truly exclusive, she would have opted for the sixth arrondissement at the foot of the *Presqu'île*. Instead, the Croix-Rousse neighborhood was lively. It had the largest outdoor produce market in Lyon, and all of the bistros and restaurants made her think that here, people did not eat to live, but rather lived to eat. It would be a challenge to keep her newly slim figure—she was looking forward to it.

Her thoughts turned to her friend Blondell Royston and her death in a stupid mugging accident. She had inherited Blondell's apartment on Place des Vosges in Paris. With the proceeds from its sale, she had switched from living month-to-month to a much more comfortable lifestyle. Yet, she was still getting used to her freedom after years of financial stress.

She followed the real estate agent through the apartment, impressed by how easily the woman navigated the tiled floor in her impossibly high heels.

"Well, what do you think?" asked Madame de Prie-Louvois as they walked back into the large living room. Marie-Agnès liked the apartment very much; it was by far the nicest one she had seen. *But what would Alex say?* She thought.

"It's quite nice, but I need to think about it. The price is a bit high compared to other flats that I've visited."

Madame de Prie-Louvois smiled. "Yes, it is high, but this is a unique product. If you're truly interested, I could perhaps talk to the owner, to see if there's some flexibility."

It was Marie-Agnès' turn to smile. "Yes, please do."

One of her cell phones rang. She fished in her Vanessa Bruno tote bag and pulled out the phone she reserved for her conversations with Merv Peters. She let the phone ring and returned it to her bag.

#   #   #

Merv Peters' office, Paris

"Shit. Shit. Shit." Merv Peters stood at the window of his office. It was June. Paris should have been warm and sunny, but it was cold and overcast. Despite the early evening light, a thin grey curtain hung over the streets and buildings, depressing for even the hardiest of spirits.

Merv had arranged for Carl Weller, a wealthy American, to meet the art consultant Jacques Mornnais. That meeting had taken place at the end of April. Now it was June, and he'd had no word from Jacques, or from Mag— the girl who had introduced Merv to Weller—or from Weller himself.

10

He'd heard that Jacques' wife had been killed in an automobile accident in the South of France—but for fuck's sake, had he buried his BlackBerrys with her? And that twit Mag, Merv had tried to contact her through Blondell's new lawyers, but since they had paid his outstanding fees, they'd given him the cold shoulder. Was it because his bill was on the high side? He had to make a living. He'd tried to reach Weller as well, but the number just rang until it disconnected.

It wasn't even that he'd missed out on another commission. What pissed him off more than anything was that no one was answering his phone calls. Something was up, something was not right, but what?

Merv called Mag's number again and left a message. And although he knew it was pointless, he rang Jacques. Voicemail. All that remained was to continue to eat breakfast at La Belle Fermière: among the flow of people stopping by his table to trade gossip, perhaps someone would have news of Jacques Mornnais.

Chapter Three

Rue de Prony, Paris

"ANNE-LAURE, BRING ME A COFFEE, would you please?" Jacques Mornnais didn't look up. What was the point? He knew that the young woman was in the office, he knew that she had blonde hair, not the almost white platinum of his deceased wife, Mila, but lighter than Nathalie Martin, the girl who had worked for him until Mila fired her last March. All blondes—did it mean anything? he wondered. He didn't think so; they were just random facts, like individual beads strung together to make a bracelet. On the other hand, what *did* matter was that Anne-Laure was the daughter of Henri de Montcalm, one of the boys who had bullied him back when he was at the *lycée*, and it gave him a small pleasure to treat her no better than his maid Mercie. Of course, his classmates had known him when his name was Jean-Charles Molina.

Jacques published a bi-lingual art and lifestyle magazine—*Artixia*. He'd posted a position for an intern at one of the business schools here in Paris. It was an unpaid job, but students were eager for any kind of work that would fill out their resume. "Anne-Laure de Montcalm," he had read. When he confirmed that Anne-Laure's father was Henri de Montcalm, he called her in for an interview, but he was already determined to hire her, as long as she was able to translate from French to English.

"S'il vous plait, Monsieur." Anne-Laure placed the coffee on his desk—*"Merci,"* he grunted. For the first time that morning, Jacques raised his head and nailed her to the wall with a hostile stare. She gulped: "Shall I continue to work on my translation?"

"Yes, I'd like that."

\#   \#   \#

As Anne-Laure stared at the computer screen, her eyes filled with tears. She'd been so excited when she'd been offered an internship at *Artixia,* but the taste of metal had replaced her dream of working in the glamorous world of Culture. She had a constant lump in her stomach when Jacques was in the office. He was an ordinary-looking man, slight of build, but he frightened her: was it his eyes, blinking behind his rimless glasses, or the way he ordered her around, as though she was a maid and not a student from a prestigious *école de commerce?* All that she knew was that she could not continue to work here. She'd have to find another internship, but *tant pis.* The only problem was that she had to tell Jacques that she was leaving.

\#   \#   \#

Jacques listened to the messages on his Blackberrys. The tiresome lawyer, Merv Peters, had called yet again, but Jacques was still too angry to talk to him. Merv had arranged for Jacques to meet a potential client, a man who called himself Carl Weller. But when they met, Jacques discovered that Carl Weller was in fact only a pseudonym for an American named Eugene Spector. Jacques and the art dealer Nicolas Pagès had sold Spector's aunt a fake Poussin, and Spector had forced him to reimburse the sum paid. While Jacques had managed to remove Nicolas Pagès from the equation, Eugene Spector had outsmarted him anyway.

The more Jacques thought about it, the more he realized that he was lucky that Eugene Spector didn't seem to care about the forgery once he'd

13

paid him. It had cost him, or more precisely, his deceased wife Mila, as he'd taken the funds from one of her accounts that he controlled. As long as he never crossed paths with the American again, he'd consider that chapter closed.

Jacques turned back to the fax he had been reading. The message was short:

Dear Mr. Mornnais,

A mutual friend suggested that I get in touch with you to discuss a business proposition that I think you'll find interesting. I've tried to reach you by phone, but no success. I'd be grateful if you could call me at your earliest convenience.

Yours, Thomas Smith

"Sir?"

"Yes, Anne-Laure, what is it?" Jacques' mind was on the fax.

"I, I think I've got a fever sir, I'm not feeling well and if you don't mind, I need to go home."

She stood in the middle of the room, her body tensed to pivot out the door. He noticed that she was wearing the jacket she'd come to work in, and her purse hung from her shoulder. "Well, all right, if you're ill, then it's best that you get some rest. Let me know when you can come back, I'm counting on you to finish that translation for our next issue."

He had so much to do today: organize an upcoming luncheon, talk with his clients in Brezikstan, and find a buyer for a beautiful fake Signac. Thinking about the painting brought a smile to his lips and he did not hear the door close as Anne-Laure left the office.

#   #   #

Later that afternoon a message spilled out of the fax machine:

Dear Sir,

I regret to inform you that my health does not permit me to continue working for Artixia. I am sorry for any inconvenience and thank you for the opportunity.

Yours truly, Anne-Laure de Montcalm

How annoying. He'd have to contact the business school and post another job offer. As so often happened when he had to get involved in running the office, Jacques ruminated that this situation was something that Mila would have handled. Still, the trade-off—possession of her accounts and freedom from her nagging in exchange for handling administrative matters—was worth it. Love was not a variable in his calculations.

Jacques turned his attention back to the fax he'd received that morning. Who the fuck was Thomas Smith and what did he want?

Chapter Four

Citadel Sushi, Aigues-Mortes

MAX MARTOLLA PACED LIKE A caged animal, circling the restaurant's empty tables. He stepped outside, smoked a cigarette—Max was so angry it seemed that he would swallow it each time he inhaled. He went back inside. "Where is that fuck Filippo?" he shouted into the empty space.

Patrick, unloading the dishwasher, looked up. "I don't think he's coming."

"What?" screamed Max. "What's that supposed to mean?"

"His locker, it's empty. The door is open."

Max strode swiftly to the staff room behind the kitchen and stared at the empty locker, as if willing it to tell him Antonio's whereabouts. But the locker had nothing to add, and he stormed back into the restaurant.

"I told you he'd quit if you didn't stop talking to him like that," said his wife, Emma. She had been sitting at one of the empty tables, watching her husband as he worked his annoyance into a rage.

"That's it," his voice rose into a shriek. "I'm finished with this shit hole, I'm closing it up." Tears now from Emma, who, unlike Max, actually worked in their restaurant, "No, Max, you can't do that."

He glared at Patrick, "And you, I suppose you didn't know anything about this." It was a statement, not a question. Of course, Patrick and the wait staff had all witnessed Max's tirades and heard Filippo muttering that he couldn't take much more of that.

"No," said Patrick, "I don't know anything."

"You can go home now, come back this afternoon to pick up your pay." Max walked out into the morning heat, got into his 4x4, and headed to his *mas* in the Camargue National Regional Park.

Patrick stopped what he was doing, got his backpack, and approached Emma, who sat crying softly. "I'm sorry, Madame," he said, "What time shall I come back this afternoon?"

"Oh, Patrick, you know he didn't mean it. He's just having a temper tantrum."

"Perhaps. But I need a steady job."

#   #   #

Patrick sat on the edge of his bed, hands on his knees, staring at the floor. *Putain, why hadn't Filippo told Max he was leaving? He's got another job, but we're all out on the street.* Patrick was fed up with Max and his unpredictable spurts of anger, with washing dishes, making rice, cleaning pots, everything. If he never saw another sushi or a maki or sashimi or the rest of that shit, it wouldn't be too soon.

Aigues-Mortes is like many little French towns, bringing to mind pebbles flung haphazardly by some giant striding across the countryside. Something noteworthy—perhaps a monument or a church—catches the tourist's attention. Afterward, she will stroll through the town's center, buy some postcards, and eat a forgettable meal. Aigues-Mortes' claims to fame: historic towers and majestic ramparts that circle the town's heart; Louis IX and the crusades. Tourists march along the ramparts; they explore the towers and look out over the salt plains. Ah, yes. Salt. Aigues-Mortes' other claim to fame. Perhaps the tourist will book a spot on a boat touring the salt marshes, and maybe she'll buy a pot of *fleur de sel*. But once she's walked up the main street and bought her postcards and an ice cream cone, she'll be ready to move on to Arles and Sête, which have more to offer.

Patrick Trabert hadn't come to Aigues-Mortes because he had an interest in history. He'd come because he had met a girl; she said she lived in Aigues-Mortes, and on a whim, he left Marseilles and followed her there. But whatever spark had been lit, it soon fizzled, and she was off to Montpellier. It turned out that she had never intended to stay in Aigues-Mortes for very long. In the meantime, he'd found a job at Citadel Sushi, and he thought to stay on and give it a try.

But he found the people small in mind and spirit, hypocrites who'd smile at you and then say nasty things behind your back, or they were choleric, like Max. No, the welcome mat was worn beyond repair; it was time to move on.

Before he'd worked in a bookshop in Marseilles, and he regretted having left. He decided to call his friend David, to see if his old room was free. Surely he'd find work—it was only a matter of time. *I just need a small loan to tide me over,* he thought, and planned to call his mother tonight.

Chapter Five

EVERY MORNING SANDRA PICARDEAU LEFT her apartment on Montée de la Grande-Côte and walked to the Alpine Trading Bank, a discrete private mansion near Place Bellecour. On a clear day, she could see the Fourvière Basilica, but today the pointed spires were shrouded in fog, a fog so thick that even the buildings further down the hill were hidden behind a soft grey veil.

The morning walk was a time to prepare for the coming day, doing her best to let go of negative thoughts and unpleasant images. Usually, it worked, but this morning she felt troubled by her brother Bruno's sudden appearance last winter. She had had no news from him for years, and now here he was, like a phantom out of the blue, a ghost who seemed to have trouble remembering his name. He hadn't said very much. His response to her questions was, "I don't know," or "I don't remember." After a while, she gave up trying to find out where he had been and what he had been doing since he left Lyon some twenty years ago.

Sandra arrived at the bank, an automatic door opened and she walked through the entry and up a winding stairway, covered in dark green carpet.

Like the fog outside, the carpet seemed to absorb the noise, silence hung in the air. There was a corridor at the top of the stairway, she followed it, stopped at a heavy metal door, punched her code into the keypad, and entered the ATB back office.

Caroline Trabert, small and bird-like, was already at work in the cubicle next to hers. Thick brown hair, having an off and on relationship with comb and brush, stood out from her head like an open nest for a sparrow.

She was not a particularly attractive woman, but she indulged her sense of coquetry by wearing the shortest possible skirts with lace top stockings. When she was seated, as she was most of the day, her skirt rode up to barely cover her underwear, leaving an exposed band of white, slightly dimpled flesh. If Sandra found Caroline amusing, their male colleagues, focused on the time remaining until they could retire, probably would not have noticed if she wore her skirt around her neck.

Sandra didn't know much about Caroline. The woman kept to herself, seemed uninterested by politics and current events, occasionally mentioned her son, who was living in Aigues-Mortes. He was a nice boy, he had done well at university, but he was drifting, washing dishes—wasting his life away. Sandra never asked, but she was sure that Caroline was sending him money from time to time.

This morning, though, she would need to talk with Caroline. The summer holiday season was approaching, and everyone in the back office had scheduled their vacations, everyone except Caroline. The HR manager didn't ask Caroline for her plans outright. Instead, he had grumbled to Sandra that he would arbitrarily assign Caroline time off if she didn't submit a vacation request form.

"Caroline, you must let François know when you want to take time off."

"Oh yes, sorry about that. I'll let him know right away."

Why is she waiting, wondered Sandra. *Well, I have other things on my mind, like what to do about Bruno.* It did not occur to her that Caroline had no money to spend on a holiday.

#   #   #

20

Later that day, Caroline's phone rang. 'Patrick' flashed on the screen, and she knew, before answering, that he was calling to ask for 'help.' This time it meant money to move back to Marseilles. She stepped outside the back office into the hallway.

"Patrick, this has got to stop. You're squeezing me like a lemon."

"Sorry, *Maman*, this will be the last time, really."

"That's what you say every time."

"No, really, the last time, I promise."

"I hope so because who knows how much longer I can stand doing this dreary, boring job."

"I'll call you once I'm settled."

"Yes, it would be nice if you called just to say hello."

"I will, I promise. Bye."

"Bye," she replied, but he had already rung off.

#   #   #

Sandra was on the phone as well, trying to make an appointment for a neurologist to examine Bruno. After months of nagging, he had agreed to consult a doctor. Everyone was booked solid until September, and the thought crossed her mind that she might have to take him up to Paris; at least there, doctors were available. And then, through the friend of a friend, she found a neurologist in Lyon and made an appointment to take Bruno to see him at the end of the week.

Chapter Six

Lyon

BRUNO LEFT THE DOCTOR'S OFFICE on the fourth floor of the Cour des Voraces. He made his way down the broad exterior stairway to the *traboules*—or passageways—below. The doctor told him that he did not appear to have any permanent brain damage—but he did have an enlarged liver, the sign of an alcoholic.

"That's funny," said Bruno, "I can't stand the smell of wine."

"Just as well, my guess is that you blacked out, or perhaps some traumatic event occurred. Your sister says you grew up in Lyon, so my advice is to walk around and hope that seeing familiar places from the distant past will reawaken memories. It may take some time."

As Bruno walked through the passageways, he saw a boy run past, ducking into the shadows. He heard the sounds of steps as three older boys ran past him, continuing straight ahead, and then the smaller boy emerged from the passageway, laughed, and ran away. Bruno realized that he was the little boy, but as he tried to follow him, the image faded, and the passageway was quiet once again.

\#   \#   \#

When he first arrived in Lyon, Bruno needed money—money to buy an identity card and pocket money until he could find a job. But he didn't want to take money from Sandra. Instead, he would go to the Part-Dieu train station, mingle in the compact crowds, and lift a wallet from an unsuspecting tourist's backpack. Unsuspecting—no, stupid—it amazed him how people paid so little attention to their surroundings. Or he would hang around Lyon's Old Town, with its picturesque buildings and overpriced trinkets and souvenir shops. It was such a small area, he had to be careful, but the motions seemed to come naturally to him, and he imagined that sometime in the past, he had been a petty thief. And after that? He hoped time would tell.

A few months ago, he had climbed the hilly streets in *Les Pentes* and stopped in front of a bar. It wasn't so much that it was familiar—the façade had been painted a few years ago as the area gentrified—but somehow, he felt drawn to it. And the inside did have a comfortable feel: a worn tile floor, scruffy tables, and chairs in dark wood. Behind the counter, Jean-Pierre was removing glasses, cups, and saucers from the dishwasher, stacking them on the shelves behind him. Thick grey eyebrows hung over his small, deep-set eyes, his hair and beard needed a trim: he fit in perfectly with his surroundings.

Bruno stood at the counter, waiting for the man to look up. When he did, the man smiled, exposing teeth yellowed from years of smoking: "Well, if it isn't Bruno! You haven't changed much, just fatter around the middle. Back for a visit?"

"Maybe for a while." He stared at the barman, trying to remember his name and how he knew him. He came up blank. It was difficult to follow along as the fellow made small talk, and he interrupted: "I need to find work, know anyone who's looking for someone like me?"

It was Jean-Pierre's turn to stare. He remembered Bruno when he was young: tough and athletic, smart too, but a heavy drinker from an early age. The man in front of him was like an empty shell: the same on the outside, but something missing on the inside.

"You could try the café across the street, Chez Michel. Ask for Michel.

Say that Jean-Pierre told you that he's looking for someone. But are you still drinking the way you did before? That might be a problem."

"No, I don't drink." So, it does look like I was a drinker. "Thanks…Jean-Pierre." And I must have known him when I lived here. It was a start.

Bruno began to work for Michel the following day. Each morning he would set out the tables and chairs on the little square in front of the café. He'd unload supplies, mop the floor, clean the toilets, wash dishes, and wait on tables. In return, Michel paid him in cash, asked no questions.

He looked at his hands; they were not the hands of someone who had done manual labor, although he seemed to fall quite easily into the rhythm of his new job. He wondered what he had been doing since he left Lyon. Sandra had told him that his last name was Picardeau, the same as hers. He thought it best to avoid any connection to Sandra. When he bought his identity papers in the outskirts of Lyon, he became Bruno Leblanc.

Chapter Seven

Arlington, Virginia

EARLY MORNING, THE BEST PART of the day. The sun had risen, but the air was still fresh, the silence broken only by birdsong, or an occasional passing car. Eugene ran past the solid houses with neat lawns, vivid flowers, flags hanging limply; occasionally a dog barked as he ran by. He circled a gated community, ran down to the Metro and back up the hill, took another street past other houses—different yet the same.

The run completed, he stood in front of his sister's garage. He let the sweat run down his body, his breathing slowing, the red flush gradually leaving his face. When he had cooled down, he went inside, showered, dressed, and headed for the kitchen. His sister had already made coffee; he poured himself a cup and sat down at the table.

Eugene Spector's leave from the FBI would be over at the end of the month: that meant returning to work in July. The fourth of July fell on a Sunday this year, so he'd have to go back to work on the sixth. He was not tired from his run, but thinking about returning made him feel weary: the politics, the rules and regulations, his boss Pascal Navarro.

Truth be told, he had enjoyed the six months he'd spent in France. It hadn't been a waste of time: he'd helped to get some money for Ella, the Filipino woman (even if he'd had to dip into an off-the-books account to do it). More importantly, he'd forced the dishonest art dealer Jacques Mornnais to refund his sister money for the phony Poussin painting that she'd inherited from their aunt.

He thought about all the dead bodies: Bruno Edremal (a pity he couldn't question him), Tarek, Mila and Walter Helmann. And then there was Alex: very much alive, beautiful and strong-willed. She seemed to have led a comfortable life in Washington: what made her want to trade Georgetown for a crumbling château in a remote village in the south of France? He remembered how she'd helped him recover the money his aunt had paid for the forged painting, remembered the intensity of her desire to punish Jacques Mornnais. It had all been a bit of a roller-coaster ride, and she had seemed to thrive on the adventure. Would the quiet French countryside truly satisfy her?

His coffee had turned lukewarm. He dumped the contents into the sink, poured himself another mug, the hot liquid almost burning his lips. He thought again about the tension in the office, heard Pascal Navarro's clipped, nasal voice—*there's a reason why we have rules and regulations, Gene.* It was time to turn the page: if the Marines had been Part One, the Bureau Part Two, now he was eager to move on to Part Three, title to be determined.

Chapter Eight

Paris

ALEX HAD STARTED IN SAINT-GERMAIN-DES-PRÈS before moving on to Le Marais. As she glided from one shop to another, a thought nagged at her: *what am I doing here?* But she persevered, and two days later she ended up on Avenue Montaigne. She found a sweater at Dolce & Gabbana, and, her purchase made, she lost interest in visiting any more shops. *"I've never before NOT been in the mood for shopping, and as I've saved so much money, I deserve to treat myself to tea at the George V."*

She walked over to the hotel and settled into a fauteuil in the Galerie. The luxurious surroundings washed over her like a warm shower: the flowers, the tapestries, and the *objets d'art*. A sinfully rich pastry, tea brewed at her table: it was a delightful end to her trip to Paris.

"Bonjour, Nathalie." Alex froze, her mouth full of whipped cream. She turned her head towards the voice and saw Jacques Mornnais standing by her table, his lips forming what she took to be a smile. Alex covered her mouth with a napkin as she tried not to choke.

She tried to sound calm: "Why, hello, Jacques, what a surprise."

Three men were standing behind Jacques. He turned and said something to them that she could not hear, and they walked to the end of the Galerie.

"How have you been?"

Since when would Jacques care how she'd been? "Oh… fine. And you?"

"May I?" he asked, as he picked up the Dolce & Gabbana shopping bag that was on an empty fauteuil, placed it on the floor and sat down. "I see you've been shopping." He paused and leaned forward. "It's funny running into you here." The unspoken meaning was clear: *this place is above your pay grade.*

"Yes, I guess it is."

"Still on your sabbatical?" he asked.

"Yes, I have a few months left."

"That's good news. Unfortunately, my translator got sick and walked out on me. It occurred to me, seeing you here like this, that perhaps you'd be free to help out like you did a few months ago?"

Alex had been relieved when Jacques' wife Mila fired her; she'd been eager to leave their employ. But now, curiosity chased away her fear, and instead of refusing outright, Alex wanted to continue the conversation. She replied in a cold, metallic voice: "If I remember correctly, Mila fired me, so it's strange that you'd want me to work for you again. Even if your translator walked out on you. I'm sure Mila can find someone else—there are lots of translators out there."

"I don't suppose you know, but Mila had a fatal accident in April."

Try to look as though you're sorry. "How awful. My condolences."

"Let's forget about the past, Nathalie. Would you be free?" *I wonder what happened; he doesn't seem too broken up about Mila.* "I assume you're still living in Paris? Someplace in the fifteenth, if I'm not mistaken."

"You're right. I did live in the fifteenth. But now I'm staying with a friend." *I wonder what else he remembers?* "And I'm pretty busy right now—I'll have to see what I can do. Can you give me your card? I don't think I still have your phone number."

Jacques handed Alex his card. "Nice to see you again, Nathalie. I'll wait to hear from you." Alex watched as his fingers played on his Blackberry, "Bring the car around please, Charles-Antoine." Jacques' eyes fixed on hers, he wasn't smiling now, "Oh yes, I forgot to mention that our friend Tarek was in an unfortunate accident, although it had nothing to do with Mila. I imagine you didn't know that either." Without waiting for her to reply, he walked to the end of the Galerie and joined the three men who were waiting for him.

Alex tried to finish her dessert, but she gave it up, afraid that she'd gag on the pastry. The tea was cold now, and bitter. What was that about 'our friend' Tarek? Had he told Jacques about the night he had attacked her and the real Nathalie? She didn't think so, but Jacques had an angry look in his eyes when he mentioned Tarek's name. Perhaps it had nothing to do with her.

Her thoughts went back to last spring. Had Eugene Spector forced Jacques to reimburse the money his aunt had paid for that phony Poussin painting? She hoped so. With Eugene's help she had gotten a reward for the maid Ella, who had found a stolen painting. But Alex hadn't made Jacques Mornnais pay for the attack on her friend, Marie-Agnès, not really. If she went to work for him, without Mila and Tarek watching her, perhaps she'd find a way to punish him.

If only she could get in touch with Eugene. But he was back with his wife; she would have to figure things out without him. Should she tell Mag or Richard or Charlotte about her encounter? She remembered Richard's warning: *you need to stay away from Jacques Mornnais— he's a nasty piece of work and he has friends in high places.* No, for the time being, she wouldn't let on that she'd met Jacques. The pianist was playing "My Way." Yes, she would do it *her way*. Once she figured it out.

She heard her phone buzzing, but by the time she extricated it from her bag, it had stopped ringing. No Caller ID. It was probably a telemarketer, she thought. *They find you no matter where you are.*

Chapter Nine

July 2010
Croix-Rousse, Lyon

IT HAD STARTED TO WARM up right after sunrise and by eight a.m. Marie-Agnès had closed the interior window shutters, put on a loose-fitting dress, and turned the fan on to LO. She started each day by checking her email. She deleted messages that promised riches, happiness, good health, making the Law of Attraction work, all for a price, of course. The subject *Summer in Lyon* caught her attention, and she opened the message:

Do you like to read? Want to meet with like-minded people? The Lyon Anglo-French book club will get together next Thursday evening at 8pm at Le Chanteclair, boulevard de la Croix Rousse. We'll be discussing Doris Lessing's brilliant first novel, The Grass is Singing. Hit the Reply button to RSVP.

The title sounded familiar. One wall of her workspace was lined with books, all carefully arranged in alphabetical order. In the L's, she found 'The Grass is Singing,' alongside 'The Golden Notebook' and 'The Good

Terrorist.' Marie-Agnès leafed through the book; she had a vague memory of the story of a white woman's descent into madness in Southern Rhodesia. It was a short novel, and she would have time to re-read it before next Thursday.

Disparate images from last winter bubbled up: being mugged, Bruno's henchmen, getting the reward for Ella. She saw the faces of Blondell Royston, Jacques Mornnais and Mila, Eugene Spector, and, of course, Alex, who was off renovating the family château. Bruno. She knew he was dead, yet her stomach clenched, just thinking about him. But it was all over now: Marie-Agnès had had quite enough excitement, and she looked forward to the uneventful experience of sitting around discussing books.

On a random page, her eyes fell on a description of the austral summer, the stultifying South African heat, and instantly she felt cooler.

#   #   #

Summer in the Croix-Rousse neighborhood was like one big, endless party. The broad sidewalks were packed with people eating and drinking, laughing, and having fun. Unlike Paris, where everything was small and cramped, here there was room to spread out, to relax.

Tonight it was Caroline Trabert's turn to lead the book club discussion, and she arrived early at Le Chanteclair. In front of the restaurant, tables had been lined up for the book club. She took her place at the center, spread her reading notes on the table, and waited for the others to arrive. A wave of nervous energy—invisible yet intense— wrapped itself around Caroline. As the others came, a seat next to her remained vacant.

Marie-Agnès had been working on a translation, and she had lost track of time. While she no longer had to work, she believed that she needed a reason to get out of bed each morning, and going shopping was not enough. She had walked up the boulevard slowly—no need to rush in the still thick heat. When she got to Le Chanteclair, she had a choice: a place on the outer edges of the group, or one in the center. She chose the latter (*I need to be in the middle if I'm going to meet people*), and sat down next to Caroline Trabert.

Eating well being a primary preoccupation, the group ordered, ate, and energized by generous but not unreasonable servings of wine and beer, they turned their attention to the book. Caroline went through her list of talking points: the personalities of the characters, in particular, the hapless Mary; the structure of the book; what was the grass singing for (rain, someone suggested).

As the alcohol loosened tongues, Marie-Agnès listened intently, trying to understand the mentality of the people she had wanted to become friends with. The group discussion had morphed into sub-groups arguing with each other. No one paid attention to Marie-Agnès. She turned to Caroline, "And what do you think, " she asked her. "Are the French attitudes to the Arab population like those of the whites to the blacks in the story?"

#   #   #

For the first time that evening, Caroline took a closer look at the woman sitting next to her. It crossed her mind that she wished that her hair were like the red cloud that framed her neighbor's face. A long flowing dress (Caroline thought she had seen it in the window of a shop on Rue du Président Edouard Heriot) followed the curves of her body. And without meaning to, Caroline tugged at the hem of her short skirt but to no avail. She smiled at Marie-Agnès—this woman would be a welcome addition to her book club.

"Are you new to Lyon?" she asked. Marie-Agnès omitted the story of her good fortune. She had just moved to Lyon from Paris, where she had lived and worked as a translator and was continuing her work here in the Croix-Rousse neighborhood.

When no further information was offered, Caroline asked, "Are you free for a coffee this Saturday afternoon? There's a charming little café with a lovely terrace in *Les Pentes* called Chez Michel, on Place Sathonay. Marie-Agnès hesitated, then agreed to meet Caroline at Chez Michel.

#   #   #

It was after midnight when Caroline returned to her home on Rue Crillon, a quiet street in an upper-middle-class neighborhood. The apartment was cramped: she was on the losing end of a prestigious-location-for-space trade-off. With made-to-order shelves and cabinets, she had put every square meter to best use, but the customized furnishings had come at a cost.

When she turned on her cell phone, she saw a missed call from her son. As she listened to the message—another request for money 'really, the very last time'—her eyes fell upon the pile of bills on the table, and she started to cry. Overdue income tax, real estate tax, a bill for improvements to the building, her revolving credit statement, and now Patrick was hounding her for money. The least he could have done was to ask how she was doing. Even if he didn't really care.

Chapter Ten

Chez Michel, Les Pentes, Lyon

ON PLACE SATHONAY, PURPLE, PINK and green tables were spread out under the shade of plane trees. Michel greeted Caroline warmly—she had been a client for years—and shook hands with Marie-Agnès.

"Have you tried a *Praluline* yet?" asked Caroline. The delightful brioche, flavored with pieces of rose sugar-coated pralines made from almonds and hazelnuts, was a Lyonnaise specialty.

"I try to avoid pastries. I love them, and they love me too much," laughed Marie-Agnès.

"Let's share one, just this once," insisted Caroline.

Marie-Agnès managed a tight smile, trying not to let her annoyance show: "I'm sorry, but I'll have to pass."

Unlike Marie-Agnès, Caroline remained rail-thin no matter what she ate. It was apparent that she took a small pleasure in ordering the *Praluline* and eating it down to the last crumb. "You don't know what you're missing," she said between mouthfuls.

The waiter brought two small cups of coffee and two glasses of water: "You have lovely hands, Madame," he said, as Marie-Agnès raised her cup to her lips. The cup remained in mid-air, then fell to the ground; the china was so thick that it remained intact.

The waiter bent down to pick it up, "Let me, Madame."

Marie-Agnès felt disconnected, as though she had entered a parallel universe. Bruno Edremal was dead, yet he had spoken to her. She forced herself to look at him: it was Bruno all right, but his face was expressionless. Her mouth was dry; she felt her heart pounding so strongly that she feared it might burst. Bruno brought her another cup of coffee, this time he did not even look in her direction.

"Are you okay?" asked Caroline. "Your face is so red, are you feeling ill?"

"No, I'm fine. I guess it must be the heat."

"Don't pay any attention to Bruno, he's really quite harmless."

"Bruno?"

"Yes, the waiter, Bruno Leblanc, his sister Sandra is one of my colleagues at the bank. He turned up on her doorstep one day after having been away for years. It seems that he's lost a good part of his memory, they don't know how or why. Sandra found a specialist who agreed to treat him, but it's apparently very slow going. So don't pay any attention to him."

The coffee felt like a solid fist in the pit of her stomach. Marie-Agnès wanted to go to the toilet, but she was afraid that she'd cross paths with Bruno inside the café, so she sat and tried to ignore the pain in her belly.

"You're really not looking well. What's the matter?"

"I must be coming down with a summer flu. I hope you don't mind, but I think I need to go home and rest."

She stood up, removed a ten-euro bill from her wallet, and placed it on the table. "Please forgive me." She left Chez Michel and climbed up the hilly streets as quickly as she could, her breathing shallow, her mouth parched.

When she closed her apartment door, hot salty tears ran down her cheeks, falling on her chest, leaving dark spots on her dress. The anger and fear that she had left behind in Paris had returned. She needed to call Alex.

Chapter Eleven

Trubenne

ALEX WAS BACK TO PEELING wallpaper. As she rubbed the wet sponge over the wall, the water ran down her arm, through the hollow of her armpit and trickled along her ribcage. Her sense of gratitude had evaporated, replaced by thoughts of Jacques Mornnais. She knew that she didn't have to accept Jacques' offer, or what if she put a limit on her involvement, and told him she could be free for only a week? Either she'd find something, or she wouldn't and that would be it.

But first, there was the problem of Nathalie Martin, the girl whose identity she had borrowed. They hadn't parted on the best of terms—that was for sure—and Alex could hardly tell Nathalie that she was using her name again. Still, shouldn't she try to find out what Nathalie was up to these days?

As for Tarek and Mila, Alex couldn't pretend to be sorry that they were no longer around. Especially Tarek. She remembered the night he had shown up at Nathalie's apartment. In the ensuing struggle, he'd never caught on to the fact that she wasn't Nathalie Martin—at least she didn't think so.

Alex dropped her sponge into the bucket, dried her hands and went into her bedroom. *Let's get this over with.* Nathalie picked up on the third ring:

"Hello Nathalie, it's Alex, Alex Thornhill."

"Oh… hello, Alex," Nathalie answered. No love lost there.

"I'm just calling to see how you're doing. After everything that happened. I thought you might have wanted to get away from it all, go back to India."

"Really, Alex? Is that what you thought? You're right about one thing—I definitely wanted to get away. From that apartment. I guess I should thank you."

"Thank me? I don't understand."

"After, as you say, 'everything that happened,' I put the apartment on the market, and along came this couple who thought it was perfect, and the closing was last week. So I'm out of there, thank goodness."

"Oh, that's great. Where are you living now?"

"You don't seriously think that I would tell you, do you? Just in case you decided to be me again."

"That's the farthest thing from my mind. And you cannot imagine how glad I am that you were able to sell so quickly. Take care, Nathalie."

#   #   #

Nathalie Martin paced back and forth in the two small rooms in her furnished rental. She had put her belongings into storage and moved here after selling her apartment. The memory of being attacked by Tarek had lingered; *I need some space to decide what to do next*, she had told herself.

And now, out of the blue, Alex had called. "I'm just calling to see how you're doing," she'd said, before asking where Nathalie was living? Why? What was Alex up to?

With trembling hands, Nathalie Martin slipped a meditation tape into her tape deck. Alex's phone call had upset her, and she needed to calm her mind. She put her hand to the cheek where Tarek had struck her; it could have been much worse, but Nathalie could still not forgive Alex for having stolen her identity.

By the time the tape finished, Nathalie had made a decision. It was time for a new beginning. She had an aunt who was living in London; with the funds from the sale of her apartment she'd be able to quit her job and move in with her aunt until she could find work.

It would be a fresh start—maybe Alex's call was a good thing after all.

\#   \#   \#

Alex was torn between the thrill of the chase and fear of the unknown. Perhaps it wasn't such a smart idea to go back to work for Jacques. She had kept the phone she'd used when she was Nathalie Martin; she called Jacques' number and left a message: "Hello Jacques. This is Nathalie Martin calling. I'm sorry, but I'm tied up right now. I'll call in a week if my schedule opens up."

Alex's phone rang and she saw MAG flash on the screen. She hadn't spoken with her friend since her return to France, and she answered eagerly, "Marie-Agnès, what a nice surprise, how are you?"

Chapter Twelve

HE HADN'T EXPECTED IT TO be easy, and it wasn't. Pascal listened to him, unblinking, as Eugene explained his decision to leave the Bureau. "I don't think I can continue," he said, "I've never been good at office politics, dotting the 'i's' and crossing the 't's.' I'd just create more problems for you and for me if I came back."

Pascal was not surprised, and he was relieved. Gene had many good qualities: he was smart, intuitive, and courageous. But being a team player was not part of his skill set, nor was abiding by rules and regulations. Pascal started to go through the motions to convince Eugene to give it one last try. Then he presented him with the solution he had already worked out: an indefinite leave of absence in exchange for some help on a special project.

"What kind of special project?"

"Yeah, well, the problem is, you know the ten K that I released to you, upstairs they weren't too happy about that. They feel that you owe us something more, that kind of thing." Pascal told him what they had in mind: they wanted Eugene's help in getting their hands on the files Jacques Mornnais was rumored to be keeping on French politicians.

"I don't know how you expect me to get close to him; we're not exactly bosom buddies."

"Yeah, I know that, but we're sure you'll find a way. No rush, just keep me posted."

Eugene had been told once before that his help in getting the Mornnais files would be appreciated, but he'd put that request to the back of his mind. Now, the request sounded more like a demand, and he doubted that he could continue to ignore it.

"Okay, Pascal, let's get on with the paperwork. I've got plans to do some summer skiing in the Alps."

#   #   #

Quai de Saone, Lyon

Travis Bartlett's wife Julie had aired out the guest bedroom. She closed the interior shutters to block the blindingly bright sunlight. They were expecting Travis' friend, Eugene Spector, to arrive today. The trio would leave tomorrow and spend a few days at the couple's chalet at La Clusaz in the French Alps, before driving to Tignes for summer skiing.

It was too hot to eat the rich dishes that Lyon was so famous for. Instead, Julie had prepared a tomato and mozzarella salad and a large platter of avocado, shrimp, and smoked salmon, along with crusty four-grain bread and butter from Jean-Yves Bordier. For dessert, there would be peaches poached in red wine.

Eugene's flight arrived mid-morning, and he took a taxi to his friends' home, a spacious apartment that overlooked the Saône River. After dropping off his bags, he went out for a walk. He crossed to the opposite riverbank, admiring the pastel-fronted buildings on the river's graceful curve.

Alex kept intruding on his thoughts. He remembered their going to dinner after they had attended a concert at Salle Pleyel. He relived the night when Tarek had attacked her: she'd managed to stick a knife in his back and later on felt remorseful. Eugene knew she had tried to contact him when she returned to Washington; at the time, he didn't want distractions in his life. But that was months ago, and now that he was free from the Bureau, he wanted to see Alex, kiss her, hold her, see where things went from there.

On his way into Lyon's Old Town, he bought a cheap cell phone, sat on a café terrace, and stared vacantly at the people—mostly tourists—streaming by. A broadly built man caught his attention. He didn't look like a tourist, and as he sidled up to a woman carrying a large backpack, Eugene thought he could be a pickpocket. He lost sight of the man as the waiter brought his coffee. When Eugene saw him again, the man had turned to walk in the opposite direction, disappearing into the crowd. But before he did, Eugene caught a glimpse of his face.

He sipped his coffee and recalled a photo of Jacques Mornnais with his inner circle: his wife Mila, his driver Tarek and his right-hand man, Bruno Edremal. The Bureau had sent the photo when he was in Paris earlier in the year. Eugene was sure that the man he had just seen in Old Town was Bruno Edremal. Yet that was impossible: Bruno had been found dead, floating in the river Arroux.

Eugene thought about Alex again, moving Bruno Edremal to the back of his mind. He dialed her number, no one answered, and his call went to voicemail. He didn't leave a message but would try her later.

Chapter Thirteen

ATB Bank, Lyon

IT WAS GOING TO BE another sweltering day. Caroline Trabert couldn't bear the thought of wearing stockings, but with her short skirts, she felt naked without them. She rummaged through her closet, guided by an image of Marie-Agnès in her long, body-skimming dress. She found a pale blue ensemble—a top, and a long skirt. It wasn't exactly her friend's look, but it would have to do.

She arrived at the bank early, entered the back office space, and booted up her computer. The silence was broken by the sound of her cell phone ringing. *Not Patrick again.* 'No Caller ID' flashed on the screen. She answered anyway: it was someone from *Bordeaux Recouvrement,* one of the finance companies that she'd borrowed from to furnish her apartment.

"Madame Trabert," the voice was flat and stern, "We didn't receive your payment for June. You know, Madame," the voice continued, "You must make your monthly payments on time, and if payment is not made today, there will be late charges. Can you give me a credit card number that we can charge?"

"I'm sorry, I'm going into a meeting. Can I call you later today?"

Caroline knew her credit card was already maxed out, but at least she'd have a few hours to find a solution.

Her co-workers had started to arrive as she sat in front of her screen, mechanically inputting transactions. In a few years, she suspected, she'd be out of a job, replaced by a computer program that had no financial problems, that never got depressed, that was never tired.

"*Bonjour,* Caroline, did you have a nice weekend? Sorry I couldn't come to the book club meeting last Friday." It was Sandra. "Have you thought about your vacation plans? We really have to complete the holiday schedule."

Caroline smiled, a weak turn-up-the-corners-of-your-mouth kind of smile. "I think I'll go in September, after the rest of you have returned." She spent the rest of the morning processing her assigned transactions that would then be approved by Sandra.

ATB Bank held the accounts of the upper-class Lyon residents. They declared a part of their revenues in France, enough to keep the tax authorities from taking a closer look at their affairs. It was an old bank, set in its ways, and not quick to change and update rules and procedures. There wasn't any reason to do so: the bank didn't engage in sophisticated financial structuring, so there was no need for what the Directors considered excessive oversight. But even ATB had a rule that passwords were never to be left in one's desk,

Midday. To save money, Caroline brought her lunch from home. She sat at her desk, slowly chewing her sandwich, and watched the office empty out. Sandra's cell phone rang as she was getting ready to leave. "Yes, I'll see what I can do," she said and hurried out of the room. Caroline looked around the empty back office. As if pushed by an unseen arm, she walked over to Sandra's desk and tried the drawer in the center. *Well, well, she's forgotten to lock her desk.* Caroline rummaged through the open drawer—there was a collection of pencils, pens, and post-it pads. She opened another drawer, this one on the top right. *What's this? Could it be Sandra's password?* She copied down the series of numbers and letters on one of the handy post-its and closed the open drawers. It was hard, but she resisted the temptation to rifle through the remaining drawers—*who knows what else I might find?* Caroline took her place behind her desk just as some of her male colleagues were returning from lunch. As she finished her half-eaten sandwich, previously inchoate thoughts started to take form. She smiled and resumed entering data.

When Sandra returned mid-afternoon, Caroline looked up from her work and asked: "Is there a problem, is everything okay?"

"It's my brother. The doctor called. He had made an appointment for Bruno to have some tests, and Bruno had forgotten to go. I had to run over to Chez Michel, explain the situation, and drag him away to the hospital. They can't tell when his memory will return, it could be tomorrow, or it could be never." She sighed. "Speaking of Chez Michel, would you like to go for a drink after work tomorrow?"

"Why not? I met an interesting woman at the book club meeting—the one that you missed. I think you'd like her, why don't I invite her to join us?"

At the end of the day, Caroline remembered that she'd told the collection agency she would call them back this afternoon. They would just have to wait. She needed more time to work things out.

#   #   #

Rue de Prony, Paris

Jacques found the number of the translation agency that Mila had sometimes used. He would have preferred to have Nathalie working in the office—he wouldn't hesitate to ask her to perform additional tasks as needed—but he had to get the text translated now. He had just finished making the arrangements when his other Blackberry rang. He saw "No caller ID" on the screen, but he answered anyway.

"Oui."

"Mr. Mornnais?"

Jacques thought he recognized the American accent. "Oui."

"Thomas Smith here. You're a hard man to get a hold of."

"What do you want? I don't have time to waste."

"Yes, of course. Like I said in my fax, we have a mutual friend who suggested that I get in touch with you.

"And who might that be?"

"I'd rather not talk about it on the phone. All I can say is that it's a friend

44

of Tony Perryman, and that it would be better if I met you."

Tony Perryman. A trader who had been featured a few months ago in *Artixia*. Maybe this friend wanted to appear in the magazine and, if so, it might be worth his while to meet with Mr. Smith.

"I can meet you next week. I'll text you the time and place."

Thomas started to say, "looking forward to meeting you," but Jacques had already hung up. Jacques realized that there was no point in calling Tony Perryman—what would he say: I heard that a friend of yours asked someone to call me? No, it would be best to meet Thomas Smith in Babs Thomason's apartment, keep things private and see where that went.

Chapter Fourteen

Croix-Rousse, Lyon

MARIE-AGNÈS COULD BARELY SPEAK, HER breath coming in short bursts, her heart beating to a staccato rhythm. Terrified, she relived the last time she had seen Bruno in Paris—they'd met for coffee in the Hôtel Lutétia. He had been pleasant, and he had paid her for the work she'd done for Jacques.

Right after their meeting, she'd been mugged in the metro, and someone had searched her apartment. After that, two men had shown up at her sister's house in the south of France, bringing a bouquet from a mysterious donor. Her sister had unwittingly told them that she was at Trubenne, and the next day, the *sangliers* had attacked a man in the woods that surrounded the château. He had been carrying a gun, but that hadn't helped with the wild boars. All because of those damn photos that she had taken. Now, all the happiness she felt had evaporated, replaced by a cloud of terror. Despite the heat, she was shaking.

"You're probably mistaken," Alex tried to reassure her.

"If only."

"I just realized that we haven't seen each other since last spring. How about if I come for a visit? I'd love to see your new apartment, and we can do a catch-up."

Marie-Agnès' voice cracked, "Could you, really? That would be great."

The following day Charlotte drove Alex to the train station in Nîmes. Alex was fond of the nineteenth-century stone building, its vaulted arches echoing the architecture of the city's Roman coliseum. A little more than an hour later, she had arrived at Lyon's Gare Part-Dieu. Unlike Nîmes, everyone here seemed to be in a rush, jostling each other as they hurried to make their train or leave the station.

Bruno was amongst the crowd, not so much like a bird of prey as a large rat, scavenging for a tasty morsel. Marie-Agnès waited for Alex at the head of the platform. For a moment, she thought she had seen Bruno, but when she looked again, he was gone: *My imagination is running wild, I've got to get a grip on myself.*

Alex emerged from the throng, pulling a black overnight bag. Her hair was slicked back into a ponytail, her blue eyes shining in her tanned, rested face.

"Oh, Alex," Marie-Agnès threw her arms around her friend, tears of relief, of release, streamed down her cheeks. Alex was always slightly uncomfortable in the face of Marie-Agnès' emotional lows. But she felt empathy for her friend, hugged her, patted her back, "Don't worry, everything is going to be all right."

As they walked through the crowded station, Marie-Agnès kept looking for Bruno, but he had already transacted his business there and was on his way back to *Les Pentes.*

#   #   #

The two friends went to *Jutard*—it was just up the street from Marie-Agnès' apartment —for lunch. They sat on the terrace, ordered large salad plates, and a pitcher of slightly chilled Côtes du Rhône. Here, even the inexpensive wine was excellent. As always, when she was with Alex, a sense of calm came over Marie-Agnès, taking the edge off her fear.

"He works at a place not too far from here, waiting on tables, washing dishes, sweeping the floor. When I remember how he was at Jacques' château—arrogant, his pocket always bulging with a wad of bills, the boss' right-hand man—it's incomprehensible. And he only said, 'You have lovely hands, Madame.' There wasn't even a glimmer of recognition in his face."

Alex picked at her salad, pushed the food around with a piece of bread. "So you're *sure* it's him, you couldn't be mistaken?"

"Of course, it's him. And he's called Bruno. But there's something wrong with him, that's for sure."

"Didn't you say he works nearby, why don't we stop in there for a drink?"

"I can't."

"Yes, you can. Remember those two men who mugged you in the metro?"

"How could I forget that!"

"Well, this may be a chance for us to question Bruno about the men who mugged you. And do you remember my telling you about the man in the shit-green car? Well, when he showed up at the château, that man said he was looking for Bruno. That is, until he saw me, and then he followed us to the train station in Dijon where Tarek dropped me off."

Marie-Agnès reached to pour herself another glass of wine. She held onto the pitcher for a moment and put it back on the table. *Empty calories, I'm not going down that path.*

"The truth is, I want to forget everything that happened, and now I cannot."

"Look at it this way: this is a great opportunity for us to find out what really happened, who those men were."

"Maybe. Anyway, let's stop talking about me. Tell me how you're doing, tell me about Trubenne."

"I'm doing great. We're renovating the château and Richard is going to put in new vines; I feel like I've started a new chapter of my life. At first, I wondered how I would like to live in a secluded French village. For now, I'm loving it, although I do wonder if my destiny is to spend the rest of my life listening to the grass grow! And, I have to confess: I did go up to Paris for *les soldes.*" She wondered if she should add that she'd seen Jacques, and then dismissed it. No need to worry Mag. "But I bought only one sweater. How times have changed!"

Marie-Agnès' phone rang. "Oh hi, Caroline." Her brow furrowed as she listened. "Oh, I'm not sure that I can make it. I have a friend visiting…Yes, well, I'll let you know."

"You look troubled. Is everything okay?"

"Not really. That was the woman with whom I went to Chez Michel—the café where Bruno works. And she's asking if we can meet for drinks there."

"And…"

"And I don't think I can do that."

"Sure you can. Anyhow, let's talk about it later."

Chapter Fifteen

Chez Michel, Les Pentes, Lyon

BRUNO STOOD IN THE KITCHEN doorway, watching Ahmed the cook as he peeled potatoes, the skins dropping onto the counter. An image of other hands peeling potatoes passed before his eyes: smaller and a lighter shade of brown. The picture faded, and Ahmed's hands came into focus. Bruno felt a throbbing in the space behind his eyes as he tried to remember where he had seen those other hands. To stop the pain, he stepped out of the doorway and into the dining room. He cleared away the dishes from breakfast, started to set the tables for lunch, waiting for the throbbing to fade away.

The doctor had told him that his memory might return slowly, disparate images would eventually come together to form a coherent picture of a part of his past. But for the moment, his mind was a maze of random forms. He seemed to notice hands. As for faces, he had seen a woman with platinum blond hair—the hair was familiar but not the face. And once, he thought he recognized a face among a group of North-Africans hanging out in front of the train station, but then the man's features seemed to morph into nothingness.

He sat down at a corner table to eat an early lunch. Michel wanted him to wait on the tables this afternoon, and in the evening, so he'd better hurry up and eat while he had the chance. There was an open bottle of wine on the table; he found the odor nauseating, and he put it on the counter on his way into the kitchen to pile more food on his plate.

#   #   #

After much coaxing, Marie-Agnès had agreed to accept Caroline's invitation to meet for a drink at Chez Michel.

Michel came out to greet the women, air kisses were exchanged, and he took their orders. Caroline had pulled her hair into a messy topknot, and Alex could not help thinking how unkempt she looked. Sandra, matronly chic in a Gérard Darrel ensemble, conformed more to her idea of what a bank employee should look like.

Bruno shuffled over with their order. Marie-Agnès sat motionless while Alex looked straight at Bruno and smiled, "Thank you," she said, as he placed a *Kir* in front of her. He stared at the white-blond streaks in her hair, and then turned his gaze down towards the table, where Marie-Agnès was resting her hands. He nodded to his sister and walked slowly back into the café.

Sandra and Caroline were gossiping about members of the book club, oblivious to the other two women who were seated with them. Alex thought them rude, but this gave her a chance to lean towards her friend: "That wasn't so bad, was it?" Caroline, listening to Sandra with one ear and Alex with the other: "What wasn't so bad?"

Alex replied with the first thing that came into her head: "Oh, I'm afraid that Marie-Agnès is suffering from the heat today. She wasn't sure that she wanted to walk all the way down here, but I convinced her that it wouldn't be so bad." *Nosey little woman, isn't she?*

Painful small talk. Marie-Agnès' drink didn't do much to dissipate the anxiety that stiffened her body. But the *Kir* did take the edge off Alex's nervousness, and she felt more curious than ever. Ideas bounced inside her head: *was Bruno connected to the two men who had mugged Mag? Were they the same men who had delivered the mysterious flowers? And what about the man in the woods at Trubenne, and the driver of the metallic green Peugeot? Bruno's apparently lost his memory, I wonder how we can pry*

51

open his mind and uncover this part of his past. Eager to discuss her ideas with Marie-Agnès, she wondered how much longer they would have to stay. When Michel came to ask if they would like another round of drinks Alex shook her head, "I'm so sorry, I have a terrible migraine, I hope you'll excuse me, but I have to go lie down."

They started to walk back as the color leached out of the sky. The temperature had dropped. But the friends still breathed heavily as they climbed the flights of stairs that led up to the top of the hill. Stopping to catch their breath, wiping the perspiration from their temples and upper lips, for Marie-Agnès, the tension was unbearable.

A torrent of words: "Did you see him staring at you? You never met him; maybe he thinks you're someone else. And I felt him looking at my hands again! What does it mean? What the fuck is going on in his head?"

"That's what we have to find out. Bruno's kind of weird—sort of here and not here at the same time. We need to find a way to talk to him, without those two gossips listening to everything we say."

She felt her cell phone vibrating in her Bottega Veneta bag. She was thinking about how to approach Bruno when she took the call. It was from Eugene Spector.

Chapter Sixteen

Saint Germer-de-Fly

DAWN. A PALE BLUE SKY, streaked with ribbons of pink. Merv Peters rose early, walked in circles through the grass in front of his house. His pajama pants, wet from the morning dew, stuck to his ankles. Thinking, ruminating: his calls to Jacques had remained unanswered, although there were rumors that he was back in France. The sale to Carl Weller was dead in the water, he was sure of that. He had let it go, only to be replaced by a much more troubling preoccupation: the provenance and authenticity of all the paintings Jacques had sold to him.

Despite the warmth of the summer morning, his feet were numb with cold, and he went back into the house. After breakfast, he methodically went through the records of his purchases. For the first time, Merv looked more closely at the provenance of his paintings: the dead Russian's estate, a reclusive collector in Switzerland, trusts in a variety of tax havens. In other words, he had no idea where the paintings came from. The familiar wave of anxiety rose up from the pit of his stomach, constricting the muscles in his back until it reached behind his eyes. The throbbing was so intense that he popped an ibuprofen pill the size of a bullet.

An art dealer, Nicolas Pagès, had prepared many of the certificates of authenticity. He recalled a meeting at Pagès' gallery when he had started his collection: walls covered with paintings, a multitude of *objets d'art*, and bibelots. This memory reassured Merv, the muscles in his back loosened, and the pressure behind his eyes disappeared. He was confident that the art dealer would be able to give him more information on the origin of his paintings, but he was unsure of the man's relationship with Jacques Mornnais. It would be best to drive down to Fontainebleau unannounced. His workload was lighter in mid-summer, and he planned to go next week after he returned to Paris.

#   #   #

Fontainebleau

Merv got an early start, keeping to the speed limit on the A6 motorway. In the past, he would have raced down the highway, knowing that Jacques would have his speeding tickets taken care of, but he doubted that would still be possible. Merv arrived at Fontainebleau mid-morning, and without any difficulty, found a parking space near the gallery. Walking up the gravel path, he was surprised to see that the lawn was overgrown, the garden unkempt.

The shutters were open, though, and he rang the bell, waited and rang again. *Strange,* he thought, just as a young woman opened the door. She was wearing jeans with artful rips in the knees and a crop top, leaving an expanse of flat mid-section visible.

"Yes," she said. It was not exactly the welcome Merv had been anticipating.

"I'd like to see Mr. Pagès, please, I'm an old client."

"I'm afraid that won't be possible. He's not here."

"Oh, when will he return, I can come back."

"I doubt that he'll be coming back."

"And you are...."

"I'm his daughter, Véronique, and...."

Merv interrupted her. If he was good at anything, it was dealing with troubled women: "Véronique, I'm pleased to meet you. My name is Merv

Peters. I'm a lawyer, and I was one of your father's clients." He handed her his card. "May I come in?"

"What do you want?" she asked, unmoved.

"As I said, I was one of your father's clients, and I wanted to ask him about some documents he prepared for me. I'm a bit concerned with what you said about his not coming back."

"My father went off one day and never came back. We've checked hospitals and airports, even the morgue, but there's no sign of him. The police say that he's an adult and if he wants to go away, there's nothing to stop him."

Merv felt his head starting to spin: was it because he had missed breakfast, or because his plans were going entirely off the rails, or both?

"Well, Véronique, I'm going to sell a few of my paintings, and I need some further proof of the provenance, so do you think I could come in and have a look through the files that deal with my purchases? You can stand right next to me, make sure I'm not touching anything that I shouldn't."

She sighed, "I can't help you there either—it looks like my father packed up his files and took them away with him."

Her eyes glistened with unshed tears. Before Merv had a chance to calculate, figure things out, he heard himself saying, "I'm starving. Would you like to join me for lunch to make up for my having wasted your time?"

A tentative smile, "Yes, please wait here, I'll only be a minute." Ten minutes later, Véronique reappeared. She had combed her hair, put on lipstick and mascara, and exchanged her jeans and crop top for a Saint James *marinière* and white pants. He could see the outline of her pointy little breasts under the thin cotton, and tried not to stare, reflecting that he was old enough to be her father.

#   #   #

La Table du Parc, Fontainebleau

At lunch, Merv employed his considerable abilities to make small talk and draw his partner out. Véronique, he learned, knew almost nothing about her father's business. In fact, they had not been very close. She let slip that he had helped her to overcome what she referred to as her "problems," but Merv couldn't get her to say any more about what those problems were.

They shared an iced *Saint-Honoré* for dessert. Merv, no longer hungry, picked at his pastry, while Véronique dug into the whipped cream with relish. When a waiter removed the remains of the desert, Véronique wiped her mouth delicately and placed the napkin on the table.

"I've been thinking, my father bought a house in Marseilles a few years ago, I don't know how often he used it, but maybe I should go down there and see if there are any papers...."

He tried to contain his excitement: "Good idea, perhaps we could fly down together, I'll pay for the tickets."

"That's okay. I'll call you if I find anything useful."

Merv didn't intend to wait for Véronique to call him, and as he drove her back to the gallery, he was already thinking about whom he knew in Marseilles.

Chapter Seventeen

Marseilles

AT DAYBREAK, PATRICK TRABERT WAS seated in the "Micheline," a little railway that connected Aigues-Mortes to Nîmes. He had made it a point to take an early morning train. It was the best way to avoid the groups of unruly adolescents, frequently prone to gratuitous violence, who had nothing better to do during the summer months than look for trouble. When he reached Nîmes, he boarded the TER train for Marseilles. Short on funds, he took the chance that the under-staffed French railway wouldn't bother with ticket collectors on this secondary route. He arrived in Marseilles no poorer than when he had left Nîmes.

Marseilles may have been France's second-largest city, but Gare Saint-Charles reminded him of a country train station. The crowds seemed less dense, slower, the departing trains headed towards a mountain vista. The station stood atop a steep hill—probably the only French station so situated—with a view of the omnipresent Notre Dame de la Garde silhouetted against a cloudless sapphire blue sky.

Patrick walked down the long stairway that led to Boulevard d'Athènes. At the bottom, he stopped to catch his breath; he'd been going since early morning, and carrying a heavy backpack and dragging an old suitcase had tired him out. A bus pulled up, and he hopped on. No need to buy a ticket for the short ride to the Canebière and the Noailles neighborhood. Here, the market streets were crowded and noisy. Men sat at tiny tables outside hole-in-the-wall cafés, sipping coffee. Side-by-side in the narrow streets were butchers, greengrocers, shops selling nuts and grains, straw baskets, kitchenware, and cosmetics. Diners in cheap couscous restaurants, kebab, and fast-food joints spilled onto the sidewalks. The sights and smells were light-years away from Aigues-Mortes' tourist center.

He slipped past the women on Rue d'Aubagne, some pushing baby strollers, others pulling market caddies behind them. Many had their heads covered: hijabs or abayas. Patrick turned onto a narrow side street, found the building where he had lived before he left for Aigues-Mortes. As he pushed open the unlocked front door, he was hit by the familiar smell of fried fish and urine. Holding his breath, he climbed the wooden stairway to the top floor and rang the bell outside a reinforced door. A rangy youth, his scraggly hair pulled back into a ponytail, opened the door.

"*Salut* Patrick, I was expecting you."

The apartment hadn't changed since Patrick had lived there. David was a graphic designer, and there was the full panoply of electronic equipment to accompany his profession. The rent was cheap—the neighborhood could be rough—but the reinforced door and barred windows made the flat a safe haven.

David was glad to see Patrick. One of his apartment-mates had left, and there was a room available, but…It was a big but: he would have to pay his share upfront, said David—in the past it had sometimes been difficult to squeeze the rent money out of Patrick.

"No problem, my mother is going to help me until I find work. I'm sure something will turn up soon."

#   #   #

David had done some work for a lawyer with offices near the *Préfecture*. *Mâitre* Sauveur Paoli specialized in real estate transactions, and through his network of government officials, he was able to obtain permission to build in places where development was prohibited. He worked closely with builders and promoters, creating the opaque financing structures necessary to smooth the way to completion of their projects. And he turned to David to design many promotional brochures and posters for his clients.

When David saw *Maître* Paoli's caller ID on his screen, he imagined that another design project was in the offing. But the lawyer had something else in mind. A colleague in Paris had heard that a property in Marseilles might be coming on the market. Rumor had it that the house was uninhabited, and he had asked *Maître* Paoli if someone couldn't take a look around, to see if anyone lived there. He knew how busy David was, but perhaps he had a friend who'd like to earn one thousand euros for an hour's work?

"I might know someone. Can I call you back?"

Chapter Eighteen

Rue Lalo, Paris

BABS HADN'T HEARD FROM JACQUES since Mila's accident, and she had started to wonder if he would ever again rent her apartment for one of his meetings. She perked up when he called to say that he'd like to meet a colleague at her place one afternoon. Still, it was disappointing that he hadn't wanted to meet at lunchtime—she would have been able to tack on a little extra to her fee. Coffee, tea, and mango juice—that was all that would be needed. The apartment, like Babs, needed some rejuvenation: the Persian rugs were worn thin in spots, and the furniture dated back to the 1980s. Yet the shabbiness lent an authentic charm to the place. It said to all who noticed, *I am what I am, I'm not some arriviste that needs your approval.* If Jacques heard the message, he didn't let it bother him; when he was chez Babs, he focused on the business at hand.

Babs had a ritual before her guests' arrival: she would pummel the pillows that needed no plumping, straighten the paintings that weren't crooked, rearrange the fruit in a large cloisonné bowl. She had just nipped an overripe grape when the intercom rang. That must be Jacques' colleague; Jacques himself never arrived on time. Two minutes later the elevator arrived at the door to her penthouse.

The visitor, a deeply tanned young man, introduced himself and shook her hand. "Hi, I'm Thomas Smith."

He looked more like a surfer or a waiter than a businessman, and as his rough palm scraped against hers, she wondered what Jacques was up to with a man like that.

He walked around the room, looking at the paintings. "You've got a nice collection here. Especially the Turner—it is a Turner, isn't it?" He flashed her a dazzling white smile.

"Oh, absolutely. I inherited the paintings from my father. If you don't mind my asking, where are you from—New York by any chance?" she asked. "How did you guess," he laughed, making direct eye contact.

"I have so many friends from New York—were you born there?"

The intercom buzzed, and Babs was stopped from probing any further by Jacques' arrival. Thomas strode across the living room, his arm outstretched.

#   #   #

So this is Thomas Smith. A little young to be a friend of a friend of Tony Perryman. And he has the hands of a tradesman, not a trader.

Babs brought in a coffee for Thomas and mango juice for Jacques and retired to the kitchen. While the men sipped their drinks, the only sound was the distant hum of the refrigerator. Jacques got up, walked to the kitchen, where his hostess was standing just inside: "Please Babs, close the door, I can hear your refrigerator in the salon."

He returned to the living room, perched at the edge of the sofa, as though he was ready to spring up and depart on a moment's notice.

"So, Mr. Smith, tell me what this is all about."

Thomas Smith sat on a fauteuil facing Jacques. He took another sip of his coffee and lowered the cup gently to the occasional table next to him. His gestures were assured, elegant: they didn't match his rough hands.

"Where to start? I was living in New York City, studying art history, and I decided to take a year off to travel the world. When I ran out of money, I got a job in the south of France, with a company that services ocean-going yachts. There was this guy—a Middle Eastern prince—he had a big party and we came in to clean up afterward. Now, I'm a big fan of your magazine *Artixia*. Read every issue. You know the spread you did on Tony Perryman? In one of the photos, you could see part of a painting and I recognized it right off the bat: Mondrian."

Thomas Smith paused, as Jacques replaced his glass of mango juice on a side table, never taking his eyes off the man in front of him. "Yes, go on."

"The next time I saw that painting, it was hanging in the super-yacht we were cleaning. Of course, at first I wasn't sure that it was the same painting, but I did some research, and I learned that the Mondrian in Mr. Perryman's apartment had been stolen. There was another big party on the ship—these folks sure know how to have fun—and when we went in to clean up, I took a closer look, and it did look like that was Mr. Perryman's painting hanging on the wall. I figured that if I helped to find his stolen painting, he'd give me a reward.

"Now a guy I went to school with met Mr. Perryman once—I guess it's a slight exaggeration to say that he's a friend of Tony Perryman"—he rubbed his hands and smiled— "and he suggested that I get in touch with him. But no joy. In any event, I realized that I needed help in finding out if that painting is the same as the one that was stolen. And I figured that being the publisher of *Artixia* and part of the art world, you'd be the right person to turn to. I was thinking that if we could establish that the painting on the ship is Mr. Perryman's, you could contact him, and that we could share the reward."

Jacques had leaned back against the rigid cushions, and for a moment, he felt irritated by how uncomfortable Babs' sofa was. Then he sat upright and returned his attention to Thomas Smith.

"That's an interesting story. If I understand correctly—you'll have to excuse me, English is not my mother tongue and sometimes things escape me—you've not finished your studies?" Thomas Smith nodded. "*Alors*, I don't imagine that you're an expert on the painter Mondrian?" Another nod. "So, how do you know that the painting you saw was the one stolen from Mr. Perryman? Perhaps it is not exactly the same, or perhaps it is a copy, or perhaps both?"

"Well, maybe I can't be 100% sure, but don't you think it's worth looking into, and then we could let Mr. Perryman know what we found?"

"Know what, exactly?" That you were snooping around on a yacht, looking at things that didn't concern you? I'm sure that Mr. Perryman has engaged art detectives who will help him recover his painting. And how do you think the owner of the yacht—an Arab prince, I think you said— would react if you accused him of possessing stolen goods? Trust me, you don't want to play this game."

Jacques took a last sip of mango juice and pushed himself up from the sofa: "If I were in your shoes, I would steer clear of that ship." Thomas stood up and Jacques patted him on the back, gently propelling him towards the elevator door: "And if you'll accept a further word of advice: go back to New York and return to your studies."

#   #   #

The meeting hadn't gone according to Thomas Smith's expectations. Instead of congratulating him on his sleuthing, Jacques Mornnais had poured cold water on his idea of investigating the provenance of the painting and recovering a reward from Tony Perryman. It was as if he didn't care that the tableau on the yacht might be Perryman's stolen painting.

When he left the building, Thomas Smith noticed two men leaning against a black Mercedes parked further up the street—one man was a head taller than his companion. As he started to walk up Rue Lalo towards Avenue Foch, Thomas felt that he was being followed—like most New Yorkers he had an extra eye at the back of his head. When he heard footsteps, he stopped suddenly and retraced his steps, brushing past a tall man striding up Rue Lalo. Thomas Smith crossed to the other side of the street and stepped into a small grocery store. He pretended to examine the bottles of wine while he called for a taxi. He lingered for a few minutes before stepping outside. A black Mercedes drove past, its windows were tinted and he guessed that Jacques Mornnais was inside. When his taxi came, Thomas Smith gave the driver the address of his hotel on Rue Boursault in the seventeenth *arrondissement*. The taxi headed up Avenue Foch toward Etoile, and he wondered what had happened to the tall man.

#   #   #

No sooner had Jacques settled in behind his driver, than he was on the phone. "We agreed that you would hang the Mondrian in your private apartments, not on the walls of your ship, where anyone can see it."

"Why, my friend, is there a problem?"

"Nothing that I cannot take care of, but please, take down the painting and put it away until you're ready to hang it in a safe place."

Chapter Nineteen

French Alps

EVERY MORNING EUGENE AND THE Bartletts rose at daybreak. By seven o'clock, they were skiing down the icy slopes of the glacier at Tignes. In the afternoon, they would hike along the mountain trails, swim, or sit in the shade, reading, snoozing.

It had been an idyllic two weeks. Eugene had tried to reach Alex a few times. But his calls went to voicemail, and he was starting to wonder if she hadn't changed phones. It was their last day in the mountains when he decided to give it one final try.

"Eugene Spector, what a surprise!" He heard the excitement in her voice.

"I've been trying to get back in touch, but you're not an easy lady to reach. Are you in France? I remember you talked about a family château in the Languedoc region."

"Yes, that's right. We're renovating Trubenne. But what about you? Are you still doing your secret government job?"

"Not really. I'm on leave, and I'm here in France. I've been skiing with some friends in Tignes. They live in Lyon, and we're leaving tomorrow to return to their home."

"You're kidding! I'm in Lyon right now!"

"What a coincidence—can I invite you to lunch or dinner? I'd love to hear all about Trubenne."

"Yes, that would be lovely. But Eugene…"

"Yes, Alex…"

"There's something I need to tell you. I'm in Lyon because I'm visiting my friend Marie-Agnès, the one who arranged for you to meet Merv Peters."

"Of course, how is she?"

"Well, that's just the problem. Mag bought a flat here in Lyon and went with a friend to a café, and you'll never guess who is working there: Bruno Edremal."

Eugene felt the familiar tingling behind his ears. "I thought Bruno was dead, thrown into the river by the maid and the painters. You told me all about it."

"I know, that's just it. Bruno's very much alive. But there's something wrong with him. He's lost his memory. He told Mag she had beautiful hands, but he didn't recognize her. And she took me there today, and I saw him for myself."

How incredible, thought Eugene. He'd be able to see Alex, and if Bruno Edremal was indeed alive, perhaps he could lead Eugene to Jacques Mornnais.

"Why don't we talk this through when I'm back in Lyon?"

"Yes, I'd like that."

The three friends drove back to Lyon via La Clusaz, and as the majestic mountains faded in the distance, Eugene felt that he was being sucked back into reality. He called Alex the evening they returned to the apartment on Quai de Saone. She was delighted that he'd called and asked if he could stop by Marie-Agnès' apartment tomorrow.

Eugene had never met Marie-Agnès, but he knew all about her involvement with Jacques Mornnais. He was aware that she had been mugged following her meeting with Bruno Edremal. Also important to him, she had been instrumental in introducing him to Merv Peters, who had, in turn, arranged for him to meet Jacques. He smiled, his eyes a golden brown, and embraced her: "Well, the famous Marie-Agnès, at last, we meet!" He hugged

Alex, "It's great to see you again," his eyes shining, alive with possibilities.

They pieced together what they knew: While trying to rape Ella, Bruno had passed out in the kitchen of Jacques Mornnais' château. And Ella and the painters, thinking (hoping?) that he was dead, had dumped him in the river Arroux behind the property. A body had been found floating in the river and it was identified as being Bruno Edremal. But apparently that had been someone else. For it looked like Bruno had somehow escaped the clutches of the river and made his way to his sister's home in Lyon. His body was intact, but the same could not be said for his mind.

Marie-Agnès had at first been shaken by Bruno's reappearance. Still, Alex's excitement was contagious, and now her fear had given way to anger. Chez Michel would be closing for a week in mid-August; Eugene wanted to meet Bruno that afternoon, but the women thought it would be better to go after dinner. They would try to engage him as the tables thinned out.

\# \# \#

The sun had set, the color slowly fading from the sky. Bruno was clearing the tables when Marie-Agnès called to him, "Do you know who I am?

It was the first time he had heard her voice, and he stared at her even more intently than before. "Yes, you're a friend of Sandra and Caroline."

"Yes, I am their friend. But *who am I?*"

"You are the red-haired cow," he said, with as much emotion as if he had said *this table is painted green*. Marie-Agnès' neck turned crimson, the flush mounting to her face. Alex placed her hand on hers and squeezed it, and Marie-Agnès asked in a voice as flat as Bruno's, "And who else calls me the red-haired cow?"

"I don't know," he replied.

"Maybe you know who mugged me in the metro, maybe you know who sent me flowers?"

Bruno shook his head, "I don't know."

Alex said gently, "You keep staring at me, do I remind you of someone?"

"Mila," he said, his gaze riveted on her hair.

"And who is Mila?"

"Tarek's lover."

"And who is Tarek?"

"I… don't know," he replied again, starting to walk away.

Eugene got up and hurried after him. "I know you've lost your memory, but we can help you. We knew you when you were called Bruno Edremal. Does that ring a bell?"

Bruno turned to look at Eugene. "You're not French," he said, "You can speak to me in English. And my name is Bruno Leblanc."

"Okay, Bruno, have it your way for now. But the woman who you called the red-haired cow, the last time she saw you was in Paris when you had coffee in the Hôtel Lutétia. We can help you to fill in some of the blank spaces in your memory: wouldn't you like that?"

Bruno approached him, his face inches away from Eugene's. "And who are you?"

"I'm a friend of the two women at the table."

There was a sour smell about Bruno: body odor, onions, and garlic, "Leave me alone," he hissed. "I don't want to talk to any of you." He turned and again started to walk away.

"Are you afraid of what you might find out? " Eugene called after him. "For now, you might be interested to know that Tarek is dead. And when you're ready, I have a lot more to tell you." He didn't add that he had a lot of questions as well.

It was Eugene's turn to walk away as Bruno disappeared into the kitchen. The pounding behind Bruno's eyes had returned. He wanted to go back to Sandra's apartment, take a pill, try to sleep, and wait for the pain to fade away.

Chapter Twenty

THE NEXT DAY ALEX WALKED up Boulevard de la Croix-Rousse to meet Eugene. The words *Tarek is dead* echoed through her head. How did Eugene know that?

Eugene was waiting for her at Bistrot Jutard. His first words to her: "Let's forget about Bruno Edremal for a while, shall we? I'm much more interested in knowing how you're doing."

It was the moment she had been dreaming about, and in that instant she looked around for something to say; her thoughts about Tarek's death had evaporated into the warm summer air.

"Oh, I'm doing great. We're renovating the château from cellar to roof, and my uncle Richard is putting together financing to upgrade our vineyard, so it's really an exciting time. And what about you? Still the man of mystery?"

Eugene hesitated for a moment—there were the sounds of a truck passing, of birds chirping in the trees. Then he told her about his work for the FBI and his current leave from the Bureau.

"I'm sorry that I didn't tell you earlier, but I just could not."

"And your wife, doesn't she mind you being away so much?"

Eugene looked at Alex sheepishly: discomfort and relief fighting for control. Relief got the upper hand. "I… I'm so sorry. I don't have a wife. I

don't! The woman you met when we rented your house was my sister. Kate."
He held up his hands in surrender.

Alex could feel the edges of her ears tingling, and she hoped they were
not red.

"Wow. I can't believe the lies you fed me."

"Not lies, Alex, omissions. I really had no choice."

"And how do I know that you're telling me the truth now and not just
more bullshit?"

"One of the reasons I came to Europe was to find you, to make a clean
breast, to start things off on the right foot. I want to earn your trust, just give
me a chance, okay?"

Under her deep suntan, the tingling had spread to her neck and face, but
she didn't care.

"Well, I suppose you could start by telling me why you're so interested
in Bruno Edremal. Are you still chasing after Jacques Mornnais?

"No, I forced Jacques to reimburse me for the fake Poussin his dealer
sold to my aunt." His light brown, gold-flecked eyes met her blue ones.
"Really, I'm done with him."

"Then I'm asking you again. I'm sorry, but I just don't understand why
you're interested in Bruno Edremal. Of course, Marie-Agnès and I would
like to know if he had anything to do with her mugging, not to mention those
men who were following us. But it's also true that we would be happy if he
disappeared forever. I mean, I reminded him of Mila— nothing good can
come from that!"

"Just idle curiosity, that's all. Really." This time the lie was one of
commission, not omission. Somewhere in the back of her mind, Alex knew
this, but in the moment, she preferred to avoid the discomfort of truth and
chose the false luxury of self-delusion.

"I'd like to see you again," he gave her his best shy smile.

"I have to return to Trubenne this afternoon, there's an important meeting
with the architects tomorrow, and I need to be there. Would you like to visit
the château?"

"My friend Travis—I'm staying with him and his wife—asked me to
help him on a case he's working on, but as soon as that's done, I'd love to

take you up on your invitation."

They walked up Boulevard de la Croix-Rousse to Marie-Agnès' building. He drew her close to him, whispered that he was so glad to have seen her again. Although he hadn't intended to, he kissed her tenderly.

"Take care, Alex. I'll see you soon." Alex stood motionless, still feeling the warmth of his body, and watched as he walked down the boulevard towards the quays.

#   #   #

Mag was on her way out when Alex returned to her apartment to pick up her bag. "As we said, you'll have to visit Trubenne, just let me know when you'd like to come down." Alex took the bus to the Gare Part-Dieu; she saw that she had time for a coffee before boarding her train. Hunched over the counter, she stared at the dark liquid, ran her finger around the rim of the cup. *Jacques in the box.* She couldn't prevent his image from popping up. Should she accept his offer to go back to work for him? She knew only too well what a nasty, dangerous man he was, and yet…The prospect of being in his office, of being closer to him and his *curious* business, was hard to resist.

"Hello, Jacques, I hope I'm not disturbing you…Good…I'm sorry I couldn't call any sooner, I've been so busy… I guess you probably found someone to do the translation you mentioned?…Yes, of course…But I wanted to let you know that I could be free to help out in September, in case you needed me then. You're probably already covered, but if not…Okay, I'll call you the first week of September."

#   #   #

After the call ended, Jacques' face was twisted into a look of annoyance. He wasn't used to translators picking and choosing when they would work for him, even if Nathalie Martin had been one of the best he'd had. He wondered if Mila hadn't fired her out of jealousy. No matter now. It was just as well that she hadn't been free to translate when he'd met with Thomas Smith.

71

Chapter Twenty-One

Traverse Paul, Marseilles

VÉRONIQUE SAT ON THE TERRACE, her legs folded under her meditation bench. She tried to focus on her breathing, but the visit to the house on Traverse Paul had unsettled her. It was evident that her father had not been there for some time. She had cleaned out the refrigerator, ordered groceries on-line, and called an electrician to repair the doorbell. Remembering lunch with the overbearing lawyer, Merv Peters—he had been so insistent about wanting to see her father's records—the first thing she did was to go into the bedroom that her father had used as his office and pack up all the files.

She gave up on meditation and spent the next half hour doing yoga. When she was done, she felt lighter, more relaxed. It was another radiant day. She took a deep breath, started to listen to Lady Gaga on her iPad, and leaned over the terrace railing, staring at the overgrown flowering bushes in the garden.

#   #   #

Patrick wandered aimlessly in Parc Borély, seeking relief from the midday heat in the shade of the park's tree-lined paths. He walked over to the lake, tried counting the ducks, but he was having a hard time calming his nerves. When David had proposed the project, it seemed like a good idea, a quick way to make some money to pay his rent for several months. But at this moment, he would have preferred to be back in Aigues-Mortes, making rice.

Oh, fuck it, let's get this over with.

He left the park, crossed Avenue Clot Bey and started walking up a narrow road, Traverse Paul. A century or so ago, this had been farmland, feeding the city of Marseilles. But today, the farms had been replaced by elegant villas hidden behind high stone walls. The leaves on the tall trees whispered into the gentle wind, vegetation spilled out onto the street. One of Marseilles' *quartiers sud*, it was a prosperous bourgeois neighborhood.

He stepped to the side of the road to let a car pass, and before he knew it, he was at number 89. He took a deep breath, pressed the button next to the nameplate 'Nicolas Pagès,' and waited. He pushed the button again: silence— it didn't seem to be working. David had said that if no one answered, he'd need to find a way to take a look around. He managed to get a toehold in the uneven surface of the stone wall, and pulled himself over the top, dropping to the ground on the other side. Once inside, he crouched unmoving, waiting for his rapid heartbeat to subside. A path ran alongside a thick hedge of glycine. There was a wooden door at the end of the path; it was unlocked, and he pushed it open. Patrick now stood facing a large house. It was composed of superposed concrete cubes, with large windows fronting the lawn and a terrace on the upper floor.

Although it was the middle of the summer, a tarpaulin was stretched across the swimming pool; it was covered with dead leaves that had fallen from a huge plane tree. He walked around the lawn, looked through the windows into a large living room. Magazines were neatly piled on the floor beneath a rectangular marble table. The furniture—sofas, occasional chairs, commodes, a buffet—looked expensive, but there were no papers, no clutter, no sign that anyone lived in the big house. As he started to turn the corner to look through the kitchen's sliding doors, he heard music—*Bad Romance* cut through the quiet afternoon.

Patrick ran to the plane tree, pressed his back against its trunk, and tried to figure out where the noise was coming from. He looked out from behind the tree. To his horror, he saw a young woman on the terrace, leaning on the railing, looking down at the garden.

He closed his eyes, held his breath. When he looked up again, the woman had disappeared. It was time to go. He made it as far as the wooden door, looked over his shoulder and stopped: the woman was pointing a pistol at his chest. She held the gun with both hands: trembling, she told him to move back and sit down on the grass.

"Tell me what you're doing here," she said. "And don't fuck around, or I'll shoot your balls off." Patrick did not hesitate: the best course was to tell her the truth, or at least the version he felt most comfortable with.

"It's a long story. A lawyer here in Marseilles asked my roommate to stop by your house to see if anyone lived here. I think the lawyer had been trying to contact the owner to see if the house is for sale. But no luck. And then, my roommate asked me to come over here and take a look around, see if anyone was at home. David—that's my roommate—he's swamped, and I had some free time…" His voice trailed off as he saw that she was no longer pointing the gun at his chest.

"What's your name?" she asked.

"Patrick."

"Well, Patrick, I don't think you were coming to steal my TV, but the house is not for sale, so you need to tell me more about this lawyer."

"I don't know anything else."

"Not even his name?"

Patrick was starting to relax. Two simultaneous thoughts; the young woman wasn't going to shoot him, and it would be fun to get to know her better— her workout clothes didn't leave much to the imagination. And what did he owe to David's lawyer anyway?

"No, but I guess I could find out."

"Would you do me a favor?"

"Depends."

"I need to put some boxes into storage; can you help carry them down the stairs? Then I'll forget about calling the police to report that you were trespassing. Do we have a deal?"

They walked back into the house. In one of the upstairs rooms, Véronique pointed to the boxes and asked if he could take them down to the driveway. When he had finished moving the boxes, he stopped to catch his breath. For a moment, they stood awkwardly, and, as if in a dream, Patrick told Véronique that he'd like to see her again. "Sure," she said, "I'll meet you tomorrow at four o'clock at the Hard Rock Cafe on Place aux Huiles."

She paused, and continued, "You'll give me the name of the lawyer then, won't you?" When he nodded she continued. "And what will you tell him about the house?"

Patrick smiled. "That no one was home, and the garden needs tending."

Véronique smiled back, "It's been a pleasure to meet you, Patrick."

He walked out onto Traverse Paul, and Véronique called for a freight taxi to take the boxes to a nearby storage site.

#   #   #

"Salut," said Patrick as he walked into the apartment. David, concentrating on a rush job, grunted, and continued working.

"I went to the house like you asked me to. No one was living there, and there were piles of leaves in the garden. Can you tell that lawyer, what's his name, so that I can get paid?"

"Yeah," David still hadn't looked up. "Sauveur Paoli."

There didn't seem to be much point in continuing the one-sided conversation. Patrick would have to wait until David took a break to again ask about getting paid.

The heavy smell of fried fish wafted in through the open window. Patrick flopped on his bed, thinking about the girl he'd just met. Too bad he couldn't tell David, but it would be best to keep the circumstances of their encounter to himself. His cellphone rang, interrupting his pleasant daydreams. The caller ID flashed: *MAMAN.* His mother, what could she want? Usually, he was the one doing the calling. The thought crossed his mind that he might take the opportunity to ask her for one more loan to tide him over until he got paid for the job he'd just done.

He made an effort to hide his annoyance. "Hello, mother, nice to hear from you. How are ya doin'?"

"Just fine, Patrick, thank you for asking. Look, I was wondering if you could do me a small favor?"

Danger here. "Sure, mother, if I can, I will. What did you have in mind?"

"I'm on vacation starting the end of August, and I was hoping you could put me up for a week or two, I've always wanted to discover Marseilles."

Oh shit. "Um, there's really no room in this apartment, mother." Silence. "But I have a friend who has a house that they're not using right now. I could ask them if you could stay there for a week or two."

"Thank you, Patrick, that would be great."

"No promises, I need to ask them first." If Véronique agreed, he could ask his mother for a small loan, but not before. "I'll call you back in a few days."

Chapter Twenty-Two

Rue Boursault, Paris

THE HÔTEL BOURSAULT, ON THE street of the same name: small, family-owned, with two stars on a white plaque next to the door. Its limestone façade, stained by diesel fumes from the railway that ran below the street, had seen better days. But the rooms, if rudimentary, were clean, the beds not too lumpy, and above all, it was cheap.

Thomas Smith stretched out on the bedspread—a dusty rose quilted satin that reminded him of his grandmother. He got along much better with her than with his parents. His parents: they sent him money every month, even now, when he didn't need it. He always felt inadequate when talking with them—he knew they didn't really approve of his art history studies. They would have preferred law, or business, even medicine. He had tried to reach his mother when he was in the south, but she was always on voicemail. Now, he tried her again.

"Hi, Mom—yes, I'm fine, and you? No, I'm in Paris right now. Listen, is Dad there? No… yes… of course I understand. Well, okay. Maybe he'll be around the next time I call. You take care, too. Bye, Mom." He looked at his phone. Two minutes. That was as much of her time as she could spare.

He lay on the dusty rose bedspread, staring at a thin crack in the ceiling, feeling the damp beneath his back. The conversation with his mother was typical—his parents never seemed to have much time for him.

When Thomas Smith had checked into the Hôtel Boursault, he had planned on staying for a few days only, before returning to the Côte d'Azur. He thought about his meeting with Jacques Mornnais: the man had been so dismissive. As for his thinly veiled warning—*trust me, you don't want to play that game*— he knew better than to trust a man who says *trust me*.

This got Thomas Smith to think that it might be wise to change his plans: there was some research that he needed to do, and instead of heading back south, he'd stay in Paris. With his good looks suggesting a romp in the surf, if not more, he found a job waiting tables in a bistro on Rue des Batignolles.

His room overlooked the train tracks leading out of Gare Saint-Lazare— it was on the cheaper side of the hotel. For most, the view was hardly picturesque, but it reminded him of a painting by Monet, and he imagined old locomotives passing under his window. Thomas Smith hung up his clothes and booted up his computer. He opened a new email account and bought a subscription to *Artixia*. He would split his time between waiting on tables and pursuing his research project. If the project worked out, then perhaps his parents would start to respect him.

\#   \#   \#

Each night when he returned from work, Thomas Smith focused on the back issues of *Artixia,* trying to match the articles featuring collectors with reports of robberies at their homes. When he found a match, he looked for more information on what was stolen and whether it had been recovered.

In mid-August, the café where he waited on tables would close for a week, giving him more time to devote to his project. He would start work in the cool, early morning hours. When the heat turned the sky white and it got too hot in his small, airless room, he would sit in the nearby Square des Batignolles, watch the ducks making lazy circles in the pond, and hear the voices of children whose parents couldn't afford to leave the city on holiday. Thomas Smith felt ill at ease in Paris: crowded, hot, and unfriendly. But he had given himself a deadline: finish his research by the end of August. In September he would contact Jacques Mornnais again; he was sure that the publisher would listen closely to what he had to say.

Chapter Twenty-Three

August 2010
Place aux Huiles, Marseilles

PATRICK DIDN'T WANT TO MESS up; he arrived early at the Hard Rock Café, wondering if Véronique would show up. Then, relief when he saw her strolling across the Place aux Huiles. She took a seat and after they ordered, he blurted out, "His name is Maître Paoli." She looked puzzled until he added, "The lawyer, his name is Maître Paoli."

"Oh," Véronique responded. "Thanks." The lawyer's name no longer seemed of any concern to her. After that, they continued to meet at the café's outmost table, each recreating the past to present a rosier picture of what might have been.

Patrick spent one morning cleaning and straightening out his room before bringing Véronique back to the apartment. He'd been to her house on Traverse Paul, and he wondered what her reaction would be. He needn't have worried. She found his lovemaking satisfactory and took note of his housekeeping skills.

"I'm returning to Fontainebleau," she announced when they again met at the Hard Rock Café, "the house is such a mess, do you want to come and help me to clean up? It should only take a couple of days."

"Yeah, sure." It was August, not the right time to look for a job, and besides, it might be fun helping Véronique. "Only a couple of days?" he asked. What are you going to do after that?

"I'm thinking of heading back down to Marseilles for a week or two."

"Maybe you'd like help cleaning up there as well? Like, I saw a lot of dead leaves in your garden."

Véronique smiled: "I don't know, Patrick. Let's see how you do in Fontainebleau."

#   #   #

At the end of three days, Véronique decided that it might be amusing to spend another week or two with Patrick. Besides, as he said, he could help to clean up at Traverse Paul as well.

She took two cans of beer out of the refrigerator. "So, Patrick, now that I'm going to go back down to Marseilles, maybe you'd like to come with me? Just for a week or two."

"Yeah, I'd love to." Véronique watched as he sipped his beer, locked his gaze on her face, and asked in an off-hand way: "Did I tell you that my mother is coming to Marseilles at the end of the month? I don't think she'd be comfortable in my small room, and I was wondering, do you think she could stay at your house, she'd be a kind of house-watcher."

Véronique had no trouble holding Patrick's gaze. "Your mother?" Her mother had slipped out of her life years ago. In her memory, her parents were talking in her father's office, not shouting, but their voices were loud enough for her to hear that they were arguing. Her mother went upstairs to their bedroom and came down carrying a suitcase. A kiss quickly planted on Véronique's head, her mother getting into her car and driving off. For a while, she would come to visit every two or three weeks, but over time, the visits stopped.

"Your mother?" she repeated.

"Yeah, if it's a problem, forget about it."

He's kind of cute, and he's going to help me clean up the house in

81

Marseilles, so why not? She could always change her mind later.

"Sure, why not?"

Véronique told Patrick about a garden supply store up the road where Nicolas used to leave a set of keys for her when he was not at the house.

"I'll do the same thing; your mother can pick them up when she arrives."

#   #   #

Traverse Paul, Marseilles

In a few hours, they removed the dead leaves, rolled back the tarpaulin, and cleaned out the pool. They rose early every morning and drove to the beach, returning to the house at midday. Afternoons were spent making love and lounging poolside. With day after day of cloudless blue skies and bright sunshine, they put off the return to Fontainebleau. But the idyll came to an end on the sixteenth of August, when they closed up the house and returned to Fontainebleau, leaving the house for Patrick's mother.

#   #   #

Saint-Germer-de-Fly

Merv was snoring gently, the book he had been reading lying face down on his lap. The hammock was stretched almost to the breaking point, but it held fast as he rocked ever so slightly. His cell phone, never far even on vacation, rang, jarring him awake. It was Sauveur Paoli; he had sent someone on the errand they had discussed, but no one was home.

"Well, I'd like to be able to take a look for myself," said Merv.

"That will have to wait until September, my friend. I'm practicing for a regatta all month, and anyhow, none of my associates would be available in August. "

Fucking French holidays, no wonder nothing gets done in this country.

"Of course, I understand. Well, good luck with your race, I'll call you in September."

The hammock made a squeaking sound as he rocked, and he sat up. His ample buttocks almost touched the ground. *I wonder if this fucking thing is going to break—probably made-in-China crap.*

He pushed himself up, afternoon clouds had rolled in, and it looked like it was going to rain. He went into the house, poured himself a glass of his favorite calvados, and wondered what that little minx Véronique Pagès was up to. His vacation had only started, and he was already bored—he might as well have stayed in Paris and worked, but that just wasn't done.

Why not take a drive down to Fontainebleau, he thought. He didn't care to wait until September, and if he found Véronique at home, he'd try to be more persuasive. But no one answered when he rang the bell. The shutters were closed, and the weeds had continued their invasion of the garden. He consoled himself with lunch at the Table du Parc, intent on calling Sauveur Paoli the first week of September.

Chapter Twenty-Four

ATB Bank, Lyon

THE HEAT LAY OVER THE city like a blanket of lethargy. The streets were emptier, stores closed for the month; one had to map a route to find a bakery or an open butcher shop. But Caroline Trabert always looked forward to August. She took comfort in a feeling of spaciousness, of tranquility, that was missing during the rest of the year. And she was particularly looking forward to August this year.

Her colleagues in the back office did not all leave on holiday at precisely the same dates, but by the tenth of August, only three workstations were manned. Sandra would be away for the last three weeks of the month. Caroline knew that the bank's internal audit program would sweep through the accounts weekly, except in August. Then the sweep would take place only twice, providing her with a window of opportunity in the second half of the month.

Each day, as the lunch hour drew near, she would go into the kitchen, take her sandwich out of the refrigerator and bring it back to her desk: it was the routine that she had followed for years. When she was sure that her colleagues were enjoying lunch on a café terrace, she entered a few transactions on her computer. Afterward, she sat for several minutes at Sandra's desk, keying in the required authorizations. And so, over eight days, Caroline closed out many of the ATB inactive accounts, transferring the funds to an account she had opened at BRG Bank International in Luxembourg. By late Wednesday afternoon, she had quietly cleaned out her desk. On Thursday morning, the twenty-sixth of August, she called in sick and took the bus from Lyon to Luxembourg.

Caroline was thrilled to be on her way. A brief thought for the dull grey men in the back office. How nice never to have to see them again. And poor Sandra, I'm afraid she's going to have some explaining to do. She nagged me about taking my vacation, and so now I am. A permanent one. She pulled her sweater closed. It was hot outside, but inside the bus, the AC system was on full blast. She felt as light as a feather floating on the chilly air.

The following day she closed her account at BRG, loaded forty packets of five hundred euro bills, one hundred bills to a pack, into her overnight bag.

Dobrin Frères International Bank was a short walk from BRG. It was a small bank, specialized in using Luxembourg's bank secrecy laws to protect the privacy of their depositors. No questions would be asked about the origin of the funds. Caroline made her deposit and left the bank with an account number and twenty thousand euros in cash. She could have flown, but instead, she took the train to Metz, boarded the night train to Lyon, where she changed trains again to arrive in Marseilles mid-afternoon. She resisted the temptation to take a taxi to Traverse Paul, and bone-tired took the métro to the Rond-Point du Prado station where she caught the number 44 bus for the last leg of her trip.

It was late in the day on Saturday the twenty-eighth when she put her feet up on the coffee table and stared at the overgrown garden and at the dead leaves on the lawn. She felt safe, her whereabouts known only to her son and his friend, and it seemed to her that she could hide out here as long as necessary. Two million euros was a very small sum for ATB, and she suspected that they might not even go to the trouble of trying to locate her. *Let those shits just try.*

Chapter Twenty-Five

Croix-Rousse, Lyon

BLONDELL ROYSTON WAS NEVER FAR from Marie-Agnès' thoughts. She felt guilty that Blondell's death from a freak accident had resulted in Mag inheriting the apartment on Place des Vosges in Paris. She felt guilty about enjoying the financial freedom that the sale of the apartment had provided. Guilt and happiness, an incompatible mixture.

She had disposed of Blondell's clothing as well as the furniture and tableware—she had wanted none of it. There remained the rare book collection of Blondell's late husband, binders with paid bills and other records, and several photo albums. Mag had had the movers pack them all up and put them into storage. She had sold the apartment on Place des Vosges but she couldn't shake the image of her friend in her fake leopard coat and hat, carrying the ill-fated Murakami handbag. Today, several months after the accident, she found a new reason to feel guilty. She had packed away the last evidence of Blondell's existence, and she felt that was not right.

A phone call to the movers, asking them to send the storage boxes down to her in Lyon. She would go through everything, see if Blondell's family wanted any of the photos, although she had not heard much from them since her death. They were, it seemed, involved in squabbling over her substantial American estate.

The storage boxes arrived a week later. Mag had them placed in the guest room, and early each morning, she would open a box and sift through its contents. She called the lawyers and asked what documents they might need. The rare books quickly found their place on her bookshelves. Reading was Marie-Agnès' preferred activity now that she had ceased to treat food as a refuge. That left two boxes of photo albums, and she procrastinated about opening them, busying herself with sorting through the documents to be sent back to the lawyers in Paris. But once that was done, she couldn't put it off any longer.

The photos were the last link with Blondell. Her image had already started to fade; yet Marie-Agnès could still hear the slow melodic whine of her voice. Reluctantly, with a sense of foreboding, she opened the first box. She realized that she must have packed up in a hurry or without paying much attention. Two wedding albums were buried under takeout brochures (sushi, Indian, Italian), copies of U.S. Vogue, catalogs from the frozen food chain Picard, coupons from Carrefour, and other junk. The wedding had been a very large, formal affair. John Royston, with piercing black eyes under bushy eyebrows, looked—what was the right word? Not *happy,* but perhaps pleased, yes, pleased to have his much younger bride next to him. In a few photos, Blondell had been caught unawares, her face set in a *'when will this be over'* mask. Marie-Agnès recognized the family members she had met when she had traveled to the U.S. with Blondell. They, at least, looked as if they were having fun.

She threw out everything except the two wedding albums, which she placed next to the rare books. Alex might like to look at them, or she could write to Blondell's cousin Claudia to ask if anyone in the family was interested.

One box left. *Let's get this over with.* Unlike the first box, this one was tightly packed with four albums and manila envelopes containing loose photos. These were John Royston's business photos, showing him shaking hands with the good and the great. She looked at the date stamps and realized that these photos all predated Blondell's marriage. Without looking at all of them, she slid them back into the manila envelopes. Should she throw them out with the rest of the junk? No, the photos were a memory that would have meaning to someone, she didn't know to whom right now, but she felt it would be wrong to destroy them.

The photos in the four albums were more recent. Almost all showed Blondell, sitting next to her husband at a dinner table. Marie-Agnès was sure she could sense the sadness under the fake smile that her friend put on for the camera. In each photo, John Royston had the same empty expression on his face—was he bored, happy, angry? Impossible to tell. Marie-Agnès was starting to lose interest as she felt the apartment heating up. In the kitchen, she poured herself a glass of water. It was time to go into her bedroom, and turn on the air conditioner, letting the cold air waft down the hallway and into the guest room.

A pink post-it stuck out from the last album, decorated with a cloud of question marks. At first, Marie-Agnès looked past the post-it to the image of Richard Vesla de Trubenne sitting at a circular dinner table with Blondell and her husband. She looked again at the post-it; its edge was on another table further to the back of the room, and she stared at Mila Korsikova's perfect profile. *The man with his back to the camera must be Jacques*, she thought. Just seeing Mila and Jacques troubled her.

That doesn't compute, Marie-Agnès thought. Richard had seemed genuine when he said he'd never heard of Jacques Mornnais, that he would ask his friends if they knew anything about him. Yet there he was at a business dinner attended by Jacques. Was it possible that Richard was simply not acquainted with everyone in the room?

Marie-Agnès suddenly felt cold and went into her bedroom to turn off the air conditioner.

Chapter Twenty-Six

JUST IDLE CURIOSITY, THAT'S ALL, he had told Alex. Eugene found the Bureau's request challenging, and if he could unlock the door to Bruno Edremal's memory, he might find a way to get what they wanted. But Alex had no need to know about any of this.

Eugene had been to Lyon several times, but always only passing through. Now, he wanted to make the most of his time in the city. Following Travis' suggestion, he had already strolled along the quays and wandered in Lyon's Old Town. Next on his list was the *Cour des Voraces,* one of Lyon's most famous *traboules.* The covered passageways linked one courtyard or building to another, offering protection from the elements when precious silk had been transported.

This morning he walked to Place Colbert and entered the *Cour des Voraces* through a doorway at n°9. He followed the passageway and came face-to-face with the building's famous façade: an imposing six-story external stairway. The stark, geometric lines of the stairs and guardrails made him think of an uncoiled ribbon frozen in place.

He stood still for a moment, trying to imagine how the *traboule* looked almost two centuries ago. There would have been groups of workers milling around, grumbling about being exploited, plotting their ill-fated revolts.

A tour group in front of him descended the stairs to the courtyard below, and he followed them. His mind was still on the *canuts,* as the silk workers were called, when he looked up again at the massive staircase…and saw Bruno walk out of an apartment on the fourth floor. It looked like the big man was in a hurry as he ran down the stairs with light, sure steps. Eugene melted into the crowd until Bruno passed.

What's the rush? Is he late for work? Meeting a woman?

Bruno pushed past the group, turned, and ran down another flight of stairs. It was hard to keep up with him, but Eugene saw Bruno exit the building. They were in a narrow alley. At first, Eugene headed towards another flight of stairs on his right. But then he looked to his left and caught sight of Bruno's back as he exited the door at the end of the alley. Eugene followed him and found himself on Montée Saint-Sébastien.

Once on the street, Bruno stopped running. He now walked with a slow, purposeful gait.

Maybe he was running away from something and not to it, but what could that be? Who knew? The guy was a bit crazy, after all.

Eugene followed Bruno down Montée Saint-Sébastien until he reached the Croix Paquet métro station. He continued on to Place des Terreaux where he started down Rue du Président Herriot. Then he made his way through a series of side streets until he reached the stairway to Place Bellecour.

Is he fucking taking me on a tour of Lyon? But then Eugene realized where they were headed.

Bruno was now crossing Pont Bonaparte and continued on to Rue Saint-Jean, the pedestrian thoroughfare of Lyon's Old Town. Eugene watched as he walked slowly past a group of tourists outside a souvenir shop.

Then it happened. A girl—she looked like a high-schooler—stood holding her backpack, screaming, "Thief, thief!"

Eugene no longer saw Bruno. As he approached the screaming girl, he saw a sign pointing to the entrance to a *traboule.* But once he stepped inside, the passageway was empty. *Was there another passageway further on?* But it didn't matter. Bruno was gone. *He may have lost most of his memory, but there are still some things he remembers pretty well.*

The girl was surrounded by a small crowd. Two policemen joined the group, asking, "Are you all right, Mademoiselle?"

"I'm okay," she sniffled. "But that fucker stole my wallet."

"You need to be more careful," they told her. "There's a gang of petty thieves operating around here."

Eugene wondered if it was not a gang of one. He'd have a topic of conversation when he saw Bruno later that day at Chez Michel.

#   #   #

Marie-Agnès had spread the photos from the manila envelopes on the floor. Like doing a puzzle in reverse, she removed all the images of John Royston by himself or with someone she did not recognize. That left four photos: three with Richard Vesla de Trubenne, and one with Jacques Mornnais.

She looked again at the business photo album. There was Richard, seated at the same table as John and Blondell. Marie-Agnès remembered that she and Alex had talked about Blondell when they were in Richard's presence. He'd even intimated that he might have known John Royston. He was getting on in years, and he had seemed uncertain. And then there was the photo of John Royston with Jacques. Had Jacques known all along that Blondell was John's widow?

Logically, if John knew both Jacques and Richard, then must Jacques and Richard know each other as well? She didn't know, but it occurred to her that it would be an excellent time to take Alex up on her standing invitation to visit Trubenne. The fifteenth of August was approaching when the country came to a Christmas-like standstill. She would call Alex and book her ticket to Nîmes.

Chapter Twenty-Seven

CHEZ MICHEL MAY HAVE BEEN a small café, but the *salade lyonnaise*—a perfectly poached egg, croutons, salt pork, and dandelion greens, seasoned with a mustard vinaigrette—along with a pitcher of slightly chilled Côtes du Rhône, was as good as it gets. Eugene thought about all the pretentious, over-priced French-style bistros in D.C. and Alexandria—they couldn't hold a candle to this place.

When Bruno came to take his order, Eugene murmured that he'd seen him that morning in Old Town, and perhaps they could talk? He had kept his voice low and friendly, Bruno nodded and walked back to the kitchen. Eugene ordered a coffee, skimmed through a free newspaper, and waited until Bruno had piled up the tables and chairs.

"Let's walk," Eugene said. "I saw what happened in Rue Saint-Jean this morning. You used to work for Jacques Mornnais, but I can't figure out why you now would turn to pick-pocketing."

Bruno stopped and turned to face him: "My sister told me my name is Bruno Picardeau, you tell me it is Bruno Edremal. But until I learn what I did before I lost my memory, I prefer to be Bruno Leblanc. I have no bank account, no social security. So I need extra cash. It's that simple."

"Like I said before, I can tell you some of the things you did before you lost your memory, not all, but some. But if I do that, and if you start to remember things, will you share that with me?"

"So you're offering to help me if I help you, is that it?"

"Yes."

"Why? What is it you want to know?"

"I know some things about the people you worked with. But I would like to know more. Do we have a deal? You have nothing to lose but your amnesia."

Bruno gave a wry smile: "Maybe I don't want to know who I was. Maybe I'd rather be just who I am right now."

It was Eugene's turn to give his best, timid smile, nodding his understanding.

"I know what you mean. When I was in the military, there was an explosion, and for a week, I had no idea who I was. Totally disconnected. I found that I had no past to judge things against, and that made me feel uncomfortable. Don't you feel that way sometimes?"

Eugene had never experienced memory loss, but in the time-honored tradition of hucksters from carnivals to the internet, *I feel your pain* was often an excellent way to soften up the target.

"Yes, I guess I do. Okay, let's see how it goes."

They agreed to meet tomorrow at the main entrance to Parc de la Tête d'Or. They would find a bench in a quiet place and talk undisturbed. Eugene had brought a file of photos with him, and he would show them to Bruno as they progressed. He had planned to be done by mid-August, but perhaps he'd have to put off his visit to Trubenne. It depended on how things went with Bruno. He was on a roll.

Chapter Twenty-Eight

ALEX AND CHARLOTTE WERE SITTING at the long table in the kitchen at Trubenne.

"More coffee?" asked Charlotte, already poised to refill their cups. "How was your trip to Lyon? And how is Marie-Agnès? Will she be visiting anytime soon?"

"So many questions! Where to begin? Let's see. First, Mag bought a beautiful apartment in a very charming neighborhood. All was going well until she ran into Bruno Edremal—you remember who he is, don't you? He's alive and working in a café not too far from her place. Only he's apparently lost his memory."

"I thought that they found his body in the river?"

"It looks like they found *a* body, but it was someone else's. Anyhow, I went with Mag to the café, and it was clear that Bruno didn't recognize her. But he told her she had beautiful hands. At first, she was upset, but now I sense she's angry about what we think he did. You know, having her mugged, and then sending those two thugs after Mag and myself. But if that wasn't enough, guess who called me while I was in Lyon? Eugene Spector! We met for a coffee, and he told me that he wasn't married—the woman I had met when they rented my house was his sister. And that he'd come to

Europe to see me. All three of us went to the café where Bruno works so that Eugene could see him for himself. When I asked Eugene why he was interested in meeting Bruno, he said it was just idle curiosity. But of course, I don't believe him. It's just like last winter—I have the feeling that there are things he's not telling me."

"But you find him attractive, don't you?"

"Yes, and I wish that I didn't. Maybe it's Eugene's air of mystery or his beautiful eyes. I don't seem to have much luck with men, do I?"

Charlotte sipped her coffee. "Perhaps he'll share more as you get to know him better."

"You'll have a chance to see for yourself. He'll probably be coming for a visit one of these days. And I've asked Mag to come—I think she needs a change of scenery."

"I'd love that—especially seeing Mag again."

"She's so changed from the girl who I dragged in here last January. She was already transformed when she came back to Paris, but inheriting Blondell's apartment has changed her life even more."

Alex stared at her coffee cup, then looked up at the ceiling. A large fly circled overhead, the only noise in the room was a loud buzzing. "But there's something else. I keep thinking about Blondell. Mag said she sounded upset the last time they spoke, and I can't help wondering what she had on her mind. With Eugene and Bruno both showing up so unexpectedly, I completely forgot to ask her about that. Maybe we can figure it out when Mag visits."

Chapter Twenty-Nine

A FREAK COLD FRONT SENT the temperature plummeting, bringing temporary relief from the air that had felt too hot to breathe. Marie-Agnès slipped on a long silk and linen knit cardigan that she had bought on sale at Claudie Perlot. She enjoyed being able to spend money without always calculating whether she could afford it. But she didn't feel more carefree than a year ago. Mag had exchanged one set of preoccupations for another.

And now, Mag was having second thoughts. She kept returning to the photos as if to reassure herself of John Royston's connection with Alex's uncle Richard and Jacques Mornnais. Adding to her discomfort, she had found Richard's visiting card stuck into the front of the photo album. Did it really make a difference now? John Royston was dead, the dinners had taken place years ago, what did she hope to accomplish by stirring things up at this late date?

She returned to her first thoughts, and it boiled down to this: Richard owed them an explanation of his relationship with Blondell's husband, and why not, Jacques Mornnais. Before the doubts could return, she had called Alex; "Why don't you come tomorrow," Alex asked, "We need some downtime together."

\#   \#   \#

Three men wearing black tuxedos are seated at a table. They have their backs to her, she tries to get up to glimpse their faces, but her legs feel so heavy that she can barely budge. At last, she finds the energy to move.

"Ladies and gentlemen, we'll be arriving in Nîmes in a few minutes, please make sure to take all your belongings when you leave the train."

Marie-Agnès awoke with a start—it seemed that she had only just settled into her seat, and she was already at her destination.

Alex, in a white t-shirt and cut-off jeans, was waiting for her on the platform. They embraced; Alex could feel her friend's ribs through her colorful mid-calf dress.

"My god, you're so skinny, have you lost more weight?"

"I don't know. I haven't had much of an appetite recently. Must be the heat."

"I love your dress."

"Proenza Schouler."

But despite the beautiful dress, Alex saw that her friend's face was set in the same anxious mask that she had worn following the attack in the Paris *métro* last January.

\#   \#   \#

Alex's cousin Charlotte, her face as brown and textured as a walnut shell, her blue eyes bright and lively, greeted Mag: "I'm so glad to see you again, my dear."

Last January, after Alex had spirited Marie-Agnès out of the hospital, she had driven her down to Trubenne to stay with Charlotte. The visit had marked a starting point in Marie-Agnès' quest to recover her self-esteem, aided by Charlotte's quiet serenity.

Much had changed at Trubenne since Mag had been there last January. The roof had been repaired, the electrical wiring had been brought up to standard, the kitchen expanded and modernized. The floors were covered in sheets of plastic as the workmen renovated the bedrooms, the dining room, and the reception areas.

As she followed Alex, Marie-Agnès asked if Uncle Richard was around. "Of course, he's the guiding spirit behind this project!" Right now, Richard was taking his afternoon nap but would be with them shortly.

Alex showed her to her room: the exposed beams had been cleaned and restored, the grime had been removed from the floor tiles, the walls covered in a blue *toile de Jouy*, and the same fabric had been used for the bedspread. It was a definite improvement over the room Mag had occupied at the beginning of the year.

Charlotte had put her new kitchen to good use. The three women sat at the long wooden table—a slab of oak two meters in length that had first seen service in a convent—drank green tea and ate warm slices of *Tarte Tatin*. But today, while the pastry was delicious, foremost on Alex and Mag's minds was Bruno Edremal.

Alex mused, "Ella said that the painters threw him into the river. It was freezing that night, how did he survive? And how did he make his way to Lyon?"

"Do you think he's truly lost his memory? How convenient is that if we tried to ask him about the men who mugged me? And what about the two men who came looking for me at my sister's house, with flowers no less?! If you ask me, they're the same two thugs who were after us, Alex, and good for them that they're both dead."

Mag stopped talking long enough to sip some tea, and continued, "All the danger and the stress that we've gone through, it's due to that horrible Bruno Edremal."

"Let's not forget about Jacques Mornnais," said Alex. "I'm sure Bruno was just following orders, as they say. But there's a chance that we may be able to find out more."

"Oh?"

"Before I left Lyon, I met Eugene Spector for lunch. I had to leave for Trubenne right after, so I never got to tell you about it. He told me that he used to be a Special Agent, but he's no longer working for the FBI. And he said he's interested in helping Bruno recover his memory. When I asked why, he replied, *just idle curiosity*. But I cannot get over the feeling that Eugene has some special interest in diving into Bruno's memory. When I asked him if his real focus was not on Jacques Mornnais, he denied it. Of course, he's lied to me before, so I don't know. But if he is talking with Bruno—whatever his motive—then maybe he can find out about the two men who mugged you. And whether or not they're the same people who delivered the flowers and all the rest."

The mention of Jacques' name gave Marie-Agnès the opening she was waiting for.

"Oh, speaking of Jacques, let me show you something, excuse me for a moment."

She went to her room, and when she came back, she spread the photos on one end of the table, and opened the photo album to the page with the pink post-it.

"I was going through the stuff that was left in Blondell's apartment when I came across these."

Alex and Charlotte stood up to get a better look.

Marie-Agnès turned to Charlotte: "The man with the bushy eyebrows is John Royston. The woman sitting next to him is his wife, Blondell Royston. She's the one who died in a freak accident and left me her apartment on Place des Vosges. Royston died a few years before we met Blondell, and he left her a pile of money. Not that it did her any good. And this man"— she pointed to the photo album and then to the loose photos on the table—"this man is Jacques Mornnais. What's curious is that Richard is sitting with Blondell and her husband, at the same dinner as Jacques. By the way, the platinum blond with the perfect profile is his wife, Mila."

The kitchen was silent. Outside, the hum of crickets filled the air. Alex and Charlotte stared at the photos as if looking at them could provide a backstory. Mag had returned to her seat. She added a small dollop of *crème fraîche* to her slice of pie, delicately placed the pie and *crème fraîche* on her fork. And savored the taste of the rare treat she allowed herself.

#   #   #

Footsteps. Richard, smiling, walked over to Marie-Agnès. She stood up as they exchanged air kisses.

"How lovely to see you again, I'm so glad you could come and visit us."

"Yes, I'm happy to see you as well."

"Ah, you've brought some photos?" he said as he walked to examine them more closely.

As he looked at the dinner table photo showing him seated next to John and Blondell, Richard recalled her calling him, asking him to stop by her apartment. Blondell had been interested in this photo as well; Richard remembered her dark red fingernails pointing to the photo and asking about the man seated at the far table. Richard had said he'd hardly known the man, who was just another intermediary in a complex investment scheme. He had been surprised when Blondell told him that she was sure that he was Jacques Mornnais. But then, John Royston had dealt with many people, some upstanding, some less so. It wasn't Richard's problem.

Mag concentrated on eating her pie, examining the *crème fraîche* leaking onto the plate. Alex and Charlotte waited expectantly, a cloud of silence hovered over the table.

Richard was starting to wake up from his nap. His eyes, unfocused a few minutes ago, were again like two steely blue marbles in his heavily tanned face. The skin around his neck had loosened, but he held his head erectly as he spoke: "I'm sorry to say, there's not much to tell. You know, there are many levels of participation in some international deals. While I knew that your Mr. Mornnais was part of the team, I didn't know his name, and didn't deal with him directly. That would have been John Royston. If your friend Blondell hadn't recognized him and told me his name, I wouldn't know it at all. I couldn't tell her anything useful about him, either."

"Wait, when was it that you met Blondell?" Alex sounded troubled.

"She called me, said she had something to show me and asked me to stop by her apartment. I had met her a few years ago when I went to pick up John at their home. John wanted her to see our coat of arms, so I gave her my visiting card. Until Blondell called me, she had completely slipped my mind."

"But why didn't you tell Alex and Marie-Agnès?" asked Charlotte. She said it softly, as there was no point in backing Richard into a corner.

"Yes," agreed Alex, "why didn't you tell us?"

"By the time I saw the poor woman, you had already left Mr. Mornnais' employ. So what was the point in telling you? It would not have made any difference."

"I guess," said Alex doubtfully.

They cleared the dishes from the table, Marie-Agnès gathered up the photos. Alex and Charlotte went back to work in the house, and Mag stretched out under the trees and soon fell asleep.

Chapter Thirty

Parc de la Tête d'Or, Lyon

HE STOOD AT THE ENTRANCE to the park, watching the children arrive—on bicycles, on scooters, in strollers, or on foot. They wore shorts, or jeans, or sundresses or bloomers in a myriad of colors, and he tried to remember the last time he had seen such a group of children. As he watched, he saw three boys walking through the little throng. They passed out of his line of sight, only to appear again. He looked at them closely and realized that one of the boys was himself. The familiar throbbing behind his eyes returned, and the images of the three boys evaporated.

Eugene came up to him. "*Salut,* Bruno."

They walked into the park together, following the long path that led to the lake. The benches surrounding the lake were mostly empty early in the day. It was already warming up, and they found a shady spot. Eugene slowly took Bruno back in time, starting with the afternoon when he had arrived at his sister's apartment. Back to the Part-Dieu train station, the train, hitching a ride with a trucker and back to the hut along the river Arroux. Eugene had heard Ella's story of how Bruno tried to rape her and wondered if he could take Bruno back to the moment before he was submerged in the river. Bruno shivered despite the heat as he relived his escape from the river.

Eugene first showed him pictures of the two painters who had produced the forgeries, Li and Wen. Marie-Agnès had taken them when she had visited the château and explored the grounds on a snowy afternoon.

"Those fuckers were always whining about more money."

"More money for what?" asked Eugene.

"For the paintings," said Bruno. How could Eugene not know that?

"What paintings?"

"I don't know."

Eugene next showed Bruno a photo of Ella. It had been taken when she was at the airport, waiting to board her flight back to the Philippines. "This woman's name is Ella, do you remember her?"

Bruno scowled. "Peels potatoes," he mumbled.

"What did you say?"

"She peels potatoes in the kitchen."

"Where is the kitchen?"

"I don't know." A line of ducks was making its way through the lake, drawing his attention away from the photo.

To bring him back, Eugene waved the last photo in front of his face. "And do you recognize this building?"

Bruno looked one more time at the ducks, then studied the photo: "I saw it when I was outside the hut on the river." He paused. "And I saw her."

"Who is that?"

"The woman you just showed me, the one who peels potatoes."

"Do you know what this building is? It's a château called Château d'Hélène."

"I don't know anything about it. And I'm tired. My head hurts. Can we stop for today?"

"Sure," said Eugene. He hoped that this first session would begin to jog Bruno's memory, opening up some doors to his past life. "Can we meet tomorrow, same time and place?"

"Yeah, I guess so." Bruno got up and continued walking around the lake, hoping to catch a glimpse of the three boys he had seen earlier. He wondered what they were up to.

\#   \#   \#

Bruno didn't show up the next day, and when Eugene stopped by Chez Michel, he told him that he had overslept. If he felt better, he'd be there tomorrow. He didn't bother to tell Eugene that the image of the woman—Ella—had kept him up half the night.

He had flashes of sitting at a dinner table, drinking a bottle or two of wine. He wasn't feeling well, and he saw himself getting up to go to the toilet. Then he saw Ella: her hand was in the pocket of the jacket he'd hung on the back of a chair. He slurred his words: "You little bitch, what else have you stolen?" When he tried to reach her, his vision blurred, he stumbled and fell. Then darkness.

The images flashed, again and again. His head ached. He took one of the painkillers the doctor had prescribed, and at last, fell asleep.

\#   \#   \#

The same bench, the same phantom children, their features clearer. Ella had told Alex that Bruno passed out while trying to rape her. When Eugene heard Bruno's recollection, it made him wonder who was telling the truth.

Some doors were opening. Eugene had a photo of Jacques, Mila, Tarek, and Bruno: "That's Mila," Bruno said, "And that's Tarek. He was fucking her, you know."

But not all doors: "Didn't Jacques know, didn't he mind?"

"Jacques? I don't know anyone named Jacques." In the distance, a red paddleboat was moving silently across the lake. "I don't feel like talking anymore," Bruno said, watching as the boat traced a large curve, leaving little ripples in its wake.

\#   \#   \#

He was in a labyrinth, chasing the red-haired cow. Each time he caught a glimpse of her, she disappeared around a corner. Tarek was there, laughing at him as he tried to follow her. Suddenly Jacques and Mila were walking towards him, he didn't know where they were coming from. He heard Tarek's laughter, but when he turned his head, Tarek was no longer there. Jacques pushed Mila aside and took a step closer to him, his eyes like two deep black pits. "Is it done?" he asked, "Isitdoneisitdoneisitdone?" He tried to run away, but the labyrinth closed in on him, growing smaller and tighter. He woke up, bathed in sweat, his head throbbing.

When Eugene went to see him at Chez Michel, Bruno said that he wasn't feeling up to talking right now. Perhaps tomorrow. But Eugene waited in vain at the entrance to the park. The café would be shutting down for a brief summer holiday, and he was starting to feel impatient and restless. Why was he hanging around trying to bring life back to what passed for Bruno's brain when he could be spending time with Alex at Trubenne? He would give it one last shot before accepting the fact that Bruno couldn't—or didn't want to —remember Jacques Mornnais.

#   #   #

Eugene came up to Bruno as he had just finished slipping the chains around the folded tables. A cloudless night, a cool breeze swept across the square. "Do you have time for a drink?" They walked silently until they found an open bistro; Eugene ordered a beer, Bruno, a Perrier.

He poked at the floating lemon slice, pushing it to the side of the glass with the green plastic swizzle stick. Sipped the water, inhaling the tart aroma of the lemon juice.

"I had a dream about Jacques."

Eugene sipped his beer, said nothing to puncture the moment.

"It was about the red-haired cow; he was angry that she disappeared."

Eugene felt a familiar tingling at the back of his neck. "What do you mean, *she disappeared?*"

"Samuel and Cosimo, they were supposed to take care of her, but something went wrong, and after that, we couldn't find her. I told Jacques it would blow over, but he wouldn't drop it. So I called Samuel again, and told them to do it right this time." He chuckled, "They were supposed to deliver flowers to her sister, ask where she was."

"And what happened?"

"I don't know."

"But why did Jacques want her taken care of? What had she done?

"We thought she had photographed the painters, maybe she'd seen the paintings in the atelier. Weren't sure, didn't want to risk that getting out."

"The painters who were doing the fakes?"

"Yeah."

"So, you remember working for Jacques?"

"It comes back to me in bits and pieces."

"Like what, for example?"

"Picking up stuff we had ordered for clients. Things like that."

"Do you remember anything more?"

"Not so much. Just me and that asshole Tarek driving to these little shithole places all over France." Bruno emptied the remaining water into his glass, fiddling with the slice of lemon. "Why are you asking me all these questions?"

"I told you, I'm trying to help you to recover your memory, remember your past."

"Well, I've remembered as much as I want to, so you can just bugger off now."

Eugene could see that he was losing Bruno. But he couldn't let that happen. He wanted to know more about Samuel and Cosimo. And Bruno had started to remember Jacques. He'd try a little more of *I feel your pain*.

"Yeah, I know how you feel. There was a time when I didn't want to remember any more. But then, people began telling me about things from my past, and I got curious. See what I mean? Maybe you'd like to know what happened to your friends Tarek and Mila?"

Bruno nibbled on the bait. He sighed. "Sure. Why not?"

Eugene told him that Tarek had been killed in an automobile accident, without mentioning that he had been with the mercenary Walter Helmann. Bruno gave a wry smile. "He had it coming, the fucker."

As for Mila, Eugene decided to tell the truth and see if Bruno had anything to say.

"Mila also had an accident, but it was a bit strange: she was killed when a car bomb exploded as she turned on the ignition."

"Really? I guess Jacques finally got fed up with her."

"Fed up with her?" repeated Eugene.

"Yeah, once he got his hands on her money…" His voice drifted off. As Eugene had hoped, Bruno felt a need to add some new information to the pot.

"He wasn't interested in women, I don't think he was jealous that Mila had a lover, it was more that he was disappointed that she chose Tarek. Jacques managed her money in Singapore and put it into one of his companies. So he didn't need her anymore."

Eugene tried to keep Bruno talking. "But he had his own money, didn't he? Did it all come from the paintings?"

"No, he was a go-between on big deals with Eastern Europe. He dealt with some big investors. Fucking snobs."

Eugene was about to ask another question, but Bruno held his hand up. "You can stop now. I've told you all that I intend to. As I said before, bugger off. I never want to see you again.

Chapter Thirty-One

A THUNDERSTORM HAD DELAYED SOME of the trains, and passengers were gathered with eyes riveted on the information board. Eugene had found a seat in a nearby Starbucks where he could enjoy an overpriced drink and watch for a new departure time. He thought about his upcoming trip to Trubenne and surprised himself at how excited he was to see Alex.

#   #   #

Alex drove to Nîmes to pick up Eugene. Would Marie-Agnès like to come along for the ride? she asked. But Mag said no, she'd feel like a spare tire and she was sure Alex could manage the trip without her.

They chatted about the renovation of the château and the plans for the vineyard. Eugene told her about his friends Travis and Julie. They talked about tennis (they agreed that Rafael Nadal was amazing), and France's diminutive President, Bill Palmac. According to Travis, his nickname was Bonsai Bill.

Eugene said he was looking forward to meeting Richard and Charlotte, as he'd heard so much about both of them. He almost added that it was funny that he hadn't met Marie-Agnès until a few weeks ago. She had, after all, played a crucial part in arranging his meeting with Jacques Mornnais. But they avoided mentioning either Jacques or Bruno.

It was past noon by the time they reached Trubenne, where the table under the trees had been set for lunch. Richard was what Eugene had expected: patrician, friendly, but keeping his distance, his blue eyes alert and judgmental. Eugene preferred Charlotte—more hospitable, less standoffish, not a snob like Richard.

The weather was warm but not too hot, with a bright blue sky and a few fluffy white clouds. Cold salads, sliced meats, open-faced peach pie with vanilla ice cream, chilled rosé followed by coffee. It was the kind of afternoon that you want to put into a bottle or press between the pages of a scrapbook: something to remember in a less perfect moment.

After lunch, they cleared the table, and Alex took Eugene on a tour of the property. They stopped on a low rise overlooking rows of vines that would be replaced if Richard's plans worked out. Eugene put his arms around Alex, kissed her gently at first, then more intensely as she pushed her body up against him.

"I'm so happy to see you," he whispered into her ear. She shivered and whispered back, "Me too." Then she pulled away, took his hand, and they continued walking.

He followed Alex down the narrow paths alongside the vines, silent. After a few minutes, he stopped her. "What's the matter?"

"I just can't shake the feeling that you're still focused on Jacques Mornnais, and I wish you would tell me why. I sort of understand why you lied to me before, but you said you wanted to make a fresh start, and that means telling me why you're still interested in him, since you said that you recovered your aunt's money."

A light breeze crept through the vines, tickling wisps of hair that had escaped from Alex's ponytail. Eugene's better self battled with his professional self; his better self won. "Look, normally I shouldn't be talking to you about this. It concerns my work. But I told you that I wanted to earn your trust, so I'll tell you about my interest in Mornnais—but you have to promise to keep it to yourself."

"Of course."

Eugene's eyes were the color of mud, the gold flecks had disappeared. "Our friend Jacques apparently keeps dossiers on the escapades of the political and business elite in France—you know, compromising information: who's sleeping with whom, who's living beyond their means, that sort of thing. Someone in Washington would like to get their hands on those files. So guess who they tasked with doing that?"

"I see. I don't suppose Jacques would be too happy to see you after you made him pay you back. By the way, you never did say how you managed to pull that off."

"It wasn't that difficult. Remember Mélandère, his house in the south? He kept his paintings in a vault there. We were able to access the vault and photograph the paintings. I showed him a photo we took in the vault, and threatened to blow it up if he didn't pay. So he did."

"Would you have really blown up the vault?"

He smiled, "not likely."

"Now I see why you're so interested in helping Bruno recover his memory: you think he can tell you something that you can use against Jacques."

"You've got it. But it's slow going."

"Oh yes, there's one other thing I meant to ask you: how did you know that Tarek was dead?"

"A guy I know in the Interior Ministry told me, why do you ask?"

While she had been listening to Eugene, the same question repeated itself in Alex's mind: Should she tell him about meeting Jacques in the George V? It would mean opening the whole can of worms again.

"You have a funny look on your face, Alex. Surely you're not upset that Tarek is dead."

She took a deep breath; her decision had been made.

"No—I'm not upset. In fact, I learned that he was dead before I even saw you. Jacques Mornnais told me."

Eugene cracked a smile; the gold flecks had returned. "And I bet you're going to tell me all about it."

Alex described her encounter with Jacques, and how she had been uncertain as to whether she wanted to work for him again—a battle between curiosity and fear. "Maybe I could help you if I went back to work for him, to find out something that you could use to persuade him to turn over his files."

Eugene placed his two hands on her shoulders: "I appreciate that, I really do, but Jacques is a dangerous man. I don't think you should put yourself in harm's way a second time. So thanks—but no thanks."

Alex's eyes, an intense blue, the color of the sky, flashed, but her voice was soft. "Eugene, please don't take this the wrong way, but I'm not asking your permission. I wanted to punish Jacques for what he did to Mag, and even though you got your money back, I don't think he's been punished enough."

"Please, Alex, don't do it. You know the saying: if you lie down with dogs, you get fleas. Sooner or later, Jacques will get his comeuppance, folks like him always do. And you don't have to be the one to punish him."

Eugene wrapped his arms around Alex, drew her close to him, kissing her with an intensity that awakened her long-lost feelings. She savored the moment—*let it be different this time.* When she opened her eyes, his golden gaze locked onto hers, she could hardly catch her breath. He planted a last kiss on top of her head, took her by the hand, and they walked silently back to the château in the soft early evening light. When they arrived, Charlotte and Marie-Agnès were already setting the table for dinner.

Chapter Thirty-Two

SANDRA SPENT THE FIRST WEEK of her vacation at home, catching up on the household tasks that had fallen by the wayside as she tried to cope with Bruno's presence. She gave the apartment a thorough cleaning, enjoying the physical effort that took her mind off her job at the bank. Bruno came and went as he pleased, he had found work, didn't ask her for money, and there were no more missed doctors' appointments. It was just as well that she didn't know that Bruno had stopped seeing the doctor altogether.

It was mid-week when she drove to the A6 motorway. She would go to Paris, spend the night with a girlfriend and then continue her journey to a yoga retreat near Roscoff, on the English Channel.

Sandra arrived at the end of the afternoon, unpacked her few belongings—this was not the place for making fashion statements. A walk along the grassy cliffs, watching the tides come in, swirling around the rocks that stood like ancient sentinels near the beach. It amused her to imagine Viking ships on their way to the Atlantic coast; it was a moment to enjoy the stillness and stark beauty of the place.

Smoking was not allowed, no meat, no seafood, no wine: just grains, algae, vegetables, and water. No matter, Sandra thought, she would skip lunch one day, drive into Roscoff and treat herself to a seafood platter and some chilled white wine. Otherwise, this was a good break from Lyon's delicious but rich cuisine.

They started each morning with the sun salutation followed by an hour and a half of postures. It was a mixed group: young, not so young, old, skinny, fat. Through her mostly closed eyes, Sandra watched a heavyset young woman execute the most challenging postures with ease—it was so demoralizing. Slender and rigid as a board, she squeezed her eyes shut.

Afterwards, they ate breakfast and spent the remainder of the morning chopping vegetables and preparing lunch. In the afternoon, there were meditation classes, walks along the cliffs, swimming, and sunning. Every evening, the group trooped to the edge of the cliff and watched the sunset, applauding as the fiery red ball dropped into the sea.

Sandra was at peace. Or almost. At odd times, when she held a pose, or during meditation, a flicker of anxiety rose from her abdomen to her chest. She felt her heartbeat increase, and then it passed. Was it Bruno? Or the bank? She didn't know and tried to ignore the fleeting moments of unease.

She treated herself to the promised lunch in Roscoff, sipped her coffee in the shade of a red parasol. The terrace had emptied out. A waiter was clearing away the dishes when a man sat down at a nearby table, carrying with him the aroma of tobacco and leather.

Sandra turned her head towards the smell, her sunglasses hiding her eyes. He was not bad looking: his face was deeply tanned, most likely from living rough, not from sunbathing. Although it was summer, the man wore a leather jacket, and she could now smell his body odor as well. He lit a cigarette, the waiter approached, and he ordered a coffee.

"I'm sorry, sir, but these tables are reserved for people ordering food." He handed him a menu. The man sighed and stood up, "I just want a coffee," he said as he slung his backpack over his shoulder.

Sandra watched as the man walked away. There was something about him that reminded her of Bruno—another soul living on the margins of society. The thought expanded, she recalled Bruno sitting in the doctor's office for their first appointment, how disconcerting to have forgotten everything, even his name.

During meditation, Mathilde encouraged them to examine their emotions.

I'm feeling anxious again, she thought, the acknowledgment taking the edge away. She paid for her meal and returned to the center, looking forward to another meditation session.

\#   \#   \#

As always, when you're doing something you enjoy, time passes too quickly. It was now the end of August, and Sandra, looking healthy and feeling fit, packed her bag and began the trip back to Lyon. She again spent the night in Paris, got an early start the next day, and a few hours later, she was back in Lyon. Feeling full of energy despite the long drive, she put up a load of laundry and set about cleaning the apartment.

The return to work—to her dull, boring job—loomed like a dark cloud on today's pleasant horizon. She tried to take comfort in Mathilde's words: *the past is memory, the future is imagination, only the here and now is real.* If only.

Chapter Thirty-Three

Trubenne, France

AT DINNER, MAG'S DISCOVERY OF the photos seemed to flutter at the edges of the conversation. Eugene told them about the progress he was making with Bruno. He turned to Mag: "I have the names of the two men who mugged you in the metro—Cosimo and Samuel."

"And what about the flowers—were they the same two men?" asked Mag.

"Yes. Bruno never found out what happened to them—he'd had his encounter with the river by then."

"At least we know now," said Mag.

"But we don't know everything. The man in the shit-green car, the one who was crushed by the train in Montbard—why was he following me?" asked Alex.

"Sometimes you have to accept not knowing," said Charlotte. As the telltale buzz of a mosquito pierced the warm night air, Charlotte slapped her arm. "Got it," she laughed. "I wonder whose blood this is. It's time to clear the table and move indoors."

#   #   #

Richard could see the attraction between Alex and Eugene. He decided that he needed to get to know this man better and invited him to take a walk through the vineyards.

Alex had told her uncle the truth, at least in part. She explained that Eugene had rented her house in Washington DC and that she had literally run into him while jogging in Parc Monceau. He was currently on leave from his job at the FBI. When she met him, Eugene had come to France to return a fake painting that his late aunt had bought from an art dealer who worked with Jacques Mornnais — nothing more than that.

"I understand you worked for the FBI," Richard began. Eugene launched into a description of his work in international drug trafficking, and how he had felt the need to take some time off.

"And Alexia tells me that you came to France to recover the money your late aunt had paid for a fake painting. So you got your money back?"

"Yes, I did."

"From the dealer or Mornnais?"

"Mornnais."

They continued walking. Richard knelt to examine a cluster of grapes: "If all goes according to plan, we'll be improving the quality of our wine over the coming years." Then, an awkward switch: "You met him, then, Mornnais? What did you think of him?"

"An intelligent, dangerous man."

"Can you tell me how you managed to get your aunt's money back?"

"Well, you know the saying, 'I made him an offer he couldn't refuse.'"

Silence again, the red and gold leaves stirring in a gentle breeze. Richard, thinking, seemed to have come to a decision. " I met Mornnais years ago. At the time, I didn't know his name; he was a go-between one of my business partners used when dealing with eastern European countries. He was not someone I'd associate with outside of business. But it looks like he's a man of many talents, isn't he?" They turned and walked back to the house.

#   #   #

One morning at the end of August: Charlotte had taken Eugene to see the market in Nîmes, Richard sat in the shade, reading *Valeurs Actuelles*. *It's now or never,* thought Alex, as she and Marie-Agnès cleared the table from breakfast.

"Marie-Agnès, I don't want to upset you, but that last phone call from Blondell—do you ever wonder what she wanted to talk to you about?"

Mag sighed, "All the time. I cannot get her voice out of my mind. She sounded—what is the right word—distressed, distraught. She said something about an email, but my mind was elsewhere, and I don't remember anything else. I wish I had insisted that she tell me what was wrong."

"I was wondering if you hadn't found anything in her papers."

"No, only the photos."

"I mean, doesn't it bother you, not knowing?"

"A lot. On top of how guilty I sometimes feel."

"Mag, it was a freak accident. It wasn't your fault. But I can't escape the feeling that there's some clue right in front of our noses that we're overlooking. Do you think it could have had something to do with her buying the Signac?"

"I cannot imagine what that could be. I remember once when we met for a drink, Blondell told me that she was having second thoughts. And there wasn't any painting by Signac in the apartment, that's for sure."

"Do you think Merv Peters might know what happened?"

"I hope you're not suggesting that I contact him! Leave him with Bruno and Jacques. I hope I never see that man again!"

"No, you've done quite enough. Actually, I think that *I* might call Merv Peters, you know, on behalf of the family. Just to ask if he knew if Blondell went ahead with purchasing the Signac."

"Oh, Alex, do you really want to do that? I wouldn't be surprised if you discover that Jacques Mornnais is somehow involved, and I thought that you wanted nothing further to do with that man."

Alex had a determined look on her face. She'd had seen that expression before: when Alex had spirited Mag out of the hospital, or when she'd told her that she was going to work for Jacques Mornnais. "It looks like you've already made a decision."

"Yes, I have. We need to find out what was on Blondell's mind when she called you."

When Mag didn't respond, Alex continued: "Are you still thinking about the photos, or about Bruno?

"No, not really." Marie-Agnès had finished loading the dishwasher, and she started to wipe down the table. "You know, when people have asked me why I moved to Lyon, I just said that I thought it would be fun to experience a city other than Paris."

"Yeah, I was kind of curious about that as well."

"The truth is, inheriting Blondell's apartment has given me the financial freedom I could only dream of, the freedom to do something else."

"Something else?"

"Don't laugh, Alex, but I've taken so many cooking courses over the years, what I really want to do is open a restaurant."

"I'm not laughing, I think that's great!"

"For me, Lyon is the gastronomic capital of France, not Paris. And I've enrolled in a course in restaurant management—I can't stop thinking about it! The classes start in a few days, and I am so excited."

"Wow, a restaurant! That will make quite a change from translating."

"Indeed! So, I hope you understand, but I'm off to Lyon tomorrow. I want to get my apartment organized before I begin. And Alex, don't worry, I'll try to remember if Blondell said anything that could help us."

#   #   #

Alex and Eugene had spent the remainder of August working on the renovation of the Trubenne château. As it turned out, Eugene was a skilled carpenter, and enjoyed painting: he found working with his hands very relaxing. He got along well with François Tran and his two sons, he got along with Richard and Charlotte—he seemed to have the knack for getting along, full stop. Eugene even got on with Alex. She could be prickly when she felt insecure, remembering not only her failed marriage but all her failed relationships as well. On her good days, she let herself believe that this time it was different.

One evening, as the end of summer drew nearer, Eugene announced that he would be returning to Lyon. They had been sitting around, playing Scrabble, when a thunderstorm broke. The night sky was streaked with purple as the thunder rolled in giant claps, and rivulets turned the cracked ground into a sea of mud. The game over—Charlotte had won, as usual—they all retired to bed.

Eugene kept his window closed to avoid the mosquitos. But the room got so stuffy, that he opened the window, letting in the fresh night air. When it got too bad, he pulled the sheet up to his nose and closed his eyes. Eugene wondered if tonight Alex would be there—summer was winding to a close—and then he heard the door gently open. She stood at the foot of his bed, illuminated by a shaft of moonlight. Eugene smiled, the golden flecks danced in his eyes, Alex pulled off her long t-shirt and slipped into bed next to him. A lone mosquito had flown in through the open window, but they took no notice. Later, laughing, they pulled the sheet up over their heads.

"Is something on your mind, Alex," he asked as he ran his finger down the bridge of her nose.

"I suppose you're going back to Lyon to see if you can squeeze anything more out of Bruno."

"Yup, I'm gonna give it one last try before I give it up."

"And then what?"

"I don't know. Why do you ask?"

"I've decided to go back to work for Jacques," she said. "I called him again, and he said he could use me in September. I probably won't get another chance to be in his office, and hopefully this time I'll find proof that he's up to no good, something to punish him. And who knows, maybe I'll come across something that can help you as well."

"I don't suppose you'd listen if I asked you not to do this? I don't like the idea of you putting yourself in harm's way. Certainly not for the Bureau."

"I'm not doing it for the Bureau, Eugene, I'm doing it for myself."

"You know the saying, if you seek revenge, dig two graves?"

"I'm seeking justice, not revenge. It just pisses me off to think that there are men like Jacques, who do whatever they please, with no consequences for their bad behavior."

"Please, Alex, stop thinking about Jacques. He'll get what's coming to him one of these days. You don't have to be the instrument of his downfall."

She snuggled up closer, her mind made up. "Whatever you say, Eugene. Anyhow, I'm tired of talking. Let's get some sleep."

#   #   #

Rue Boursault

By the end of August, Thomas Smith had completed his project. A single sheet of paper lay on the tiny table that served as a desk. It had three columns: the first one listed the date and number of the issue of *Artixia;* in the second column he'd written the name of the collector featured, and in the third, the artwork stolen from their collection. The chart was handwritten, printed in almost child-like block letters, for he had no printer. But it was legible, that was what counted. And while not conclusive, the chart pointed to troubling coincidences. He gathered up his notes and put them into a manila envelope to take to the post office tomorrow.

Thomas Smith sighed—it was a sigh of contentment. He was done cleaning up other people's shit, whether on a yacht or in a café. But most importantly, his parents would be proud of him.

Chapter Thirty-Four

September 2010

PATRICK AND VÉRONIQUE HAD SORTED through the papers in Nicolas' office in Fontainebleau. Weeded and cleaned out the garden and threw out the junk that had accumulated in the garage.

"This is one of my favorite times of the year in Marseilles," Véronique told Patrick, "Warm days, cool nights, just the way I like it. Let's go back down to enjoy the end of summer."

"Are you sure?" he asked. "I mean, we're having a great Indian summer right here in Fontainebleau." Patrick would have been happy to spend September in the North Pole if he could avoid Véronique meeting his mother.

"Oh right," she laughed. "I'll bet you don't want me to meet your mother. Not to worry, Patrick, it will be fine, I promise!"

They drove south leisurely, avoided the A6 motorway—an unnecessary expense—and took the longer route via the secondary roads. It was not until the end of the first week of September that they arrived at the house on Traverse Paul.

Caroline had lost no time settling in. She collected the dead leaves that littered the garden, rolled back the tarp, and spent hours by the swimming pool. On some days, she walked to the Prado beaches, marveling that France's second-largest city was, at least for her, a beach town. As for shopping, there was a large supermarket up the road, where it was unlikely that anyone would remember her. She called Patrick to give him her new phone number (she had thrown her old cell phone into the sea). When he announced that they would be coming down for a visit, Caroline was not overjoyed, but she could hardly complain.

It was while they were barbecuing chicken shish kabobs that Patrick's phone rang. It was David, with news that *that man* (he didn't want to mention his name on the phone) had called and asked if Patrick could run the same errand as before.

"How much?" asked Patrick.

"The same as before."

"Okay, I'll go over there and let you know."

#　　#　　#

Véronique went to bed early one evening, pleading too much sea and sun. Patrick and Caroline sat by the pool, sipping chilled rosé, listening to the crickets' incessant hum. Patrick had given David half of the first payment from *Maître* Paoli, and he'd do the same when he had been paid again. That would take care of his rent for a while, but Patrick still needed money to live on. So he once again broached the question, could Caroline help him with one last loan to tide him over until he found a job, which he was sure to do now that the summer was coming to an end?

Caroline didn't launch into her usual lecture. Instead, she told him that she would give him one thousand euros, that she had resigned from her job, and had to be careful about money. She would be leaving France very soon, and he might not hear from her for some time. When she was settled, she'd be back in touch. A pendant hung from her neck, nestling between her breasts. She twisted the chain around and unhooked it. "Here," she said as she pushed it into his hand. "I want you to have this, it will be a reminder of your mother." Caroline took a last gulp to empty her glass, placed a moist kiss on Patrick's forehead and went up to her bedroom.

\#   \#   \#

"It's been great, hasn't it?" Véronique murmured to Patrick one night as they lay in bed. It was now mid-September. "But it's time to close up the house and return to Fontainebleau—I need to look into my father's affairs."

"I guess that means my mother will have to find another place to stay."

"Yes, I'm sorry, but she's been here for a couple of weeks. You know, she reminds me of a nervous little bird—did you notice how she seems startled when there's noise from the street? Anyhow, you know that saying: *all good things must come to an end.*"

Caroline agreed reluctantly to leave. Once she was gone they closed the shutters, piled the garden furniture inside the garage, and once again stretched the tarp across the pool. Patrick called David.

"I've been by the property again like you asked me."

"And?"

"The place is deserted. No one's living there right now." At that moment, he was telling the truth. "And David, I'll be over later."

Patrick had decided to stay in Marseilles to look for work. Véronique dropped him off at the Rond-Point du Prado and continued to Fontainebleau. They promised to see each other very soon.

As the car drove up Traverse Paul and turned right onto Avenue Clot Bey, Caroline came out from behind a cluster of trees by the roadside. She had made a copy of the key to the house and let herself back in. She had planned to leave in a few days, and that little snip of a girl was not going to make her change her plans. Patrick's truthfulness was short-lived.

Chapter Thirty-Five

SANDRA'S SUNTAN HAD STARTED TO fade. And by the end of the week, the dark circles under her eyes had returned. Caroline was still on holiday, and if she examined her thoughts more closely, Sandra would have realized that she felt lighter in her colleague's absence.

The back office had a nickname for their boss: *le basset*. With his jowls and drooping eyelids, he resembled nothing so much as a basset hound. Cyril de la Forest du Maine was not happy, and his face drooped even more. It was not a week since he had returned from his summer holiday on the Ile de Ré, and already *les emmerdements* had commenced. After the summer break, the bank's internal audit system had swept through the inactive accounts, picked up the transfers done by Caroline and approved by Sandra, and issued an alert. Cyril was perplexed: the women knew the system would pick up the transfers, yet Sandra was back at work. He had her summoned to his office.

"I didn't do anything," she screamed. Cyril looked at the head of security, seated next to Sandra. The man, dressed in a dark suit, white shirt, and black tie, reminded Sandra of an undertaker. If Sandra had nothing to do with the theft, then how was it that Caroline had her access code?

Her face felt hot; she trembled. "I don't know," she croaked. "I have no idea."

"For now, I think you must go home. We'll call you."

"But…" Sandra started.

"That's quite enough for the moment, Madame Picardeau. This is a very serious matter. We need to investigate further, and we'll let you know."

The two men rose, Sandra felt pulled to her feet by their movements, although no one had laid a hand on her. She returned to her desk to collect her affairs, followed by the head of security.

#   #   #

It felt strange, being at home midday. Walking in circles around the living room, she tried to calm her racing pulse. Something was missing, but what? As a last resort, she sat on a straight-backed chair, closed her eyes, and concentrated on her breathing. After a few minutes, when nothing happened, she stopped and made herself a sandwich. As she chewed, she thought of Caroline, eating lunch at her desk. *Caroline at her desk.* And then she knew the buried thought that had disturbed her at Roscoff: Caroline had watched her when she had hurried out of the office, leaving her desk unlocked. She needed to find Caroline, get her to tell what she had done with the money. And, more than that: get her to share her ill-gotten gains with Sandra.

Cyril might fire me, but after that, he'll soon tire of the chase: he'll never find Caroline. But I will.

#   #   #

She waited up for Bruno to return from his work at Chez Michel. He hadn't told Sandra about his meetings with Eugene. Nor had he confided in her that new images flashed through his dreams and in his waking hours. He remained mostly silent, but it seemed to her that Bruno was more alert, more alive than before.

"I need your help," she said and told him what had happened. "Caroline's not answering her phone, and I need to find her. I know that her son Patrick works at a sushi place in Aigues-Mortes. How many sushi restaurants can there be? Do you think you could go to Aigues-Mortes, and get a hold of him? He may know where his mother is. Right now, that's the only thing I can think of."

Chapter Thirty-Six

BRUNO SAID HE'D ASK MICHEL for a few days off. He borrowed Sandra's car and drove to Aigues-Mortes to look for Patrick Trabert.

He had gone online and noted down the sushi restaurants in the town. He would start with the ones on his list, and, if necessary, cast the net wider. Memories of doing similar work for Jacques—tracking people down—came back to him.

At the second restaurant on the list, he talked to a chef named Filippo, who remembered that he had worked with a guy named Patrick at a place called Citadel Sushi. Bruno was in luck. Citadel Sushi was on the outskirts of the town—it was not on his list, so he would have gotten to it much later.

Max Martolla had hired a new sushi chef once his temper tantrum had passed. When Bruno walked into the restaurant, Max was draped over the counter, pouring water into a glass of pastis. "I'm trying to locate my nephew, Patrick Trabert. His mother is quite ill, and I need to find him."

Max studied the milky yellow liquid in his glass. "The little shit doesn't work here anymore."

"Oh, do you think you could give me his address, his phone number?"

"Doesn't his mother …" He stopped in mid-sentence. "Look, you're not his uncle, but I'm sure he owes you money. So what the fuck, I'll give you his phone number. Lots of luck to you."

He called out to Emma, "Give this guy the phone number and address for that asshole Patrick." He offered Bruno a glass of pastis; Bruno said no thanks, he didn't drink, but he'd take a glass of water if that were all right.

Bruno went to the address Emma had scribbled on a slip of paper and learned that Patrick had left a couple of months ago. There was nothing further to do here, so he decided to visit the famous ramparts. He joined a group of tourists and listened to the guide explain the history of the Tower of Constance. Standing there, he had an urge to lift the billfold from the back pocket of a man in baggy shorts and sandals in front of him. But now he was beginning to know his true self. He felt that being a pickpocket was beneath him, and he concentrated on the sad history of the Protestant martyr Marie Durand. At the end of the afternoon, he was on the road back to Lyon.

#   #   #

"What now?" asked Sandra. "He could be anywhere."

Bruno waited to see what his memory would cough up as a template.

"You should call him and say you have a message from his mother. We don't know what she's told him, so keep it vague. It would be great if you could go to his home, but I doubt that he'll want to do that. Try to arrange to meet him someplace."

"And then what?"

He explained the next steps, and Sandra prepared to call Patrick.

Chapter Thirty-Seven

Paris

WHEN MERV PETERS WASN'T THINKING about Nicolas Pagès, he replayed his last meeting with Blondell Royston. They had argued about his Picasso, "Woman in Red." She'd insinuated that the painting had been stolen from her uncle. It was a ridiculous accusation, but he'd panicked and taken "Woman in Red" to his country house, where he'd hidden it in the barn.

This morning, as he did almost every day before he left for work, he'd climbed up the stairway to visit the room that housed his collection: his secret garden. Looking at the empty space where 'Woman in Red' had hung, he felt that he'd over-reacted. Blondell had had her fatal accident two days after the meeting at his office, and he'd heard nothing further about the painting. She was dead, the accusation had died with her, and there was no need to keep the Picasso hidden at his country house. In fact, the more he thought about it, he wouldn't return "Woman in Red" to his secret garden. Instead, he'd hang it in his office, it was sure to impress his clients. Merv closed the door to his gallery and set the alarm.

#   #   #

On Saturday, he made a quick trip to St. Germer-de-Fly. He had lunch in a café in the village, drove out to his house, and slid open the doors to the barn. Merv avoided physical activity whenever possible. "Oh fuck," he muttered as he opened a rickety ladder and climbed up to reach the ledge where he'd hidden the painting. Wedged behind a box of old magazines, "Woman in Red"' was almost beyond his reach. He extended his arm, the ladder tottered, but in the end, he managed to bring the painting down without falling off the ladder. He drove back to Paris the same day and carried the tableau up to his office. *By any chance, was the office handyman around?* His phone call went to voicemail: the man was still on holiday. *Tant pis,* he unwrapped "Woman in Red" and leaned it against the wall beside his desk.

Merv thought once more about the chain of ownership of his painting. He'd sent a copy of his records of provenance to his sister, and he was suddenly anxious to be sure that she'd put the envelope in a safe place. It seemed like everyone was still on holiday, he had time on his hands, and he decided to take a short trip to visit her.

#   #   #

Merv's sister Phyllis lived in Fresh Meadows in the New York City borough of Queens. It was the same housing project where they had grown up: a vast expanse of houses, garden apartments, and towers. Merv's parents had been resolutely middle-class—his father was an insurance salesman, his mother a bank teller.

Merv sneered as he got out of his taxi and walked to his sister's building. He had come a long way from this dreary outpost. It was a far cry from his penthouse apartment in Paris' upscale sixteenth arrondissement.

Phyllis, a grammar school teacher, had been surprised when he announced that he was coming for a brief visit. She did not hear from him very often— just a card at Christmas most years—and she wondered what he wanted. It did not take long for her to find out:

"Do you still have the package I sent last spring?" he asked.

"Of course," she replied as she opened the doors to a carved wood buffet. "I have it here for safe-keeping."

"If you don't mind, I'd prefer for you to put the package in a safe-deposit box. I'll pay whatever it costs."

"No problem, what's in it anyway, plans to build a bomb?"

He pretended to laugh, "No, just a back-up copy of a project I'm working on."

"Don't they have safe deposit boxes in France?"

"Look, will you just do me a favor, or not?"

She avoided conflict whenever she could, that was why she had chosen to work with small children, and they went to the bank that afternoon.

The next day they drove to Jones Beach, where the family had gone on weekends during his childhood summers. He remembered the sandwiches his mother hand made. Bologna and mayonnaise on white bread, tuna fish salad on rye—and he could still smell the suntan cream she had smeared over their backs. Another curl of the lip as he compared the vast, crowded expanse of sand to the private beaches in the south of France.

His sister didn't enjoy cooking, and they ordered out for pizza and sushi or went to the local Italian and Asian restaurants. At the end of five days, he planted a kiss on each cheek, thanked her, and was off to the airport, his business in Fresh Meadows taken care of.

La Belle Fermière had reopened, but the room was half-empty—Paris was still deserted. On edge, he called Sauveur Paoli, and left a message. *Damn holidays.* Sauveur returned Merv's call a few days later—he had sent someone to check on the property again, and it still looked like no one was living there.

"Listen," said Merv, nervously clearing his throat, "the guy who the house belongs to has some papers of mine. He's disappeared, and…and I want to visit the house to see if my papers are there."

"I see. I'll ask one of my consultants to look into your problem."

Before Merv had a chance to respond, Sauveur Paoli ended the call.

I'll bet this guy is in some sort of trouble, thought Sauveur when he made the arrangements for Merv to visit the house to look for his documents. But he was too busy to give the matter any further thought and contented himself to add the visit to Merv's bill.

Chapter Thirty-Eight

Château d'Hélène

JACQUES WAS PACKING A SMALL suitcase when his phone rang. It was Nathalie Martin. *If you still need me, I could help out next week,* she'd said. That might work, he replied. I'm on my way to Brezikstan, but I'll be back next week. Why don't you plan to come out to the château?

"I'm afraid that won't be possible — I have plans here in Paris. I'm sorry Jacques, but it looks like it's not working out."

"No, wait, I guess you could work at Rue de Prony that week. Okay, I'll see you then."

He grabbed a few pairs of socks and stuffed them into the suitcase. What a mess—this is something Mila used to do. Although even if he had to pack his own bag, it was worth being free of her.

He thought about his conversation with Nathalie Martin. Somehow he'd been manipulated into coming to Paris. Did he really need Nathalie? Should he call her and say never mind, he too had plans? But then he'd still need a translator, and he really didn't have the time to look for one. But he wasn't in the habit of being pushed around by a woman, and he wouldn't let it happen again.

Chapter Thirty-Nine

IT WAS CAROLINE'S LAST NIGHT at the house on Traverse Paul. She had carefully gone through the house, throwing any traces of her presence into a plastic grocery bag. She would leave early tomorrow morning and dump the bag in a garbage bin up the road. Too nervous to sleep, already dressed, she sat in a chair in the bedroom, staring at the already made bed, waiting for the sun's first rays, when she would leave the house for good.

In the still night, she heard a noise; it sounded like the metal door in the wall in front of the driveway. *Could it be Patrick and Véronique, were they coming back for something they had forgotten, but what?* She stood to one side of the window overlooking the gravel path that ran alongside the house. It was not Patrick and Véronique, instead, two youngish looking men carrying sports bags, followed by a heavy-set older man. They were heading towards the back of the house, with its big glass windows overlooking the garden. The men were probably robbers, Marseilles was full of them, but she was not going to risk her life confronting them. *Let them take what they want; it's not my problem.*

As the men walked across the lawn, she grabbed her small suitcase, tiptoed down the stairway and slipped out through a door at the front of the house, then continued out to the street through the door in the wall. Caroline had opened the door to the street as quietly as she could. She was afraid to close it, figuring if she had heard the noise, then the men inside might hear it as well. She walked briskly up Traverse Paul. As she passed one of the big plastic refuse bins, she remembered that she had left her little garbage bag in the bedroom. *Too late, it won't make any difference anyway.*

At daybreak, with the brightening light stinging her eyes, Caroline enjoyed a last breakfast in a café on the Prado beaches—she would not be back any time soon. From there, she made her way to the Rond-Point du Prado to continue on the next leg of her journey.

#   #   #

Merv and the two 'consultants' entered the house. Where would Nicolas have kept his records? After a quick look around the living room, they went upstairs.

Other than a bag of garbage—not what they were looking for—the first two rooms held no secrets. The last room was more promising: it looked like a bedroom that had also been used as an office. There were piles of art magazines next to some S.A.S. paperbacks on the bookshelves. But it also looked like someone had been there before them. Papers were scattered on the desk: electricity bills, bills from the gardener, old tax statements—otherwise, nothing.

"Shit," exclaimed Merv, shaking with rage.

One of the men put a finger to his lips. "Be quiet," he hissed, "We need to leave now."

As the visitors left, one of the men noticed that the door was open—hadn't they closed it when they entered? Then he remembered the bag of garbage in the bedroom—had there been someone in the house after all? Had the person managed to slip away while they were searching for the documents?

That morning he had started to say to Sauveur Paoli, "Boss, I was thinking…."

Sauveur, his mind on a court case, had cut him off in mid-sentence. "You're paid to do, not to think." He'd follow his boss' words and gave it no further thought.

Chapter Forty

HE HAD PARKED HIS CAR in the circular drive in front of the château, and an instant later, he had walked through the carved wooden doors of the entry, facing an imposing stairway. He looked to his left: now he was in an office, standing in front of Jacques Mornnais.

"Well, if it isn't Bruno."

"I've come for my money."

"Of course," said Jacques, holding an envelope. He put his hand out to take the envelope, but it had disappeared.

"You'll have to try harder," laughed Jacques, still holding the envelope.

He tried again. And again. Jacques kept laughing, and he felt frustrated and then angry.

Bruno could feel his heart thumping, and as his anger mounted, he woke up and looked around the dark room. Then he remembered that he was in Sandra's apartment and waited for Jacques' image to disappear. But it remained, even though Bruno knew it was only a dream. He buried his head in the pillows and fell back to sleep. When he awoke, the room was bathed in sunlight.

He walked into the dining area, where Sandra was chewing on a piece of toast. *"Bonjour,"* he grunted. She wiped some crumbs from her mouth: "It feels so strange, not getting up early and hurrying off to work. I wonder how long before Cyril makes up his mind about what to do with me. Probably as long as possible, not that he cares that he's keeping me dangling." Bruno poured a cup of coffee:

"Do you want to call the kid?" he asked.

"Yeah, I guess so. I hope this works."

"Oh, it will, just do like I said."

#   #   #

It was a sunny day in Marseilles as well. Patrick lay back in bed, staring at the shadows that the windows' bars cast on the ceiling. He wished Véronique were here beside him. Maybe he should go up to Paris, look for work there. His phone rang—it was some woman who said she was a friend of his mother's. They had worked together at the bank. Suddenly he was wide-awake. "They asked me to clear out her desk, and I found something that I think you should have. Are you still in Aigues-Mortes?"

"Uh, no, what is it?"

"It's an envelope with your name on it, and I didn't want to open it. You're not in Aigues-Mortes?"

"No, I'm living in Marseilles right now."

"This might be something important, and I'd prefer to deliver the envelope to you personally. You know you can't trust the post office these days. I live in Lyon, but I'll be happy to bring the envelope to you. Your mother was a good friend of mine—it's the least I can do."

Patrick did not want his mother's friend—what was her name again—coming to David's place: "Well, uh, they're painting my apartment right now. It's kind of a mess. Could you come to the Hard Rock Café in Place aux Huiles tomorrow at two-thirty?

"Place aux Huiles?"

"Yeah, it's right behind the Vieux Port. Just ask anyone."

"And how will I recognize you?"

Patrick looked around the bedroom. In one corner, there was a rolled-up AC/DC t-shirt. He told her he'd be wearing it.

"Okay, see you tomorrow at two-thirty, then." Sandra rang off before Patrick could change his mind.

"That wasn't so hard, was it?"

"Yes, it was. I'm shaking all over. What now?"

Chapter Forty-One

THEY TOOK THE TRAIN FROM Lyon to Marseilles. The smell of fish—strong but not unpleasant—hit them as they emerged from the Vieux Port metro station. Place aux Huiles was so huge that even with the lunchtime crowd, lingering over a last espresso before returning to work, there was a feeling of spaciousness. Bruno pointed to a café at some distance from the Hard Rock Café. "Sit there," he told her. "Call Patrick when I send you a text."

Patrick was late. He'd started to get cold feet and almost called Sandra to cancel, but curiosity got the better of him, and he pulled on the wrinkled, musty-smelling t-shirt and walked rapidly to his destination. Bruno, examining postcards in front of the Arcenaux bookstore, recognized him as he went by. Patrick sat down at one of the Hard Rock Café's tables and ordered a Coke. Bruno sent a message to Sandra: "*Now.*"

Patrick's phone rang.

"Is that you, Patrick?" It sounded like the woman who'd called him the other day.

"Yes, I'm waiting for you."

"I'm so sorry, Patrick, but something has come up, and I wanted to let you know that I can't make our meeting today. Can we do it tomorrow?"

"No, we can't. Sorry, but I'm busy. Good-bye."

What could he expect from someone who was a friend of his mother's? Patrick finished his Coke: *shit, on top of everything else, I've got to pay for this.* He played with his cell phone, walked over to the Vieux Port, and sat on a bench facing Notre Dame de La Garde.

Bruno mingled with a crowd waiting to take their places on a tourist train, watching his quarry from a safe distance. Patrick got up and headed for La Canebière. It had been a shitty afternoon, and he was going home—he'd call Véronique and take a nap.

Bruno was not far behind when Patrick pushed open the door next to a shop displaying Tunisian ceramics. Bruno stood in front of the ceramics shop for a moment before entering the building. He slipped behind the stairwell and listened as Patrick climbed to the fourth floor and let himself into his apartment. A man, his hair pulled into a ponytail, hurried down the stairs, passing Bruno, who was on his way up.

Chapter Forty-Two

CHARLES-ANTOINE NASRI LEFT THE BLACK Mercedes in the VIP parking space at Charles De Gaulle airport and went inside to await his boss. Several minutes later, Jacques Mornnais exited the arrivals zone.

"Good morning, sir. Nice flight?"

"Yes," he said, as Charles-Antoine took the handle of his carry-on bag.

The inside of the Mercedes had that new car smell of leather and wax. Its predecessor had gone up in smoke and flames some months earlier, the result of an unfortunate car bomb exploding when Jacques Mornnais' wife Mila turned the key in the ignition. Jacques ignored this morning's newspapers. With his feet on the footrest, he leaned back, listening to the strains of Handel's Water Music, letting his mind wander.

A thought for Mila. He couldn't say that he missed her, with her constant questions about her investments *(After all, Jacques, it IS my money.)* He was perfectly happy without a woman, but perhaps he'd need to find some arm candy for when he attended dinners. In the meantime, he'd have to content himself with taking possession of the rest of the money she had inherited from her late husband, the plastic wrap titan, Pavel Korsikov. Mila. He had been disappointed when he realized she was sleeping with his chauffeur Tarek. He would have expected her to do better than that.

From Mila, his thoughts moved to Tarek. He, too, had died, along with the mercenary Walter Helmann, victims of a collision with a motorcycle. It was a freak accident—Jacques had had nothing to do with the crash. He probably should never have sent Helmann to try to get his paintings back from the American, what a balls-up that had been.

He'd always had a chauffeur. Of course, Jacques knew how to drive a car, but he'd never gotten around to getting his license. He'd have to remember to ask someone at the *Préfecture* to take care of that. Chauffeurs. The new man seemed adequate although he was amused by his first name: an Arab called Charles-Antoine, how pretentious! He pushed to one side his own origins: he'd been Jean-Charles Molina before he became Jacques Mornnais.

And then there was Bruno. He still found it difficult to believe that Bruno had drowned in the river Arroux. But there had been no doubts, and the body had been cremated. Bruno had mentioned a sister once, he had made inquiries, but he'd never found her. The ashes were in a polished wooden container sitting on a shelf in his office. It was probably time to get rid of them.

After all these months, he remained annoyed at how Bruno had failed to dispose of the red-haired cow. Of course, in the end, it hadn't mattered, but Jacques felt that Bruno had started to slip, that never would have happened in the past. So was it not just as well that Bruno was dead and gone?

Mila, Tarek, Bruno: all dead. Then he saw the American's face again: the deep-set, mud-brown eyes, the sensual mouth, and heard the deep voice. You had to be careful when dealing with the Americans, at least with the Americans that he knew. It was true that he'd exacted petty revenge once on a fund-raiser, but the pleasure had been short-lived.

A thought of vengeance gave him a satisfying feeling—this was about as close to sexual pleasure as he would get. Then the anger welled up as he recalled the art dealer, Nicolas Pagès. Because of his ineptitude, he'd been forced to refund the American for the forged Poussin. The American had cost him money, but he hoped never to see him again. Better to cut his losses. As for Pagès, he wouldn't be causing Jacques any more problems; he'd seen to that.

The sound of the tires on the gravel drive woke him. The Château d'Hélène, a nineteenth-century neo-gothic jewel, gleamed in the afternoon sunlight, surrounded by trees and shrubs, some of their green leaves already turning gold and russet. A gardener was bent over a flowerbed, trimming dead blooms.

As the car pulled slowly around the circular drive, a young Filipina opened the front door. "Welcome home, Mr. Jacques."

"Hello, Mercie," he said. "Get my bag from the trunk, will you?"

Mila had fired Ella, the previous maid. "My name is Mercedes, but you just call me 'Mercie,'" the new one had said with a gap-toothed smile. He didn't think about Ella—for him, the maids were interchangeable, beneath his awareness.

He went into his office, Mercie brought him a glass of freshly squeezed mango juice, and he checked the emails on his two BlackBerrys. Unbidden, an image of the two Chinese art forgers arose—not their names or even their faces, just an inchoate idea, really—and he again experienced the feeling of extreme annoyance that he had felt on their disappearance.

Shaking his head as if to rid it of unpleasant thoughts, he turned his attention to a thick folder. It held plans for the indoor swimming pool he planned to install at one end of the château's vast wine cellar. As he looked up from time to time, smiling as he thought about the project, his gaze fell on the small, polished wooden box on the shelf opposite him.

Chapter Forty-Three

ALEX HAD CALLED MERV PETERS' office to make an appointment. "He's traveling right now," said the secretary, "but I have an opening in ten-days' time. Would that work?"

"Yes, thank you."

"And you are…"

Alex had decided to use her grandmother's name. She was sure that the aristocratic–sounding name would impress a man like Merv Peters: "Nöelle Vesla de Trubenne."

"May I ask what it is that you want to see Mr. Peters about?"

"It's personal. I'd rather discuss it with him if you don't mind."

#   #   #

Alex spent the night in Richard's apartment in Neuilly. Tomorrow would be a busy day. In the morning she would go to Merv Peters' office, and in the afternoon, she would start work at Rue de Prony.

It felt good to be back in Paris, shedding her t-shirt and jeans for a beige linen pants suit and low-heeled sandals. A Cartier watch, pearl earrings, and a gold necklace. She even took the time to apply some make-up. She felt it was the right look to approach Merv Peters; but she'd need to take off her jewelry before going to see Jacques.

#   #   #

Nöelle Vesla de Trubenne he read on the appointment sheet that his secretary had prepared. Sounds like an old family. I wonder what she wants with an American lawyer. Alex was shown into his office: Definitely old money. Let's see what's on her mind.

Merv didn't have long to wait.

"Thank you for seeing me. I'm a friend of the Whittaker family—they're relatives of the late Blondell Royston. I believe she was your client?"

A sharp pain in his abdomen. *Will I never be free of that wretched woman?* "Terrible thing, her accident. Yes, she was my client, but I'm afraid I cannot tell you anything more than that. Attorney-client privilege, you know."

"Yes, I understand. But please allow me to explain. Blondell had told her cousin Claudia that she was contemplating buying a painting by Paul Signac. But when an inventory of the estate was done, there was no trace of the painting. We were wondering if you know whether she went ahead and purchased the painting. Surely, that's not confidential information, is it?"

That fucking Signac. If only she had bought it. Merv cleared his throat, smiled at Alex, and shook his head: "Madame de Trubenne, I don't think I can be of much help to you there. To the best of my knowledge, Madame Royston did not purchase the painting."

"I see. But I'm wondering *why* she changed her mind. She seemed quite upset only a few days before her accident, and we were asking ourselves if it had something to do with the purchase of the painting."

No smile this time: "I'm sorry, but I have no idea. And now if you'll excuse me…"

"Of course, I'm sorry to have bothered you."

"No bother at all," he said, although his tone of voice implied the opposite.

Alex stood up and turned to leave Merv's office. He saw that the painting leaning against the wall had caught her attention: "Oh, are you a collector?

Is that a Picasso by any chance?" Alex took a step to take a closer look at the painting. "Cubism was such an influential movement…"

Oh, fuck. "Yes," interrupted Merv without answering her questions. "Very influential." He touched Alex's elbow ever so gently, directing her to the door. "It's been a pleasure to meet you, and I am truly sorry I could not be of more help."

The door closed behind Alex. Merv dropped heavily back into his chair. Once again, he wished he'd never met Blondell, and now Merv added purchasing the Picasso to things he wished he'd never done. *It never ends, does it?*

#   #   #

Alex went to a nearby café and called Mag.

"He was exactly as you described. And I don't just mean physically. He managed to be pleasant and condescending all at once, implying that I was wasting his precious time. He practically threw me out of his office."

"I'm not surprised, but don't say that I didn't warn you."

Alex continued, "He was of no help whatsoever. Said he didn't know anything about why Blondell didn't purchase the Signac. As you say, not surprising but still disappointing."

"Alex, it was a long shot, and you did your best. I'm sure something will turn up. We just don't know what."

"I know. Anyhow, I've got to run, talk to you later."

Alex ordered lunch. She kept looking around the café, expecting to see Jacques come over to her table at any moment. *Get a grip, he wouldn't set foot in a place like this.* In the bathroom, she took a small pouch out of her purse and dropped her watch, earrings and necklace into it. *Can't look above my pay grade,* she smirked.

#   #   #

Jacques was standing behind his desk when Alex arrived. He looked at his wristwatch and frowned; *Am I late,* she wondered. *No, he's just playing mind games.* He pointed to a messy pile of dog-eared papers, there were scribbles in the margins and post-its made a colorful mosaic. "It's the document that you'll need to translate," he said with his signature smile: a slight upturn of the lips, eyes cold.

I see why he didn't give this to a translation service. They'd throw it back in his face.

"No problem, Jacques."

"I'll be on my way now, you can call me if you have any questions. And Henri here will open and close the office." Alex had noticed a tall man sitting on the sofa. His head was shaven, he had sharp, high cheekbones, and a gaze unabashedly focused on her face.

"That's great, nice to meet you, Henri."

Jacques left. Henri remained where he was.

"Are you just going to sit there and stare at me? Because if you are, then I'm afraid I'm going to have to tell Mr. Mornnais that I cannot work for him after all."

"No Alex, I've got better things to do." He stood up, said goodbye and slammed the door shut behind him.

Chapter Forty-Four

AFTER KEEPING SANDRA ON TENTERHOOKS for a week, Cyril sent word that she could return to work. ATB had found no proof that Sandra was complicit in the theft, but she could hardly expect a performance bonus at year's end. Sandra was furious. "That fucking basset hound," she snapped, then turned to Bruno: "I hope we can find that bitch." At that moment, Sandra was not an admirer of the canine race.

#   #   #

Bruno sat hunched on his bed, a small yellow notepad in his hand. He hadn't had much time in the kid's apartment; it looked like he had a roommate and he didn't know when the man might show up. He flipped through several pages that were covered with childlike doodles: nothing there. On the next to last page, in five concentric circles, he read "89 Trpaul."

He had taken the kid's cellphone and wondered if he could break into it, as he had sometimes done in the past. He'd heard about a guy who had a shop in Villeurbanne, and he hoped he could unlock the phone. It looked like a cheap model, so maybe he'd be able to do it.

The kid: as he thought about him, it was like looking at a movie.

Frightened, he had pissed himself, he'd screamed that he didn't know where his mother was hiding. Of course, Bruno had had no choice, he had a job to do, and he saw himself do it. As he stared at the two objects, the throbbing behind his eyes returned.

Then he saw himself with the American, telling him to bugger off. Maybe that had been a mistake: the American seemed to know a lot about Jacques, and that could help him to fill in the missing pieces.

Bruno left Sandra's apartment to go to Chez Michel's. Before heading up the steep street, he turned to look at the four spires of the Fourvière Basilica that dominated the skyline. Bruno saw a small boy, holding his mother's hand, in the ornate upper chapel—when he tried to follow their movements, the image faded. He turned and walked briskly up the hill.

\#   \#   \#

Eugene knew that Bruno had told him to bugger off, but he was not ready to give up. His intuition told him that Bruno knew a great deal about Jacques Mornnais' dealings—if only he could unlock his memory—and he was determined to find out. When Bruno set the café's perfect *salade Lyonnaise* down on the table, he murmured that he had something to show him. Eugene, surprised at Bruno's change in attitude, said sure, he'd meet him at the usual place, at the entrance to *Parc de la Tête d'Or.* Bruno said no, he wanted to meet outside the Fourvière Basilica.

Eugene had meant to visit the basilica, but he'd always gotten sidetracked. The nineteenth-century Fourvière Basilica provided a breathtaking view of Lyon: the city spread out below, the Saône River a wide gray-blue ribbon running through the agglomeration, pinpoints of light twinkling as the sun set, and darkness fell.

He had arrived early for the meeting with Bruno, giving him a few minutes to admire the astounding interior of the basilica's upper church. The walls and ceiling were covered with glittering mosaics, honoring the Virgin Mary, separated by six large stained-glass windows. *Ecclesiastical bling,* he chuckled.

Afterward, he stepped outside. The city, so far below, seemed peaceful in the chilly night, and he too felt calm and content. Then he sensed Bruno's presence before he saw him, and the feeling was gone.

Bruno sat down, and the thought crossed Eugene's mind that, for a big man, he was light on his feet: had he been an athlete, or in the military? At the right moment, he'd ask him. Silent, Bruno gazed at the panorama below. "My mother brought me to Mass here when I was a child." He was silent, then, "I've always found it very peaceful up here."

"Yes, it is," replied Eugene.

Bruno remained silent. Eugene had the feeling that this was going to be a long night.

Chapter Forty-Five

EARLIER IN THE DAY, THOMAS Smith stood in the shadow of a *porte cochère* on Rue de Prony, across the street from the *Artixia* offices. His calls to Jacques remained unanswered, and he hoped that he might catch him when he arrived at the office. He felt his heart thump when he saw a tall man striding up the street; it was the same man he had seen on Rue Lalo. It thumped again when he saw Henri unlock the office door and go inside. He decided to continue to wait—surely Jacques would show up. But instead, an elegant blonde woman walked slowly up the street—she seemed lost in thought—and entered *Artixia's* offices as well. A short time later, the tall man exited the building and walked up the street toward the Parc Monceau.

The concierge came out of her lodge. "Can I help you?"

"Oh, I'm just waiting for someone."

"Well, I'm afraid you'll have to wait somewhere else." The woman wore a navy-blue wrapper; dark hair, streaked with gray, was clipped close to her head. She was short and squat and she reminded Thomas Smith of a rock, solid and immoveable as water swirled about it. "Sorry, of course," he replied and walked a few doors down. He stood, staring at the entrance to *Artixia*. He made a decision: he would leave his document with the blonde woman.

Alex heard the doorbell ring, she looked out the window and saw a handsome young man, his hair bleached by the sun. "Yes?" she called out.

"I have a letter for Mr. Mornnais," he said. "He's not here, so just put it in the mail slot, and I'll see that he gets it."

After he had delivered his envelope, Thomas Smith went around the corner to the Café Vigny. As the coffee he ordered grew tepid, his stomach clenched with thoughts of self-doubt: what if Jacques Mornnais dismissed him again, or worse yet, ignored him? All around him, the waiters had started setting the tables for lunch. He ordered a *croque-monsieur*, a salad and a glass of red wine. While he was waiting to be served, he looked up from his newspaper and saw the blonde woman from the *Artixia* office. The seat next to her was unoccupied, and he got up and sat down next to her. "Hi," he said with a smile. "Aren't you the woman in the window?" He saw the waiter bringing his food and motioned to him.

"Yes, that's me," said Alex. "And you are?" Tomorrow would be her last day at *Artixia;* Jacques' workspace was locked, Henri lounged around the office, and she'd found nothing compromising. Could the young man have something of interest to tell her?

"Hi, I'm Thomas Smith." He held out his hand. "I was hoping to find Mr. Mornnais."

"I'm afraid he's out in the countryside, and I don't know when he'll be back in Paris. If you don't mind my asking, is it urgent?"

"Um, well, sort of. There's this document that I wanted him to see."

"Oh, is it in the envelope you left?"

"Yeah."

"You needn't worry, I'll make sure he sees it."

Alex picked at her salad, trying to pick Thomas Smith's brain as well. Where was he from? New York. What was he doing in France? He'd worked in the south. She told him she was a translator from Washington DC, and the conversation petered out.

The *croque-monsieur* had grown cold, the béchamel sauce and cheese were like glue on the dry bread. Luckily he had a glass of wine to wash it all down. Thomas finished his lunch: "It was nice meeting you. What did you say your name was?"

She smiled, "I didn't."

With the waiter hovering nearby, Thomas Smith reached into his pocket and pulled out his billfold, along with his room key card. He handed over a twenty Euro bill, replaced his billfold and the key card in his back pocket, but not before Alex had managed to make out the words 'Hotel Bour....' Alex mopped up the salad dressing with a piece of bread, watched Thomas Smith make his way to the front of the cafe, and made a note to Google *Hotel Bour.* A day before she was scheduled to leave, she'd perhaps come across her first lead.

#   #   #

Henri stood at the bar, nursing a beer. Out of the corner of his eye he saw Thomas Smith leaving: was he the same man that had met with Jacques on Rue Lalo? He couldn't be certain. He ordered a *jambon-beurre* and another beer. As he bit into his sandwich, Alex walked past, on her way out the side entrance by the newsstand. She nodded; it was no more than an icy acknowledgement of his presence. He took a gulp of beer and thought about what he'd just seen—or hadn't.

#   #   #

When Alex returned to the office, she picked up the envelope Thomas Smith had delivered. It was a plain tan envelope, addressed to "Mr. Jacques Mornnais, Artixia," printed in block letters. It was lying on a low table with the other mail that had arrived over the past few days. When she heard Henri opening the door, she quickly dropped the envelope on the table and returned to her computer.

On her way home at the end of the day, she stopped in a news shop, and bought a package of tan envelopes. After dinner, she sat at Richard's desk, practicing Jacques' address. When she felt she'd gotten it right, she tried it out on the envelopes she'd purchased. Alex chose the best one and put it in her tote bag. She felt a tremor of excitement as she imagined the next steps.

Chapter Forty-Six

WITH A START, BRUNO TURNED his body towards Eugene. He took the yellow notepad out of his pocket, flipped to the last pages, and asked, "What does this mean?"

Eugene shrugged, "I don't have a clue, what's this all about, anyway?"

Bruno explained why his sister needed to find her colleague Caroline. He'd managed to meet Caroline's son in Marseilles, they had a drink, but the son didn't know his mother's whereabouts. Patrick—that was the son's name—had left this notepad on the table, and Bruno wondered if it could mean something.

Eugene laughed, "He just left that notepad on the table? Okay, now tell me what happened."

"Maybe I had to rough him up a little."

"Sounds more like the truth. But never mind. You think this will help lead to your sister's colleague?"

"Maybe. I don't know."

"Why doesn't the bank go to the police, wouldn't that make more sense?"

"They want to keep it quiet; it's not good for their reputation. My sister thinks they'd rather brush everything under the rug and take the loss. It was only two million euros, which is pennies for them."

Eugene looked at the notepad. "Do you mind if I take this? I'll show it to a friend, he might know."

Bruno held out Patrick's cellphone, "I'm taking this to a guy who can unlock it. Too bad it's not like the red-haired cow; she had no password on her phone. The only problem was that I still couldn't find out much."

Eugene remembered the story Ella had told Alex, about throwing the pink cellphone into the river. He hoped that part of the story was correct and that Mag's phone was gone forever. Now Bruno had opened a door, and Eugene walked right in. "Can you tell me about the red-haired cow? How did you come to get her phone?"

"I already told you, Jacques was pissed at her, he thought she had been taking pictures at the atelier. So he asked me to take care of her and get the camera. But it didn't go as planned, we got her telephone but couldn't find the camera."

"Taking care of her, that would have been Samuel and Cosimo?"

"Yeah, two losers. I chose them to get Jacques off my back. I told him that the girl was harmless, but he wouldn't drop it. So I picked the two assholes that had the least chance of getting the job done. That way, I could tell Jacques I was taking care of things without harming the girl."

"Bruno, they tried to stick a knife in her ribs!"

"Maybe—but she survived, didn't she?"

"And they delivered the flowers, just like you asked."

"Did they? I don't know anything about that. Must have been after I landed in the river." He paused as the memory of crawling out of the river arose: "I don't want to talk about those assholes anymore."

"Okay, but what about Jacques?"

"What do you want to know? I still don't remember everything."

"Well, your job, what did you do for him exactly?"

"A lot of things. We—that's Tarek and me—we'd pick up stuff that had been commissioned, take it over to an art dealer who worked for him. Sometimes take care of people like the red-haired cow."

He said this as though he was reading from a shopping list. Bruno paused: "Jacques owes me money. It came back to me in my dreams. So I need to find him, and I was hoping you could help me. You know, we're kind of a team, aren't we?"

"Why don't you just call and ask to see him?"

"Because I don't remember his fucking telephone number, that's why."

Eugene took a cellphone out of his pocket, punched in a number and passed the phone to Bruno: "Here, it's ringing, talk to him."

#   #   #

Alone at the dinner table, Jacques had been chewing on a tough piece of roast beef. Sometimes he did miss Ella; she had been a much better cook than Mercie. One of his BlackBerrys rang. NO CALLER ID flashed on the screen. His first impulse was not to answer, but then it might be one of his associates in the Far East that he needed to talk to.

"Yes?"

"Hello Jacques. It's Bruno. Bruno Edremal."

A moment of silence, then: "I don't know how you got my number, but I'm sorry, Bruno Edremal is dead. If this is a joke, it's not funny. Good-bye."

Jacques frowned. *Who's trying to play games?* Bruno was dead, cremated, his ashes still on the shelf in his office. Did the caller even sound like Bruno? For the life of him, he couldn't recall the sound of Bruno's voice. He stood up to go into his office, called out to Mercie: "Bring me some green tea, would you please?" He had lost his appetite.

#   #   #

Bruno handed the phone back to Eugene. "He hung up on me, didn't even recognize my voice. The bastard."

"Take it easy. The authorities confirmed that the body was yours, so he has good reason to doubt you. Don't worry; we'll find a way for you to meet Mr. Mornnais."

Chapter Forty-Seven

THE FOLLOWING EVENING EUGENE AND the Bartletts walked into Old Town for dinner. The restaurant was in the heart of the tourist area, but no matter, the hearty food was delicious and reasonably priced.

Eugene didn't waste any time trying to figure out what *89 Trpaul* meant. As they nibbled on the tiny hors d'oeuvre *Canifs de Canut,* he showed Travis the yellow note pad and asked: "What does this look like to you?"

"No idea. If you wish, I can ask a friend at work; he likes solving puzzles. Where did you say this notepad was found?"

"Marseilles."

"Marseilles?" asked Julie. "I grew up in Marseilles, and there's a street called Traverse Paul, I remember it because my parents' friends lived there. It's a very nice neighborhood. So perhaps that notation means 89 Traverse Paul?"

"Nice work, Julie," said Eugene as he finished off the last little piece of toast and the flavorful white cheese mixture. He turned to Travis. "Can you ask your friend anyway, and if his best guess is that Julie's right, maybe you can get me the name of the owner?"

Now it was time to turn to the serious business of enjoying seafood washed down by an excellent white Côtes du Rhône. Eugene finished the meal with a *crème brulée*—it was an excellent evening.

#   #   #

Eugene was wondering how much longer he would stay in Lyon. He was ready to be Bruno's teammate, as he had put it, if that would get him closer to Mornnais. Trying to help Bruno and Sandra was one thing, but he didn't want to get bogged down in their problems. Then Travis returned from work in the evening and put a whole new spin on the situation.

"My pal thinks Julie's right. There's only one street in all of France named Traverse Paul, and it's in Marseilles' eighth arrondissement. And there's a house at number 89. The owner is a man named Nicolas Pagès." Eugene felt the familiar twitching at the back of his neck.

"Could you repeat what you just said?"

"The house belongs to a man named Nicolas Pagès. An art dealer. What's curious is that his daughter reported him missing a few months ago. Quite a coincidence that his address turned up in that little yellow notepad. Why don't you try to have a chat with the owner of the notepad? I'm sure he could tell you a lot more."

If only I could, thought Eugene. *Not likely, thanks to Bruno.* "Yeah, I'll have to look into that."

#   #   #

I don't know how you got my number, but I'm sorry, Bruno Edremal is dead. If this is a joke, it's not funny. Good-bye. That familiar flat voice. How Bruno hated it now. He remembered other voices: Mila and Tarek, both dead, according to the American. The maid, Ella. And the painters, Li and Wen. What did their voices sound like? He closed his eyes, and a memory arose: the crunch of something moving across a bed of gravel. Was he in a car? No, he felt himself being dragged along a rocky path. And heard voices above the sound his body made. *Dead, not dead, hurry, he's heavy, be quiet.* It was Ella and the painters; were they talking about him? And suddenly he knew: the three of them were pushing him into the river Arroux. *That's it.*

157

Chapter Forty-Eight

Rue de Prony

HENRI WAS SITTING SPREAD-EAGLED on the sofa when Alex arrived at the office. *I hope he's not going to spend the day here. That's not part of the plan.*

"Today's your last day, right? So put together whatever you want me to take to the boss—I'll be driving to the château later on today."

Alex was reviewing her translation, trying to concentrate, but frustrated that Henri, engrossed in reading *L'Equipe,* showed no signs of leaving. At last he threw down his newspaper. "See you later," he said, and left the office, as usual slamming the door behind him.

She continued to work for several minutes, then got up and looked out the window. There was no sign of Henri. She removed the pre-addressed envelope from her tote bag. Took a deep breath and picked up Thomas Smith's envelope. She slit the envelope open; it felt as though the noise of the knife cutting through the paper filled the office. Inside there was a single sheet of paper, entitled *Artixia and Art Theft.* The phrase made her heart stop. *I'll have time to read this later.* With her cell phone she took a photograph of the sheet, and then another to be sure, put the sheet in the envelope she had prepared. She folded up Thomas Smith's envelope and put it in her tote bag, and closed up the new envelope and replaced it on the low table. *If I do say so myself, I did a pretty good job of imitating his handwriting. Maybe I was a forger in a previous lifetime....*

Henri returned to the office at the end of the afternoon. A cloud of tobacco and alcohol clung to him. *He must have had a busy afternoon,* she thought. Henri sifted through the mail on the low table. He held up the tan envelope: "What's this?"

Alex had been proofreading her work before sending it to Jacques, trying to avoid eye contact with Henri. She looked up: "Oh that—someone must have slipped it through the mail slot." Henri looked at the envelope—it was only a few seconds but to Alex it felt like five minutes—then shrugged, put it with the rest of the mail that he dumped into a plastic bag.

It was time to leave. Alex shut down the computer, grabbed her coat and bag, and headed to the door. "Goodbye, Henri. Give my best to Jacques." She didn't wait for him to reply as she left the office on Rue de Prony for the last time.

Down the street, at Parc Monceau, she took the metro to Etoile. There were seats in the train, but she remained standing, remembering how Mag had been attacked in the metro. When the train reached the Etoile station, she took the escalator up to the Champs-Elysées and walked to the closest movie theater. She bought a ticket to a film that had already started and took a seat at the back of the room. It was a slow-moving Korean film, and after ten minutes, when no one had entered, she got up and left by the exit at the front. Outside, she took a taxi back to Richard's apartment in Neuilly.

#   #   #

Henri didn't care for Alex, not in the least. He knew she was the sort of woman who would never be attracted to a man like himself, and he was tempted to follow her, just to see what she was doing, to invade her privacy. But then he'd had a few beers at lunch, and he had the long drive to Château d'Hélène ahead of him. And Jacques hadn't said anything about following her. So the idea dissolved into thin air. He locked up the office and went to the car to bring the mail to Jacques.

Chapter Forty-Nine

WHEN HE CAME TO, PATRICK ached all over. He could feel that one eye was swollen, his back and shoulders hurt where the man had slammed him against the wall, there was a pain in his stomach, it hurt when he took a breath, and he wondered if he had any broken ribs. Still, Patrick was glad to be alive. The man had kept asking him where his mother was, but how should he know? She had been sort of weird at Véronique's house, and he was sure that had something to do with the bank.

His room was in disarray. The man must have taken it apart after he knocked Patrick out. He got up slowly and felt his pockets. The roll of 100 Euro bills was still there. He poked around the room. The pendant had fallen on the floor when the guy emptied his drawers—he picked it up and put it into a compartment in his backpack. Patrick couldn't imagine what he had been looking for and decided that he'd trashed his place out of pure rage. *Shit, the fucker's taken my phone.*

When David returned from his meeting, Patrick only told him that he'd been attacked at home, without going into the details. They thought that David might have passed the man on the stairs on his way out, but couldn't be sure.

"Anyway," said Patrick, "no point in calling the police."

"No, no point at all," agreed David. The police would never find the man who had given Patrick a beating, so it was better to let it go.

"I think I'll go visit my girlfriend for a while, let this all blow over." He cleaned up the mess in his room, gave David two months' rent, bought a new cell phone, and took the fast train to Paris, after which he made his way down to Fontainebleau.

#   #   #

Véronique had just returned from a long walk in the Fontainebleau forest. She loved the wooded massif at this time of year: the muted tones, the sweet odor of decaying leaves, the cycle of death and renewal playing out around her. The mellow mood that accompanied her soon changed to worry when she saw the Gendarmes' car parked in front of her house. What could they want with her? Nothing good, she was sure.

"Mademoiselle Pagès?" asked the man in a blue uniform.

"Yes?"

There were two of them, the shorter one doing the talking: "May we come in, please?"

"Yes, of course," she said as she opened the door, "Is something wrong?"

They stood in the front room, still crowded with Tiffany lamps, paintings, and furniture, the rays of sunlight making a pattern on the carpet. "It's your father," the short man said. "We think we may have found him."

"And he's…" she was not able to pronounce the word *dead*.

"We'll need your help to identify the body." Véronique sat down on a deep burgundy plush sofa, covered her face with her hands. The Gendarmes patiently waited for her to break the silence.

"Tell me… tell me what happened."

An abandoned farm was being put back into operation. A body had been found, and it seemed to fit Véronique's father's description. They'd need to take a DNA sample or check his dental records to be sure. He neglected to mention that the man's throat had been slit from ear to ear, enough time for that later.

The Gendarmes left with an old toothbrush and a comb that Véronique had found upstairs. Was the body indeed that of her father? And if so, who had buried him in an empty field, and why? Her mellow mood was gone, the familiar feelings of depression and sadness had returned.

Her phone rang. *More bad news*, she wondered. But no, it was good news, Patrick was on the line, and he was coming for a visit.

#   #   #

The Friday afternoon traffic was at a crawl, as drivers rushed to leave Paris under a heavy storm. Raindrops like bullets bounced off the windshield; Henri slipped a Miles Davis cassette into the tape deck and tried not to think about the journey ahead. Or about the man he was going to see.

It was not that he minded working for Jacques Mornnais; it was more that he didn't like to be around him. The dark eyes behind his glasses made Henri feel uneasy, as though Jacques could see right into his soul. And the way he barked *no fuck-ups!* every time he gave Henri a job to do. He didn't like the suggestion that he *would* fuck-up. So far, he never had.

Hours later, he arrived at Chateau d'Hélène. It was warm inside, and he felt the weariness of the week set in as he removed his outerwear. "Thirsty?" asked Jacques, and before he could answer, Jacques called out to Mercie. "A beer for our friend."

Clutching his beer, Henri followed Jacques into his office. "Here's the mail," he said. "And Nathalie said someone dropped this envelope off for you."

Jacques opened the envelope, glanced at the sheet of paper. "Who is 'someone?'"

"I dunno. But do you remember the guy you met at Babs' apartment? I think I saw him in the café near the office."

"Oh, really?" Jacques' black eyes bored a hole in Henri's chest.

"Yeah, actually, I saw Nathalie there too. Not together, though. Maybe it was just a coincidence."

"I do not believe in coincidences, Henri. We should talk to Nathalie. Oh shit, she's done working for me. Today was her last day."

"Why don't we call her?"

"No, I think it would be better if you went to see her, you know, have a face-to-face talk with her, find out what she knows about Mr. Smith. The problem is, I understand she's moved since she worked for us last winter." Jacques walked to a file cabinet, opened a drawer and pulled out a red folder. "Here's the last address we have for her. You'll have to go over there, poke around, see if she's left a forwarding address, ask if anyone knows where she's living."

Henri took another gulp of beer; he felt a gnawing in the pit of his stomach and he hoped they would be eating soon. Jacques copied down Nathalie Martin's address on Avenue Emile Zola and handed the scrap of paper to Henri. "Here it is. And Henri, no fuck-ups."

Chapter Fifty

BRUNO ENTERED A COMPUTER REPAIR shop on a narrow street in Villeurbanne. Keyboards, hard drives, and cables were stacked on shelves hanging over a long wooden counter. Two men were at work; the word 'depressing' seemed to float over their heads in the dusty half-light. One of the men looked up, "Can I help you?"

"Is Fahd here? I have a problem with my phone."

The man smiled. "Sure, come with me." He led Bruno into a small room at the rear of the shop. Bruno left the phone with Fahd, went to a nearby café, and walked around. He returned to the shop an hour later, paid Fahd, put the phone in his pocket, and returned to Lyon.

#   #   #

They met again at the Fourvière Basilica, Eugene, still enchanted by the panoramic view of the city below the hill. He took the notebook out of his pocket, pointed to the writing *89 Trpaul.*

"It looks like this could be the address of a house in Marseilles: 89, Traverse Paul. What's funny is that the owner of the house is an art dealer who's gone missing. His name is Nicolas Pagès. Does that ring a bell?"

"Oh yeah," Bruno sneered. "Nicolas Pagès, inventive little prick. He helped Jacques to create imaginary chains of ownership for genuine stolen works of art, or for the fake works that Jacques' painters had produced."

Bruno laughed bitterly; he had tried to get in on the act himself, but then he'd been thrown in the river. But when Eugene tried to probe, he said that he didn't remember more than that.

"All right. But let's focus on Patrick: did he go to the house on Traverse Paul? Or did he note the address because Véronique and her father were there? Is his mother connected to the house in any way? I think we need to start at Traverse Paul."

"I don't know if I can take time off. And if the kid is there, it's not a good idea for him to see me."

Eugene was relieved. "That's okay, my friend. I'll manage without you."

Bruno reached into his coat pocket, "And here, this might help. I had a guy unlock the kid's phone."

"Thanks," said Eugene. "Let's see what we can learn about our friend Patrick." He stood up. But Bruno remained seated. "There's something else. It was the maid and the painters. Ella, Li and Wen."

"What are you talking about?" asked Eugene, although he had a pretty good inkling.

"You mean you don't know?"

"Know what?"

"That the three of them threw me into the river. It came back to me last night."

"Are you sure about that?"

"Oh, yeah, I'm sure. And when the time comes, I'm going to do something about that."

"You could be mistaken. There's a difference between dream and reality. Let's concentrate on finding Caroline Trabert."

Bruno was now standing as well. "Yeah, right," he said, and he turned on his heel and walked away.

Chapter Fifty-One

A RENAULT TWINGO, ONCE WHITE but now the color of dirt, pulled up to Brussels' Gare du Midi. Caroline exited the car awkwardly, stiff after an uncomfortable twelve-hour drive from Marseilles. There had been another passenger—a twenty-something man who sat in the rear seat—but luckily he had asked to be dropped off in Dijon. In addition to his suitcase, he'd brought along a box of rabbits and the animal odor filled the small car.

The driver hadn't felt the need to make much conversation—he took passengers to help pay for the gas and tolls, not for their company. That suited her perfectly: the less said, the better. She had tried to sleep, but her cheap blond wig itched so badly that she concentrated all her energy on trying not to scratch her scalp, with only moderate success.

The area around the train station was seedy; urban renewal had yet to come to this part of the city. Many more inviting sites were within walking distance, but this was not of interest to Caroline—Brussels was merely a stopping point on her journey.

She had found a woman who rented out rooms. Caroline was relieved that the landlady was taciturn, and didn't ask too many questions. She paid for ten nights in cash and threw herself on the bed. The mattress was soft, the pillows flat, but at least the bed linen was clean. A bulb covered by a paper lampshade cast a harsh light on the patterned wallpaper. It was all so dreary, but soon she would be in a much better place, free at last. Next to an electric kettle, the fixings for tea and coffee were arranged on a tray, and when she awoke from her nap, she made herself a cup of coffee.

Her old cell phone was resting on the bottom of the Mediterranean, and she bought a cheap new one. She had been thinking about Patrick. He had no way to reach her, should she just call to see how he was doing? *I wonder if he's still with that girl, Véronique?* When she called him, there was no answer, not even voicemail, just ringing until the line cut. *He probably hasn't paid his bill, but that's no longer my problem. His girlfriend looked as if she had money—let her pay his bills.*

She went out to the airport, shopped around until she found a cheap charter to Bangkok; there was room on the flight departing in three weeks. She paid for her ticket in cash and tried Patrick again, but there was still no answer.

#   #   #

Avenue Emile Zola, Paris

Henri leaned against a car that was parked in front of the address that Jacques had given him. Seeing an elderly man stop at the door, searching for his keys, he approached him:

"Excuse me, sir, do you live here?"

Pierre Roule nodded, as he fished his keys out of his pocket.

"I'm looking for my cousin, Nathalie Martin, I think she used to live here and I seem to have misplaced her new address. Tall, blonde woman, did you know her? "

Pierre Roule looked at the stranger, a wry smile crossed his face. "Nathalie Martin, that's such a common name. But I think you must be confusing your cousin with someone else. Nathalie was short, and she had dark hair. You're right about one thing, though. She's moved away." He unlocked the front door: "Sorry I couldn't be of more help, but it looks like you've got the wrong address."

"You wouldn't happen to know where she's living? I mean, the other Nathalie Martin."

Pierre shook his head.

"Thanks anyway," but Pierre had already closed the front door behind him. *Jacques isn't going to be pleased,* thought Henri as he walked back to the metro. *But I hope he doesn't think that I fucked this up.*

Chapter Fifty-Two

Lyon

MARIE-AGNÈS WALKED BRISKLY UP THE path that bordered the sweeping green lawn in front of the Pavillon de la Roche. She stepped around the back of the elegant building, past the swimming pool's glass wall, past the patio where red parasols waited to open in time for the midday sun. At a steel door marked SERVICE—this was a less picturesque side of the building—she slipped her electronic key into the reader, the door opened, and walked into the restaurant's kitchen. Working in the Pavillon's two-star Michelin restaurant—*Aux Plaisirs des Sens*—was part of her management training program, and she arrived early each morning excited to be realizing her dream. Not even the chef's occasional verbal abuse could spoil her mood: she chose not to let it bother her.

Today she sensed that something was not right; she felt the nervous tension passing like an electric current from one of her fellow workers to the next. She turned to Jérémy, who was busy chopping vegetables. "What's going on, is something wrong?"

He didn't look up, just kept chopping: "Yeah, something's wrong, it looks like we're being sold to a group of foreign investors, and you know what that means...."

"No, actually, I don't know. What are you talking about?"

"They're sure to come in here, shake things up. We've heard that the restaurant is losing money, and you can bet they'll try to do something about that. So definitely not good."

The only rumor that Marie-Agnès had heard was that the restaurant was trying to get the third coveted star, which probably meant that they would be spending more money, not less.

In her opinion, the three-star establishments were vastly overrated. She believed that the motivation behind most of the reservations was that the diners could check off another box on their bucket list. Sure, the chefs could sometimes turn out amazing dishes, but on the whole, the price of the meal was not worth it. Marie-Agnès had treated herself to dinner in the best restaurants, and she preferred Lyon's more modest *bouchons*.

She had shared her views with one of her classmates. Tomas Grosjean had spent years working for a big insurance company, drafting and reviewing their contracts, until he couldn't stand it any longer. The work was dull, the office politics toxic. As his ample midsection attested, he found solace in cooking, and he would frequently prepare an elaborate meal and invite his friends over for dinner. The hobby gave birth to the idea of opening a restaurant.

You couldn't call Tomas good-looking. He was short and squat; his blond hair had thinned to a fringe around the lower part of his head. But his grey eyes were animated by a wicked sense of humor, and, like Marie-Agnès, he took pleasure in following his passion.

"Of course, those places are overrated, but having worked at *Aux Plaisirs* will look good on your resume when you market your own place."

"You're probably right. And I'm curious to see what happens if and when those new owners take over."

# # #

The apartment smelled stale. Mag had been so busy with her internship and her studies, that she'd let housekeeping lapse. When she returned home today, she opened the windows to give the place a good airing out. Next, she turned to dust the bookshelves, making sure that the collection of rare books that she had inherited from Blondell was perfectly aligned. One book protruded—was it out of order? She removed it and saw that she was holding a white Murakami agenda—the same iconic print as the bag that had probably gotten Blondell killed. *How did this wind up here,* she wondered.

A piece of paper stuck out from one corner. Mag placed the agenda on her desk. After a moment's hesitation she pressed the clasp and it opened: stuck inside was not one, but two sheets of paper, folded in quarters. On the open page, she looked at the agenda entries in Blondell's childish script. *Sushi Mag,* she read. *That would have been the night she had her accident.* Two days earlier, Blondell had written *M.P.*

Could that be Merv Peters?

Mag unfolded the sheets of paper. They were photocopies of a painting— not the Signac that Jacques had tried to sell Blondell, but a Cubist rendition of a woman dressed in red. *Was Blondell thinking of buying that painting from her lawyer? Somehow that seems strange.* Maybe Alex would have some idea.

When she rang Alex, the call went to voicemail. She'd try her later. The Murakami agenda slipped to the back of Mag's mind as her thoughts turned to her restaurant management course.

Chapter Fifty-Three

October 2010

EUGENE HAD DRIVEN TO MARSEILLES, left the rental car on Avenue Clot Bey, and walked down Traverse Paul, stepping to one side to let an occasional slow-moving car drive past him. He walked past number 89, glancing upward to scrutinize the windows of the surrounding houses set back from the road. When Eugene saw no movement, he walked back to number 89, rang the bell, waited, and rang the bell again. The door swung open when he pushed it—someone had jammed the lock. He walked cautiously up the gravel path and into the yard where the breeze rocked the leaves of the giant plane tree.

Next, he needed to take a look inside. He thought he might try to pick the lock on the kitchen door, out of sight of prying eyes: that was a skill he still possessed. But there was an easier way. Potted plants were arranged around the dining patio outside the kitchen. Under an empty ceramic pot, he found a key on a ring. He tried it, and the door opened.

It was obvious that no one was at home. The kitchen was immaculate, a thin layer of dust, blown in by the mistral, covered the living room. Eugene went upstairs, unsure of what he was looking for, wondering if he wasn't wasting his time. He saw the scattered bills on the office desk and noted that the bookshelves were mostly bare. He went into the master bedroom. Had Nicolas slept here? Only a few items of clothing hung in the walk-in closet. Finding nothing of interest in the chest of drawers, he went to look inside the other bedrooms. They too yielded nothing, until he noticed the only sign of life in the house: a small plastic bag of garbage.

He took the bag, let himself out of the house, replaced the key under the ceramic pot, slipped out the door to the street, and drove back to Lyon. He'd soon find out if the trip had been a waste of time.

#   #   #

Eugene had spread the contents of the plastic bag on the dining room table in the Bartlett's apartment. Two sandwich wrappers: sell-by date the 30th of September. An empty green plastic Badoit bottle. A half-eaten box of *palmiers*. Two rotting apple cores. Crumpled napkins. Eugene smoothed out two wrinkled pieces of paper; it looked like they had been torn out of a notebook. On one were scrawled the phrase *Hitch-a-ride* and a cellphone number. He turned the paper over and read *Rond-Point du Prado 8:30*. On the second piece of paper, in the same hurried scrawl were the names of airline companies.

Eugene had Googled Hitch-a-ride and discovered that it was a website that matched drivers and passengers going to the same destination, the rider sharing in the expenses. One could reserve on-line, and the driver would provide a phone number, and the parties could finalize their arrangement. Was that what Nicolas Pagès had done?

Eugene asked Travis to access the website's archive. By using the cellphone number, his friend found a record of the transaction along with the driver's name and the ride destination.

When Eugene checked the websites of the airline companies, he found that they were all charters serving Southeast Asia.

#   #   #

Sébastien Solère's phone rang as he was leaving work.

"One of my friends shared a ride with you to Brussels a week ago," said the caller. "I was wondering if you'll be going again any time soon."

Sébastien drove to Brussels every other week to visit his mother; she was getting on in years and was in poor health. Who knew how much longer she'd be around? Sébastien was glad to have someone to share the expenses. He hoped that this guy would be like his friend, that woman who had said almost nothing, leaving him in peace for the duration of the trip.

"Next Friday," he said, "Is that good for you? I guess we can skip Hitch-a-ride." They agreed on the price, Sébastien described his car to the caller—a white Renault Twingo—and gave him the license plate number; they agreed to meet at the Rond-Point du Prado.

Chapter Fifty-Four

MERV PETERS HAD JUST MOPPED up a puddle of shimmering liquid egg yolk when someone mentioned that Nicolas Pagès had been found, his throat slit. For a moment, his hand remained mid-air between the plate and his mouth, a golden strand hanging from the morsel of bread, before continuing on its downward trajectory. "Oh really," he mumbled, chewing on the toast. He wiped the egg yolk from the corners of his mouth. "When is the funeral, do you know?"

\#   \#   \#

A small group of mourners had assembled at the Fontainebleau cemetery: Véronique and Patrick, tradespeople from the town. At the outer edge of the assembly was a scattering of people Nicolas had done business with, and behind them stood Jacques Mornnais, watching as Nicolas was lowered into the ground for a second time.

Merv was there too. He tried to talk to Jacques—did he know what had happened to Nicolas' records? But Jacques hissed, "Not now, later," and turned away from him.

It had rained on and off for the past few days. Merv looked down at the soft damp earth that clung to his brand new J.M. Weston shoes. He overcame the urge to move to dryer ground when he saw Jacques saying a few words to Véronique: it might be a good idea to say something to her as well. Next to the girl was a young man—he looked as though he'd been in a fight or an accident—was he her brother or her boyfriend? No matter. He said he was sorry for her loss. She nodded, thanked him, and turned to her companion, "I think I need to get out of here." Merv picked his way back to his car, where he wiped the mud off his shoes. His feet hurt, the day had been a total loss, and he still had to drive back to Paris. He thought about his art collection. To lift his spirits, he would spend some time in his secret garden.

Another thought, this one less pleasant, crossed his mind: could Jacques have had something to do with Nicolas' death? It seemed absurd, even outrageous. Yet he couldn't shake it until he reached the ring road and turned his attention to fighting his way through a late afternoon traffic jam.

#   #   #

"The nerve of that guy. What a creep!" Véronique exploded as they were driving back to the gallery. "He came here once asking to see my father's records for the paintings he sold him, saying he needed more proof of provenance. Chatted me up with lunch in a nice restaurant. Oh *shit*, I told him about the house in Marseilles, I said maybe the papers were there. You don't think…."

"When was that?"

"In July…that's when your friend said his client wanted someone to check the house out. I think that someone was Mr. Merv Peters."

"Yeah. That's just too much of a coincidence. I guess it's a good thing that you put all the papers in storage."

She pulled the car up the gravel drive and into the garage, turned off the ignition, and sat staring at the wall. Tears ran down her cheeks. "My father wasn't a bad person, Patrick. He was pretentious, he could be a snob, but he was not evil. He helped me when I was in trouble, and I'm sorry that he's dead, even if we didn't see much of each other these past few years. And my loyalty is to him, not to that slimy lawyer."

"I know what you mean," said Patrick. He was thinking about the man who had given him a beating—he'd been asking about his mother.

"I want to go back to Marseilles, go out to the storage place, and try to see what Merv Peters is looking for."

"Maybe we shouldn't stay in the house."

"You're right. And we'll have to bring his records back here. "

Autumn had come early—it was cold, with frequent rain. For some, the contrast between the fall foliage and the unrelieved pale grey sky was a beautiful, bittersweet moment. But as they drove south the next day, the couple was happy to leave the melancholy of the north and looked forward to the mild temperatures, sunshine, and clement skies of the Mediterranean coast.

Chapter Fifty-Five

Avenue Emile Zola, Paris

PIERRE ROULE, NATHALIE MARTIN'S NEIGHBOR, was thinking about the man who had accosted him. A big man, well built, but with an evil aura about him. It was strange: the fellow had described short, dark-haired Nathalie as a tall blonde. How had he come to have the address on Avenue Emile Zola? Something didn't compute. Then Pierre remembered a night last April: there had been a ruckus in Nathalie's apartment, and the next morning he'd seen a tall, blonde woman leave the building. He had wondered if she'd had something to do with the ruckus, but when he'd asked Nathalie what had happened, she said she didn't want to talk about it.

#   #   #

London

Nathalie opened a packet of peanuts and poured a glass of red wine. Her gaze fell upon a small sculpture of a woman reclining, done by her old neighbor, Pierre Roule.

I ought to call him, see how he's doing. And I can give him my new English phone number.

"*Ah, ma chère Nathalie*, I was just thinking about you."

"Good thoughts, I hope."

"Yes, of course I was remembering all your lovely dinners, but there's something else."

"Oh? Such as?"

"A man came by the other day. He said he was a cousin of yours and asked if I knew where you were living. Nasty looking fellow. I was sure he was no cousin of yours, especially when he said you were a tall blonde...."

"He said *what?*"

"That's right—a tall blonde. Of course, I told him that he was mistaken. It's rather curious, don't you think?"

"You didn't say that I'd moved to London, did you?"

"Of course not, *ma chérie.*"

"It's probably just some mistake. But thanks, Pierre. Just the same."

#   #   #

"Alex, it's Nathalie. Nathalie Martin."

"Yes, I recognize your voice. How are you?"

"Not good, not good at all."

"Is there a problem?"

Nathalie's voice rose to a shriek: *"Yes,* there's a problem. And it's called Alex Thornhill. Some goon came to Avenue Emile Zola looking for a tall blonde woman named Nathalie Martin. Does that ring a bell, Alex? My neighbor Pierre told him that Nathalie Martin is short and has dark hair. Do you think you can tell me what you're up to now? I thought you were done pretending to be me."

Oh *shit*, Alex realized. That must have been Henri, spying on her for Jacques.

"I *am* done with all of that. Really, Nathalie. Look, you have nothing to worry about because first, the man was looking for *me,* not you. And second, no one knows where you're living these days, although I see that you have an

English phone number, so I'm guessing you're not living in France.

"This has got to stop, Alex."

"Yes, I know, and I'm sure it will. Listen, thanks for letting me know, but I've got to run now."

#   #   #

Trubenne

Alex climbed the winding stairway to the château's turret, the place she called the Rapunzel Tower. Her back to the wall, she stared out at the vivid autumn foliage glowing in the sunlight. What had happened to make Jacques send Henri to Avenue Emile Zola—had she done something to make him suspicious?

Chapter Fifty-Six

Marseilles

EUGENE SLID INTO THE TWINGO'S passenger seat. A half-empty Crystalline bottle lay on the floor; dust covered the dashboard. An unpleasant odor—dried sausage and a touch of animal stink—hung in the air. Clearly, the owner was not car-proud. Would he trade information for money? Eugene hoped so.

They shook hands, and Eugene removed an envelope from his jacket.

"I've had a change in plans, I'm afraid that I won't be traveling with you, but," he added quickly, "I will, of course, pay the amount we agreed on. I hope that's okay with you."

Sébastian had had a brief *oh shit* moment. He had been counting on sharing the trip's expenses. His anxiety dissipated as Eugene handed him the envelope. "Actually," he continued, "I was wondering if you could do me a small favor, I'm prepared to pay you for your trouble."

"What would that be?"

"My friend is not answering his phone, and I need to find him."

Sébastien smiled; he could see an opportunity to make some extra cash. "And how much would you be willing to pay for my trouble? You're asking for confidential information."

"The same as I already gave you. That's not too bad for a few minutes' talk."

"I think twice that amount would be a fair price."

Eugene opened the car door, "Sorry, pal."

Sébastien saw the extra cash vanishing, "Okay, but I need to see the money first."

Eugene held out a one-hundred-euro bill.

"First thing," Sébastien sneered, "Your *friend* is a 'she,' not a 'he.' I dropped her at Gare du Midi, so you'll have an easy time finding her, right?" Eugene ignored his question and asked him what she looked like.

"Mousey little woman, if you know what I mean. Oh, and she was wearing a blonde wig, just like my Mom does. Kept scratching her head. But she didn't say very much."

The odor had become overpowering. Eugene paid Sébastien and hurried out of the car, gulping breaths of fresh air. After doing battle with Marseilles' homicidal drivers, he took the A7 motorway back to Lyon. If the plastic bag had not been left by Nicolas Pagès, who was the woman that Sébastien had driven to Brussels? He had an idea, but he'd need Travis' help to see if his hunch was right.

# # #

Marseilles

The self-storage unit was on the north side of the building. Even when the sun was at its highest, a chill hung over the room. The silence was punctuated by the hum of the overhead fluorescent lights and the squeal of trolley wheels as other occupants moved their possessions in and out.

Véronique stood with her arms crossed, pulling her sweater closed, and stared at the boxes. "I don't know where to begin; this is so enormous."

Patrick put his hands on her shoulders: "Véro," he said. "We can't go through every single file—it would take days. Plus, this is not the right place to read through everything in those boxes. We need to concentrate on finding

182

papers relating to that lawyer—what was his name, Merv Peters? So let's see how your father organized his files."

Nicolas had a separate file for each buyer, so it was not difficult to find the records that pertained to Merv Peters, and they removed all the folders labeled M. PETERS. Nicolas had also kept separate files for each seller, with additional information. Another box held files labeled J. MORNNAIS.

"Wasn't he the little guy who came up to you at the funeral? Who *is* he?"

"I don't know. The man just said he was one of my father's colleagues, whatever that means. I wonder if we can find out any more about him."

Patrick carried the two boxes out to the car. Wedged in with Jacques Mornnais' files was a thin folder labeled B. EDREMAL.

They pulled down the storage unit's metal door, inserted the padlock, and drove to Bonneveine, where they found a room in the Ibis hotel. The next morning, a little after sunrise, they were on the road back to Fontainebleau.

Chapter Fifty-Seven

EUGENE DISLIKED THIS TIME OF year as the days grew shorter, the mornings darker. He longed to be at Trubenne with Alex, and the sooner he could take care of unfinished business, the better. When he'd called her earlier today, he was relieved to learn that she'd finished working for Jacques Mornnais. "How did it go?" he asked. And before he could stop himself, "Did you find anything interesting?"

"Ah, that's top-secret stuff, my friend. Only to be divulged face-to-face. But I can tell you this much. The answer to your question is 'yes.' Is that enough to lure you back to Trubenne?"

Eugene laughed, "Alex, *you're* enough to lure me back to Trubenne. Believe me, I'm trying to tie things up here as fast as I can."

"Okay then. You won't be disappointed, 'believe me.'" It was Alex's turn to laugh.

As he prepared to go out for drinks with Travis, Eugene imagined what *you won't be disappointed* meant, and wondered, too, what Alex had discovered while working for Jacques.

The evening was mild, and despite the crowd, they managed to find a seat on Jutard's terrace. Travis let out a beery belch. "Sorry," he said, and they both laughed. He took a cigarette out of the Marlboro pack that he'd placed on the table, lit it, inhaled deeply, and blew three smoke rings into the night air. Eugene waited patiently, practicing nonchalance. He knew that Julie had declared their home a no-smoking zone. There were very few places, other than the street, where Travis could enjoy a cigarette.

His nicotine urge satisfied, Travis smiled. It was a benevolent smile, and Eugene sensed that good news would be forthcoming. "We've found your little bird."

"Oh, really?"

"Yeah. She's reserved a flight on a charter leaving for Bangkok in two weeks. It's a lucky thing you gave us her name, as she's changed phones."

"Thanks, guess I owe you one."

"I'll remember that." Another long drag on the cigarette, Travis started to cough. When his coughing fit was over, he asked Eugene, "So what's this all about?"

"You remember the ride-sharing website I asked you to check? The name of the site was on a piece of paper that I found in a bag of garbage. At first, I had assumed that the passenger was the owner of the house where I found the garbage bag—the art dealer named Nicolas Pagès. Remember, you told me that he'd been reported missing.

"But when I arranged to meet the driver of the car, I discovered that the passenger was a female. Now, there are two kids who've been exchanging phone calls and text messages. One of them is the daughter of the missing art dealer—her name is Véronique Pagès. The other one is her boyfriend—his name is Patrick Trabert. I knew that Patrick and Véronique had spent time at the house, and I went there in hopes of finding Nicolas. Instead, I found the bag of garbage, and I had a hunch that it was left there by the boy's mother, Caroline Trabert, our little bird."

"But what made you think that it was the boy's mother who left the garbage?"

"Because she's on the run, after embezzling two million euros from a bank here in Lyon. She put her colleague, a woman named Sandra Picardeau, into a delicate situation."

"Makes sense, but what's your interest in all of this?"

"Sandra is a friend of a friend, and I told her that I'd try to help find Caroline."

Travis had stubbed out his cigarette, and promptly lit another one. What Eugene was saying had piqued his curiosity.

"Did I hear you say 'an art dealer that's gone missing?' What did you say his name was?"

"Nicolas Pagès. Why do you ask?"

"Because your art dealer turned up dead a few days ago, his head barely attached to his neck. A farmer found him buried in a field. So if you owe me one, perhaps you could tell me what you know about him?"

Eugene recounted the story of the forged paintings, how he'd met Pagès and how he had gotten Jacques Mornnais to refund his aunt's money. "That link between Véronique Pagès and Patrick Trabert was just a coincidence."

At the mention of Jacques Mornnais' name, two pink spots briefly appeared on Travis' high cheekbones. "Now that you've got your money, and with Pagès dead, I would say you could consider the painting file closed."

"Yeah, I guess so." Eugene shrugged. "And what about Caroline Trabert?"

"No one has asked for our help yet, so you're on your own."

Another round of beers, for the third time Travis smoked his last cigarette, and they ordered two-dozen oysters to take back to the apartment.

Nothing further was said about the dead art dealer. Eugene couldn't escape the realization that he had most likely put Nicolas in harm's way, another example of the law of unintended consequences. However, he didn't feel guilty: Nicolas had, after all, chosen to sell fakes and stolen goods, and he had enjoyed a lucrative income from those activities. It was more a feeling of discomfort over the excessive punishment. Jacques Mornnais would have had no second thoughts about eliminating perceived threats: Eugene knew that from his own experience. And Marie-Agnès, too, had been lucky to escape his wrath, Nicolas not so much. It made him nervous to think that Alex had gone to work for Jacques, even if all had apparently gone well.

Chapter Fifty-Eight

A CHILL HAD DESCENDED ON Trubenne. Was it the change of seasons, or something more personal?

Charlotte missed Marie-Agnès. Had only nine months passed since she'd arrived at Trubenne, overweight and overwrought? Mag had blossomed out of adversity, reminding Charlotte of the old saying about roses blooming in piles of shit, or something like that. No kitchen task was too menial for Marie-Agnès; she had been Charlotte's eager helper.

Alex missed Eugene, ached to be close to him, looked forward to his returning to Trubenne sooner rather than later. She missed the long walks through the vineyards, the warmth of his company, his gentle nature. Of course, she had seen another side of him as well, but only briefly. And now, she had something to show for the week she'd spent working for Jacques Mornnais.

It wasn't that Richard missed Marie-Agnès or Eugene in particular; instead, he missed the surge of activity, the animated chatter at mealtimes, the house filled with voices and laughter. There had been no further mention of the photos that Marie-Agnès had discovered among Blondell's affairs. But the *expectation* that a fuller explanation would be forthcoming lingered in the air.

Charlotte had made a *boeuf braisé,* the chunks of meat tender after slowly simmering, the potatoes not mealy, done just right. Alex fiddled with a potato; Charlotte had taken a knife and fork to the meat on her plate when Richard placed both hands on the table. "I want to tell you about Jacques Mornnais, it's been on my mind ever since Marie-Agnès showed us those photos."

The two women stopped eating. Like Richard, they sat with their hands on the table in the silent kitchen. "It's about time," said Charlotte, never one to mince words, "I mean, those photos sure make it look like you knew Jacques."

"In the early '90s," he began, "with John Royston and a few others, we created an investment vehicle to take advantage of the privatization of the Russian oil industry. Mornnais was one of many intermediaries, 'parasites' might be a better word, smoothing the way for the payment of what we liked to think of as a tax for doing business."

"You mean paying bribes, don't you," interrupted Charlotte.

Richard sighed, "Yes, of course, but if you keep on interrupting me, I'll never finish my story. Now, this Mornnais was a resourceful fellow. Naturally, my colleagues looked into his background before we started to work with him. They discovered that he came from rather modest origins— his parents were Portuguese, they immigrated to France after

the war. A bright boy, he got a job with one of the big consulting companies—he was called Jean-Charles Molina in those days. And then one day, (he snapped his fingers) poof…he showed up in Russia, reinvented himself as Jacques Mornnais, and worked as an advisor to some of the oligarchs. He even married the widow of a man who had made his fortune in plastic wrap. If you'll forgive my mixing metaphors, you might say he got in on the rape of the Soviet Union from the ground floor."

Like a schoolgirl, Alex raised her hand: "And what was the name of the woman he married?"

"I don't think I ever knew. The man's name, though, was Pavel Korsikov."

Alex's lips twisted into a smile. "That adds up. I met the wife when I was working for Jacques; her name is Mila Korsikova."

"After the collapse of the Soviet Union, we had some deals in the former republics, and later on in Eastern Europe. By then, our friend Jean-Charles Molina had returned to France as Jacques Mornnais, along with his wife. But you see, it was John Royston who was in contact with him, not me. I had completely forgotten about him when you and Marie-Agnès came to me with your problem. At that moment, his name meant nothing to me. And I never met the man, although I must have seen him at dinners with John Royston. I think I already told you that out of the blue, Royston's widow Blondell—your friend—called me. We met at her apartment, and it was only when she showed me the photo of the dinner that I learned that that man was our Jacques Mornnais."

"Yes, I remember you saying that you met Blondell. But I still don't understand why you didn't tell us at the time."

Richard had felt uncomfortable last August when Marie-Agnès had brought the photos of Richard, John Royston, and Jacques Mornnais. He was once again ill at ease, feeling that he had to explain himself further. "It would have raised all sorts of questions about my past business dealings, and I did not see how that could help you."

"But when I told you about Jacques Mornnais, his name really didn't ring a bell, at all?" Alex was incredulous.

"I'm afraid not. My memory sometimes fails me—old age, I guess. If I had remembered Jacques Mornnais, I would have insisted more forcefully that you not go to work for him. I do remember that I told you that Michel de Clermont d'Auvergne said to stay away from him. And now I realize why. You don't want to get caught in the web of his relationships. There's no telling where they might lead."

The food had gone cold. "Shall I heat up some second helpings?" asked Charlotte.

Still focused on Jacques Mornnais, Alex and Richard didn't seem to have heard her. Alex smiled warmly this time. "Well, this all confirms what your friend said: he called him 'a nasty piece of work,' didn't he? In any event, we're done with him." They raised their glasses and drank a toast to Jacques Mornnais' exit from their lives. *Not quite yet,* thought Alex.

#　　　#　　　#

She was in her bedroom, still thinking about Richard's disclosures when her phone rang. Was it Eugene calling? But no, she read MAG on the caller ID.

"I hope it's not too late to talk."

"No, that's fine. We just finished having dinner with Richard, and he explained how he knew—but didn't really know—Jacques Mornnais. Although at this point it doesn't make a difference."

"Yes, we need to move on. But listen, I have some news for you, though I'm not sure what it means. Do you remember Blondell's bling bag? Well, I found a matching agenda—somehow it got mixed in with the rare book collection I inherited. Something was sticking out of one of the corners, and maybe I shouldn't have, but I opened the agenda. And unfolded the papers that she'd slipped in. Guess what they were?"

"I won't know unless you tell me."

"Photocopies of a cubist painting, it sort of looks like a woman wearing a red dress. And I saw that Blondell had a meeting with someone called 'M.P.'—that could be Merv Peters, couldn't it— *two* days before we were to have dinner. I mean, it looks like she called me *after* her meeting with Merv. I was wondering, do you think he was trying to sell her that painting? Why would she find that so upsetting?"

Alex sat up in bed, pulled the down comforter up around her shoulders. "I don't know. But what I *do* know is that I saw a cubist painting—it was red—in Merv's office. I even asked him if it was a Picasso. I didn't think anything of it at the time, but he didn't answer and instead he practically pushed me out of his office. But why? What difference could it make now, whether she was thinking about buying the painting or not?"

Mag was silent for a moment. "It just doesn't compute. And I keep thinking that there's something that has slipped my mind."

"Like what?"

"If only I knew."

Chapter Fifty-Nine

THE SPEEDOMETER HOVERED AT 130, frustrating Charles-Antoine Nasri. It was a pity not to take advantage of the Mercedes' big, powerful engine. Still, Jacques was adamant: he was not to exceed the speed limit. Jacques could have his friends in the Interior Ministry take care of a speeding ticket, but he hated to waste a favor for something so trivial. Besides, the less people knew of his whereabouts, the better.

Two silhouettes stood out against the late morning sky, its gray and white undulating stripes like so many ribbons in the wind: the Fourvière Basilica and Lyon's version of the Eiffel Tower. The Mercedes sped up the Fourvière hill and entered the guest parking area of the Pavillon de la Roche. The hotel manager, a slight 1'60, was waiting for Jacques at the Concierge's desk.

"Welcome, Mr. Mornnais, did you have a pleasant trip? Good, good, if you'll follow me, please." Jacques, not very tall himself, enjoyed a moment of pleasure as he towered over the obsequious little man. *If the deal goes through, perhaps we won't be seeing much more of him.* He chuckled inwardly.

The participants had already met several times before; they were here today to hammer out the last details of the hotel's purchase by Jacques' clients. The seller had asked that the new owners promise to maintain all employees in their positions for a minimum of two years.

"We're prepared to keep current staff levels in the hotel and restaurant operations, but there will be a new management team. Your operation has been bleeding money, and we need to bring in our own people if we're going to turn things around."

"Why get rid of the management team? They're doing an excellent job in a difficult economic environment."

"I'm sorry, but that's not negotiable, my clients intend to bring in new management." Jacques didn't add that the new management would see to it that the hotel continued to lose money.

"But, these are men and women with long experience and dedication…"

"That may be, but my clients are quite clear as to their intentions. If we do not have an agreement, then I suggest that you look elsewhere for a buyer."

The seller was short of cash and needed to close the sale rapidly. He capitulated, as Jacques knew he would, and the men adjourned to lunch in *Plaisirs des Sens*.

#   #   #

Jérémy, one of the waiters, came into the kitchen: "Hey, do we have any mangoes? There's a guy out there asking for mango juice."

Like Jacques, Marie-Agnès thought as she put the finishing touches on a vegetable platter.

The kitchen was busy, and she concentrated on sculpting radishes and lemons. The time passed quickly, and she prepared to leave.

"*Merde*, it looks like the boss had lunch with some people who look like business types. I hope that doesn't mean he's selling." Jérémy sounded worried.

Marie-Agnès tried to reassure him: "I'm sure that even if they do sell, the new owners will keep the kitchen staff. I mean, you're all so good, they'd be crazy to let you go."

While the waitstaff started to clear the tables, Marie-Agnès removed her work uniform and slipped out of the restaurant's service entrance. She cut through the parking lot, walking past a flotilla of luxury automobiles.

A chauffeur was polishing the already gleaming exterior of a Mercedes. He reminded her of Tarek, although the man was taller and heavier. As she continued on her way to the bus stop, the Mercedes drove past.

#   #   #

Had she been able to look through the tinted windows, Mag would have seen Jacques Mornnais talking on his BlackBerry. He caught a glimpse of red hair but thought nothing of it at the time. The car raced forward, and he continued to report on the outcome of the meeting. Two hours later, as the Mercedes approached the Château d'Hélène, the fleeting image of the red-haired woman appeared and then faded, replaced by the figure of Bruno Edremal. Annoyance gnawed at his gut: how could Bruno have fallen into the river and left him?

#   #   #

Jacques had finished his calls and leaned back and closed his eyes, luxuriating in the Merc's smooth, quiet ride. Things had gone well and he'd been pleased to give the good news to his clients. Midway along the trip from Lyon to Château d'Hélène, one of his Blackberrys buzzed. Still groggy, he answered: "*Oui.*"

"Mr. Mornnais, it's Thomas Smith here."

"*Oui.*"

"Have you read the document I left for you? Don't you think we ought to talk?"

"Yes, I've looked at that ridiculous piece of paper. And no, there is nothing to talk about."

"Are you sure? I'll bet there are some people who would not find it ridiculous."

Jacques' mind was racing. Had Thomas Smith talked to Nathalie Martin? What had he told her? He could imagine whom the people were who would not find his theory ridiculous. Right now, Thomas Smith was in a position of strength. It would be best to meet him and then take appropriate measures.

"Look, Mr. Smith. You're wasting my time. However, I'm willing to meet with you to answer your questions, set things straight. Can you come out to my château tomorrow?"

"I'd rather meet in Paris. How about the café around the corner from your office? Le Vigny? We don't need a fancy apartment."

"As you wish. I'll be in Paris next week. I'm in my car right now—I'll call you tonight after I've checked my agenda and we'll set a date and time."

Le Vigny or Rue Lalo. It didn't matter. He'd have Thomas Smith exactly where he needed him.

Chapter Sixty

SANDRA WAS MISERABLE: WHEN SHE awoke each morning, she dreaded going to the bank. Sidelined, frozen out, her security status downgraded, she had been reduced to performing entry-level menial tasks. And why? Because the bank's internal audit system had taken a holiday in August! How was this her fault? Rarely out sick, she had spent most of her waking hours at the bank, and what did she have to show for it?

Cyril barely acknowledged her when their paths crossed. Jowls hanging like two sacks of pudding, he would frequently refer to his ancestor the thirteenth-century chevalier. *What's the big deal,* she thought, *he had probably raped and pillaged during the crusades, was that anything to be proud of?* She caught herself as her mood spiraled downward: *stop feeling sorry for yourself, do something!*

Caroline. A recurring thought had taken up residence: if they found her, she wouldn't tell the bank. Instead, she'd insist that Caroline share the funds with her. If she was going to be punished for the theft, she might as well try to profit from it.

\#   \#   \#

Bruno was restless: he hadn't seen the American for a few days. And he was tired. Tired of hearing the voices of Ella and the painters echoing in his head. The unpleasant dreams of Jacques and Tarek continued to disrupt his sleep, and even the art dealer made appearances. Last night he walked down a street in Nemours, following a gnome. Suddenly the troll turned—it was Nicolas Pagès—and walked towards him, demanding, "Where's my money?" "I lost the painting," he replied.

The painting. More than ever, he needed to find that shitty little maid, Ella. At the château, she had said very little, but he could see her looking and listening. She would know what had happened to his painting. No, Jacques must have found the painting. He felt confused: Jacques, Ella, Nicolas, he couldn't separate them. His head throbbed. He swallowed some ibuprofen and waited for the pain to subside before trudging up the hill to Chez Michel.

#   #   #

Eugene was on edge: on the one hand, there was the thrill of the hunt; on the other hand, he had come to France to look for a new beginning. Yet here he was, chasing after Jacques Mornnais and trying to find Caroline Trabert.

He wanted to return to Trubenne, spend his days painting and doing carpentry, his nights in bed with Alex. It was time to tie up all the loose ends and walk away.

#   #   #

Henri folded himself into a chair in the kitchen. Jacques didn't like him hanging around the in the château's reception rooms or in his office—Henri wasn't Bruno, after all. Bruno had brains as well as brawn, and Jacques didn't think the same could be said for Henri. So, he was sitting in the kitchen, drinking coffee, when Jacques called him into his office.

Jacques looked up, his eyes focused on Henri's face. "Nathalie Martin, did you find anything?"

Henri felt his midsection contract; he hoped Jacques wasn't going to be angry with him. "Well, it was kind of strange. I talked to a guy, an old man who lives in the building. He said Nathalie Martin was short with dark hair. And he didn't know where she was living now. Definitely not a tall blonde."

"Are you sure?"

"Yes, boss, I'm sure."

Henri waited for Jacques to react, to tell him he'd fucked-up. Instead, Jacques rolled a pencil back and forth on his desk, then broke it in two, lining up the pieces next to each other.

"Tall and blonde, short and dark?" he repeated. "We need to find the woman who *called* herself Nathalie Martin."

Chapter Sixty-One

Chez Michel, Lyon

THE CHILL EVENING AIR HAD swept the diners inside; Sandra sat with her back against the wall, waiting for Eugene. Bruno had told her that his friend had some news about Caroline.

They recognized each other immediately. Sandra saw a tall, attractive man, a fading suntan on his cheeks and forehead, alert light brown eyes scanning the room. He saw an unsmiling woman, her face set in a scowl, lines of tension etched into either side of her mouth. Bruno had taken Eugene by the elbow and guided him to Sandra's table.

"This is him," he said and shuffled away.

"May I?" asked Eugene as he sat down. Sandra cracked a thin smile. "Thank you for your help."

Bruno served Eugene a plate of *quenelles*: it was too chilly for *Salade Lyonnaise*. He didn't return to the kitchen immediately, but padded around the table, waiting for Eugene to say something.

He moved to lower her expectations: "I don't think I've been of great help, but here is what I found out. Your friend, if we can call her that, is in Brussels. Probably staying near Gare du Midi. I don't have an address, but we believe she's booked on a flight to Bangkok, leaving in ten days." The sides of Sandra's mouth drooped, the tension lines deepened. "Here's the name of the airline and the flight number. You might want to go out to the airport, try to find her when she checks in." The next steps would be up to Bruno and Sandra.

As for himself, he still needed to know how Caroline had come to stay at the house on Traverse Paul, and he intended to tie up that loose end tomorrow.

Eugene dug into his dish eagerly. For comfort food, *quenelles* were hard to beat.

#   #   #

Eugene got an early start the next day. The traffic thinned out as he left Lyon, and he was able to do what he enjoyed: driving and thinking. He had met neither Véronique nor Patrick, but he let himself imagine what they must be feeling and planned his moves accordingly.

When Eugene arrived in Fontainebleau, he drove past the house slowly. It looked like someone had raked the leaves in the front yard and cleaned up the flowerbeds. He left his car in a parking space across the street, got out to take a closer look at the house. The garage was empty, the door open. *They're probably out running errands,* he thought, and settled into his car to wait for their return. A warm shaft of sunlight poked through the clouds, and he closed his eyes and dozed briefly. He sensed Véronique's car as she slowed down to turn into the driveway, heard the crunching sound the tires made on the gravel. In an instant, he was fully awake.

Eugene watched as Véronique and Patrick unloaded grocery bags from the car. He gave them time to put things away; he wanted their full attention when he entered the house. After twenty minutes, he walked up to the front door and rang the bell.

"Hi," he said. "My name is Eugene Stokes. I had some dealings with your late father. I'm sorry for your loss."

"Yes," said Véronique, not moving. Patrick stood behind her. Eugene could see the traces of the beating Bruno had administered.

"May I come in?"

Patrick moved closer to Véronique, "What is it that you want from us, since Mr. Pagès is dead?"

Eugene sensed the boy's fear, smiled warmly. "I don't want anything *from* you, but I do have some information that could be of help *to* you. About your mother, for instance. Now, I could take my information to the police, but that wouldn't help you, would it? Don't you think it would be a good idea to invite me in?"

"What about my mother?" asked Patrick as he put his arm around Véronique's shoulders.

Eugene walked into the living room with its *mélange* of furniture, paintings, *objets d'art*. Nothing much had changed since he had been here last April.

"Let's go into the workroom," said Véronique, "I'm going to try to sell the furniture, and I don't think we should be sitting around on it."

"That's fine with me," said Eugene, and he followed her to the back of the house.

Véronique was silent, Patrick spoke with a tremor in his voice, "So, what about my mother, what did you mean by going to the police? I'm sure she hasn't done anything wrong."

"Have you spoken to her recently?"

"No, but that's not unusual. Sometimes we can go weeks without talking." He didn't add that the main reason he called his mother was to ask for money, and for the moment, that was not a problem.

"But you've seen her fairly recently, haven't you?"

"Wait a second, you were going to tell me about my mother, and instead, you're questioning me. So I'll ask you again, what about my mother?"

"Let's table that for a second. You *are* Patrick Trabert, aren't you? Just answer that, and I'll tell you where your mother is, and what she's been up to."

Eugene Stokes had a pleasant yet frightening demeanor, he didn't raise his voice, his eyes were warm, his smile gentle: he was *too* nice.

"Yes," said Patrick. "She stayed at Véronique's house in the south."

"That's the house on Traverse Paul in Marseilles?"

Véronique and Patrick stared at Eugene, their unspoken response was clear.

"Okay. Your mother embezzled two million euros from her employer, ATB Bank. She hid at the house on Traverse Paul and then left for Brussels, where she is right now. She'll be leaving soon for Bangkok."

Patrick stood up. "That's not possible," he said without conviction.

"That would explain why she was so weird," said Véronique.

Eugene remembered the phone calls from Patrick to Véronique: they had started in July. "I'd like to understand more about how your mother came to stay at Traverse Paul—have you been friends for a long time?"

The clouds had started to empty themselves, diagonal sheets of rain hitting the windows. The only sound in the room was the noise of the shower. "July," said Véronique, "Merv Peters." She looked at Patrick, and he nodded.

"Yes," he said, "it all began with this lawyer named Merv Peters." The rain had stopped by the time he finished the story.

"So, there were no files here when Mr. Peters stopped by?"

"None here," said Véronique. She pointed to the boxes on the floor: "We found many files at the house in Marseilles. I put them into storage, and we brought back the ones my father kept on Merv Peters and another man who came to the funeral—Jacques Mornnais."

Eugene had to tie up the loose end before turning his attention to the files: "So your mother didn't know Véronique's father, then. It was just a coincidence that she stayed at the house after leaving the bank."

"That's right," replied Patrick. "Just a coincidence. But what about my mother? I mean, she can't just fly off to Bangkok…."

"I think we could work something out," said Eugene. A statement positive enough to raise hopes, but vague as to the contours. "I'll have to let you know. But I'm curious about those files you brought back. Mind if I take a look?"

Véronique hadn't said much after "July" and "Merv Peters." Now she spoke: "Let me ask you a question, Mr. Stokes: what exactly was your business with my father?"

She's smart, a lot quicker than her friend Patrick. Eugene told her what she needed to hear, not the whole truth, but enough to get by. "I met your father last winter. He offered to sell me a painting by Poussin, but I thought that the provenance was questionable, so I let it drop. I came here because I thought there had been a connection between Patrick's mother and your father, and I wanted to ask you about that."

"I don't think my mother ever knew Véronique's father."

"I agree with you, Patrick, it looks like there wasn't any connection. But I find it intriguing that Véronique found no records when the lawyer came by." He looked at Véronique: "My guess is that whoever was involved with your father's disappearance also took the files."

Véronique pointed to the boxes on the floor. "But why?"

"Because I suspect that your father was part of a larger operation. I have no proof of who was behind it. Perhaps those files will provide an answer. My interest is in the mastermind, not your father. You might want to know why Merv Peters was so intent on getting hold of the documents that pertained to his purchases. I think I could help you decipher the records. But, it's as you wish. If you don't want my help, then I won't take any more of your time."

"We ought to try to find out the truth, Véro," said Patrick.

"Okay." She sighed. "Let's get started."

Chapter Sixty-Two

Château d'Hélène

IT WAS LIKE WATCHING A film in reverse. Jacques started with the encounter at the George V hotel. Remembered how Mila decided to fire Nathalie after Tarek saw her near the atelier. An image of Nathalie sitting in the kitchen with the maid, Ella: what were they talking about? Nathalie at her computer, Nathalie handing her train tickets to Mila. Tickets. Travel. The woman called Nathalie sitting next to him on the plane from Washington DC to Paris. He needed the passenger manifest.

Jacques called the airline. "I'm sorry, but we don't give out that information." He tried his contacts in the Interior ministry, but without a good reason, no one could help him. He reached for the glass of mango juice that Mercie had left for him. Brought it to his lips; his hand shook and a yellow stain spread across the newspaper on his desk. "Shit," he muttered, picking up the soggy paper. His eye fell on the headline: *Security consultants in high demand. Security consultants.* Of course. He knew who he needed. Michel de Clermont d'Auvergne.

\# # #

Paris

It was a gray, overcast day, with a hint of rain in the air. Michel de Clermont d'Auvergne watched as a *dame d'une certaine age* bent down to pick up her dog's poop on the Esplanade des Invalides. *At least some people followed the rules.* He tightened the muffler around his neck, headed towards the river Seine, and when he reached the end of the Esplanade, he turned around to walk back to his apartment. He'd felt at loose ends, and the outing filled the time. As he approached his home on Rue de Varenne, his phone rang. He saw that the caller was Jacques Mornnais, and while he found the man distasteful, he thought it better to answer. He was curious—Jacques would not be calling unless he wanted something from him.

"I'm working on a project and I wonder if you could help me."

"Sure, Jacques. If I can, I will."

"It's really quite simple. I met a woman on a flight from Washington DC to Paris last November. We had a very interesting conversation and I'd like to get in touch with her, but I've lost her card, and I don't remember her name. I thought that if I could see the passenger manifest, I'd recognize her name."

"You're asking if I can get the flight manifest? That may be problematic."

"Yes, I know, but could you try?"

"I'll see what I can do. But it may take some time, so I hope your project isn't urgent. You'll need to send me the date and flight number."

"Thanks Michel, much appreciated."

Michel was intrigued: Jacques' wife had died last spring—was he in the market for a replacement? To get the manifest, Michel would need to call in a favor. If Jacques had mentioned a man, he would have said he couldn't help, but he was curious to discover the recipient of Jacques' attention.

Chapter Sixty-Three

Lyon

THE DIRECTOR OF PERSONNEL PUSHED a set of papers across her desk: they were the documents Marie-Agnès needed to show that she had completed her internship. Mechanically, she put them into a thin dark red leather Cartier *porte documents*, her attention focused on the woman's jacquard knit ensemble.

"I hope you enjoyed your time with us."

A slight start: "Oh yes, I learned so much, and the kitchen staff was so helpful."

The Personnel Director stood up and extended a perfectly manicured hand. Her long red nails contrasted with Marie-Agnès' short, colorless fingertips that were a consequence of her work in the kitchen.

Perhaps I'll treat myself to a manicure, she thought as she padded down the corridor leading to the lobby, the thick carpet absorbing all sound.

She knew he was there before she saw the short, sandy hair, the slight shoulders, the wire legs of his glasses: a waiter had just poured tea into the cup that Jacques Mornnais was now lifting to his lips. A hot flush moved up her neck to the crown of her head, her breathing was shallow. If the sight of Bruno had frightened her, seeing Jacques Mornnais terrified her. She retraced her steps and exited the building by a rear entrance. At home some forty minutes later, she called Alex.

#   #   #

Trubenne

Alex climbed the stairway to the Rapunzel tower. Indian summer was long gone, but today was surprisingly warm, and she luxuriated in feeling the heat of the sun's rays as they pierced the tower window. She imagined that she had come here as a little girl: it was too bad that she hadn't. Her cellphone rang, breaking her reverie. It was Mag.

"Hi Mag, have you figured out what Blondell's agenda means?"

"I'm not calling about that. You'll never guess who I just saw."

"If it's Bruno, I don't want to know."

"Worse. I just saw Jacques Mornnais."

"That's funny, we had a drink the other night, toasting his exit from our lives. I guess you're going to tell me where you saw him."

"In the restaurant where I was working. It looks like Jacques' with a group that is buying the hotel." Silence. "Alex, are you there?"

"Yes. I'm trying to decide if I'm going to tell Eugene or pretend that we didn't have this conversation."

"Look, why don't I try to find out if Jacques is coming back to the hotel. If he isn't, then there's no point in telling Eugene, is there? But if he is…."

"Yeah, I guess you're right." Alex never liked to stay on the phone for very long: "Call me if you have any more news. And thanks. Be careful, though. Wherever Jacques goes, there's trouble."

Alex walked down the winding stairway: her fairytale moment had evaporated.

Chapter Sixty-Four

Fontainebleau

NICOLAS PAGÈS HAD KEPT METICULOUS records. Buyers' documents were in blue folders, those for sellers in green. On the front of the buyer's file: name, contact details, name of the object purchased, amount, and most recent provenance. Inside, the invoice, proof of payment, and more information on the chain of ownership. The seller's folders contained similar information.

Eugene started to sift through Merv Peters' folders. A wry smile crossed his lips as he remembered his meeting with the pompous, greedy lawyer, sitting behind his desk like a fat weasel. Eugene had been Carl Weller at the time. With the prospect of a finder's fee hanging in the balance, it hadn't been hard to get Merv to make an appointment for him to meet his "art consultant" Jacques Mornnais. Of course, things hadn't turned out exactly as Merv had expected.

Véronique had cut a baguette into three parts, smeared them with butter, and piled on slices of cheese and ham.

"What would you like to drink?" she asked Eugene.

"Water's fine," he grunted as he worked his way through the files.

When he was done, he found that all of Merv's paintings originated with

Jacques Mornnais. Jacques had, in turn, sold them on behalf of the estate of Pavel Korsikov, or anonymous trusts in Switzerland and Hong Kong.

Eugene shook his head, "I wonder if Merv Peters paid attention to the shady provenance of his paintings. I guess he didn't realize that it was Jacques who had provided the tableaux to Nicolas, thereby getting his cut twice: once as a 'consultant' and once from Nicolas. But perhaps Merv had become suspicious; that would explain his obsession with finding Nicolas' records."

Patrick stared ahead and said nothing.

The blue and green folders confirmed what Eugene already knew about Jacques Mornnais. But one element caught his eye: slipped in between Jacques' folders was a file labeled B. EDREMAL, with information on Bruno's lost painting, the one found by Ella. Nicolas hadn't sold the picture, but, as Eugene knew, he had prepared a certificate of authenticity and invented a provenance. He probably didn't realize that the actual owner was a tiny church in Brittany, but he could not have ignored the fact that *Storm Over the Sea* had been stolen. Eugene had brought the painting back to the Church of Sainte Marie Près de la Mer. For the frail priest, Father Jérôme, Eugene was an instrument of divine intervention.

It was late in the afternoon when he finished. "I wouldn't keep these boxes here," he told them, "You never know who else may come visiting."

"What should we do?" asked Véronique, "I can't bear the thought of taking them back to the storage unit."

"No need for that. Why don't you ask one of the shopkeepers if you can store your boxes in their basement for a little while, tell them yours has flooded. I'm sure you'll be able to work it out."

Each time he looked up from the files, Eugene had seen Patrick's battered face. And the boy moved stiffly, no doubt another consequence of the beating Bruno had administered.

Eugene stood up. Patrick's cell phone was in his jacket pocket, and he felt it touch his thigh. He'd been uncertain what to do with the phone, guessing that the cell phone was the only way for Caroline to reach Patrick. At first, Eugene hadn't wanted Patrick to be able to warn his mother that her whereabouts were no longer a secret—if Stokes had figured it out, then others might know as well. But looking at Patrick, he wondered *what would Bruno do when he gets his hands on Caroline—beat her as well?* Eugene felt that he had to try to warn Caroline, even if it meant undoing all his careful detective work. *Time for a slight change of plans.*

As he walked out the rear door, he turned to Patrick, holding out the cellphone. "Here. I believe this belongs to you. I'll bet your mother's been trying to reach you."

He waved as he got into his car, headed for Lyon. "I'll be in touch."

Chapter Sixty-Five

PATRICK STARED AT HIS OLD cellphone. *What's the point? What's he trying to tell me now?* It was a cheap black cellphone, and he had the feeling that it could only bring bad news, so he left it turned off, the digital equivalent of burying his head in the sand.

He walked into the living room, plopped down on the red velvet sofa, the cacophony of objects a blur of color. He tried to chew on his nails, but they were already bitten to the quick. He felt rough, confused, he needed some time to think things through. Véronique, stuck her head into the room: "Patrick, I've already told you that we need to stay out of the living room."

"I need some peace and quiet," he snapped. She sounded irritated and he wasn't in the mood.

"Then go upstairs, don't worry, I won't bother you." He stomped up the stairway, entered the bedroom, closed the door, and locked it to be sure he'd be undisturbed.

He thought back to last September: what had his mother said? That she'd resigned from her job, she would be traveling, and Patrick might not hear from her for a while. Véronique had said that she had seemed weird, but to Patrick, she had always been a bit odd. He remembered the one thousand Euros she had given him; he guessed he knew where that money came from.

Money. That bitch Sandra had tricked him, sent that gorilla to beat the shit out of him, trying to find his mother. Another image crossed his mind: his mother giving him the pendant. At the time, he thought that was kind of strange, part of her weirdness.

He reached for his backpack, nestled in dust bunnies under the bed. His hands were shaking as he zipped open the various outer pockets. In the third one, he found the pendant. He slid his fingers around the edges, felt a tiny bump, pressed it, and the back of the pendant opened. A piece of paper, folded tightly, was caught in the cavity.

Véronique knocked on the door, "Patrick, are you okay?"

"Yes, later," he said, his voice cracking.

It took him a few minutes to extract the paper. His fingernails were of no use, his hands started to shake again. At last, he managed to grab a ragged corner. He unfolded the little square: it was a yellow post-it. Six words: *Patrick, if something happens to me.* Under the message she had written: *Dobrin Bank,* followed by three lines of labeled numbers: *account number, ID, password.*

The rain had started again, the drops streaking the grimy windowpane. Patrick sat on the floor, his back against the bed, watching the undulating curtain of water. He started to laugh. If the guy who beat him up hadn't trashed his room, he would never have thought about the pendant. Access to his mother's bank account had been right in front of him, but the dumb fuck hadn't seen it.

He stopped laughing when he thought of Stokes. Had it only been today that he had appeared? It seemed so long ago. Stokes. Was he working for Sandra? He couldn't figure it all out. But one thing was clear: he had to safeguard the money. He stuffed the paper back into the pendant, slipped it into the zippered pocket, and slid the backpack into the nest of dust bunnies.

#   #   #

"How do you feel about a trip to St. Malo," he asked Véronique that evening.

"Yeah, as soon as we get rid of those boxes, I'd like to get away from here and all this stress."

Nicolas Pagès had been a regular at Asia Garden, a restaurant just up the street. For Corinne and Sum, he embodied the perfect French gentleman. They missed his presence even more than his patronage and were happy to do his daughter a favor. So sorry that she had been flooded, leave your boxes in their cellar as long as you like.

The following day they drove to St. Malo. At this time of year, the traffic was light, and they were greeted by the screeching of seagulls as they approached the coast. In the late afternoon, they checked into a cheap hotel with a view on the English Channel. A walk along the city's famed ramparts, then gazing at the windows of the boutiques, now closed. Véronique said that she'd like to spend some time tomorrow shopping. Patrick said he hoped she wouldn't mind if he didn't join her. He felt like hiking along the beach, and they agreed to meet up in the early evening.

#   #   #

Patrick walked to the ferry terminal and bought a ticket for a day trip to Jersey. The weather clear and crisp, the sea breeze cool but not uncomfortable as the ferry skimmed over the water. He felt the cellphone in his pocket, wondered why he was carrying it around, and he had an urge to turn it on. As if on cue, his phone rang.

It was Caroline calling to say good-bye. She would be leaving for Bangkok in three days.

"Mom, a man came to see me, he told me about the bank. They know your travel plans, so you'd better leave right now. Send me a message when you're in Bangkok."

Before she could say anything, Patrick ended the call. He looked at the phone—nothing but bad news—and turned it off again.

#   #   #

Brussels

Three days later, Bruno and Sandra waited for the check-in counter at Zaventem airport to open. They watched as the usual motley crowd of charter passengers filed by. Tour groups, backpackers, and families: over 300 people. But Caroline was not among them.

Like a deflated balloon, Sandra sat on the floor, covered her face, and lowered her head to her knees. Bruno stood by helplessly. He bent down, lifted her to her feet. "It's not over yet. We'll find her no matter how long it takes."

Chapter Sixty-Six

Pavillon de la Roche, Lyon

JÉRÉMY SLIPPED OUT OF THE kitchen and moved to the side of the building, seeking shelter from the chill wind. He lit a cigarette, inhaled deeply. Smoking might be bad for his health, but it sure felt good. It felt so good that a cough rose deep from his lungs, doubling him over. A gob of phlegm landed on the paving stones just as the phone in his pocket started to vibrate. "Yes," he gasped, still trying to clear his throat.

"Is that you, Jérémy? Are you okay?"

"I'm fine, just had something caught in my throat."

Mag overcame the urge to tell him that he should stop smoking: "So, how are things going? Any news on the new owners?"

"We heard that they're coming for a visit to take a last look at the place before signing the deal. Fingers crossed that they leave the kitchen alone."

"I already told you, I don't think you have anything to worry about. You don't happen to know when they'll be coming?"

Jérémy looked across to the space reserved for VIP parking. "I don't know. The parking lot looks like a Mercedes showroom, so maybe they're here already. Why do you care? You're out of here."

Marie-Agnès thought quickly: "Oh, a friend is writing an article for *Lyon News*, and I said I'd try to see if there is any news about the sale of the hotel."

"If you like, I can check the lunch and dinner reservations, see if there's a VIP group. Can't promise that I'll find anything out, but I can try if that'll make your friend happy."

#　　#　　#

François Tran and his two sons were bringing paintings out of storage, leaning them against the reception room's walls. Alex was curious to unwrap the portraits of her Vesla de Trubenne ancestors and have a look at the still lifes and pastoral scenes. Were there any treasures here? She remembered the meeting with Nicolas Pagès, his forehead shiny with perspiration. They'd need to find an expert—an honest one—to give them an evaluation.

Mag had just called. One of her colleagues had confirmed that the new owners of the Pavillon de la Roche had reservations for lunch today and tomorrow.

"They've reserved a table near the big windows, so Eugene needs to ask to be seated in that part of the restaurant as well."

#　　#　　#

The paintings had slipped from her mind. Alex was pacing back and forth in the château's courtyard, feeling antsy about Eugene being near Jacques. Yet that was what he wanted, and she called him to give him Mag's news.

"Good job! Thank Mag for me."

"I guess this means you'll be putting off your return to Trubenne?"

"Just for a few days. But Alex, can't you tell me what happened when you were at Jacques' office?"

"Not really; it's something that I need to show you."

"Hey, how about if you come up to Lyon for a few days? We could do some touring and you could show me whatever."

It was the invitation Alex had been waiting for, and at any other time she would have been thrilled. But now, Nathalie Martin's phone call was on her mind. There was no point in telling Eugene that she couldn't risk crossing paths with Jacques in Lyon—she was sure he wouldn't take her seriously.

"I'd love to, but I'm kind of tied up right now."

"Huh. Okay… see you in a few days." Eugene didn't get it. The last time they spoke, Alex had practically *begged* him to come back to Trubenne. And now, when he'd invited her to meet him in Lyon, she was *kind of tied up right now.* What the fuck did that mean? Well, he was *kind of tied up right now* himself, and she'd have to be patient.

#   #   #

Bruno had told Michel that he'd be back at work tomorrow evening but that he had personal business to attend to during the day.

The exhaust from an occasional motorcycle echoed off the buildings on Montée de la Grande Côte, a slit in the fabric of silence. The shaft of light from a streetlamp made a pale grey streak in one corner of the room.

Bruno stared at the ceiling: sleep would not come. His mind was a slide show. He was playing in the alleyways of the Cour des Voraces. Now, he was working the travelers in the train stations, on occasion Perrache, usually Part-Dieu. Years ago, he had grown tired of Lyon's weather—blistering hot summers, freezing winters—and hopped a train south to Marseilles. There, he had reinvented himself, moving from petty theft to property development as the right-hand man to one of the players in Marseilles' urban renewal schemes. He worked out, kept in good shape, but more importantly, he learned finance and accounting and understood how intricate deals were structured.

When his boss had some legal troubles, Bruno thought that a change of scenery was called for. One of his boss' financial backers was a man who brought funds from Eastern Europe and placed them in the Marseilles washing machine. Bruno called him and offered his services. And wound up moving to Paris to work for Jacques Mornnais, a seemingly mismatched partnership that would nevertheless last for twelve years.

Jacques took him under his wing, provided him with a room in his château, and gave him more and more responsibility as time went on. Bruno had worked with Jacques on complex financing arrangements. He supervised the painters who created the forgeries, dealt with the art dealers who sold those paintings, and liaised with the network Jacques used to procure stolen artwork.

He remembered his last trip to visit Jean-Marc, their man in Brittany. He and Jean-Marc had started to work on a side deal that didn't concern Jacques. Jean-Marc's gang had stolen a painting for him that hung in a small country church, and they left it for Bruno in a bar in Dijon. Bruno had picked it up, but the story ended there. The picture had disappeared. But how? He couldn't remember. That fucking lost painting. He thought of going to see Jean-Marc, explain what happened, but he had no idea where in Brittany the fucker lived. Tarek had always done the driving, and he'd slept off hangovers during their trips.

Drinking. That was another thing that puzzled Bruno. He remembered being a hard drinker, spending time in after-hours bars and clubs, still able to go to work the following day, although Jacques had told him a couple of times to cut down on his boozing. But now, even the smell of alcohol repulsed him. What had happened to him when he blacked out, he wondered? And there was yet another thing: women. He couldn't count the number he had had, all colors, all shapes, all ages, even though he preferred the younger ones. But now, lust, like his alcoholism, had left him.

The American. Smooth, unruffled. In a crazy way, he sometimes reminded him of Jacques.

Jacques. He heard the cold, flat voice: *I don't know how you got my number, but I'm sorry, Bruno Edremal is dead. If this is a joke, it's not funny. Good-bye.* Then Jacques walked towards him: "You're dead, Bruno, go back into the river."

"No," he screamed and opened his eyes. The back of his head was drenched with sweat. He glimpsed a sliver of light through a gap in the curtains. It was daybreak, and soon they would be going to lunch.

Chapter Sixty-Seven

Croix-Rousse, Lyon

A THOUGHT LINGERED AT THE edge of Marie-Agnès' memory, just beyond her grasp. Again, she opened Blondell's agenda and leafed through it, going backward in time. There were two appointments marked M.P. that she assumed were with Merv Peters—only a few days apart, just before Blondell's accident. She saw an entry labeled *Lawyers New York*—the word *Will* was underlined. Further back, she came across the trip they had taken to visit Blondell's family in the United States. Mag recalled the family compound at Lake Mahopac and Aunt Melissa's house in Virginia. She'd enjoyed their stay at Lake Mahopac, but the visit to Melissa had been a letdown. The old lady's memory sometimes failed her, she had rambled on about the sale of her late husband's collection, and there had been awkward silences.

Aunt Melissa, Cousin Claudia. Wait a minute. She booted up her computer. Where was the email she had received from Claudia? A few minutes later, it was on her screen:

Dear Mag,

I sent this email to Blondell, but it bounced back to me, so I guess I don't have the right address. So I'm forwarding the message on to you, I hope you will receive it and share it with her. See below.

Thanks and Warm greetings, Claudia

Then:

Dear Blondell,

I'm helping Mom to sort through Dad's papers. There's a lot of junk that we've thrown out, but we came across two photos: one that looks like a drawing, the other is a painting. Mom says they look familiar, so perhaps they are the famous "missing" paintings she talks about. They were not among the works sold at the auction. Maybe Dad was only thinking about buying them? I guess this opens more doors than it closes, but for what it's worth, I've scanned the photos and am attaching them. I hope you'll be back for a longer visit soon.

Love, Claudia

When she'd first received it, Mag had skimmed the email, only glancing at the attachments before forwarding it on to Blondell. Now she took the time to read the email slowly. She remembered Melissa insisting that there had been two paintings missing from the auctioneers' report. Mag had gone with Blondell to visit the auctioneer. He had insisted that all the works had been accounted for. She opened the attachments. The drawing was not familiar, but she felt her breath shortening as she looked at the photo of the painting: a Cubist rendition of a woman in a red dress. She unfolded the photocopies, smoothed them out on her desk. There was no doubt in her mind: she was looking at a printout of the photo Claudia had sent. But what about the second photocopy? It looked like the same painting, but this time it was hanging on a wall.

Was this the same painting that Alex had seen in Merv Peters' office? There was only one way to tell.

#   #   #

It was Mag on the line. "It's me again. I think I have an idea of what was on Blondell's mind."

Alex smiled. "Tell me all about it. I've been missing our plotting and scheming."

"Remember when Blondell and I went to the U.S., we visited her aunt Melissa? She's an old woman, and I thought she was a bit confused. She insisted that two paintings had disappeared from the auction of her late husband's collection. Blondell and I checked with the auctioneer, and all seemed to be in order."

"Yes, I recall you talking about her aunt."

"Anyhow, shortly after we returned to Paris, I received an email from Blondell's cousin Claudia. She sent it to me because she hadn't been able to get through to Blondell. What Claudia said was that she found two photos among her father's papers, and she thought Blondell might be interested. Well, I was so busy at the time that I just glanced at it and forwarded it on to Blondell. When I looked at the photos, they meant nothing to me, and I forgot about them. Until now. I'm going to forward the email to you—please open the attachments and tell me what you think."

While Mag was talking, Alex booted up her computer. She heard the ping of an incoming message, opened the email, downloaded the photos.

"Holy shit, that's the painting I saw in Merv Peters' office."

"Are you sure it's the same one?"

"As sure as I can be without having the painting in front of me."

"Alex, there's something else. There was a second photocopy in Blondell's agenda; it looks like the same painting, only hanging on a wall. What do you suppose this all means? When Blondell called me, it was just after she'd been to Merv's office. She sounded upset, and when I asked what the matter was, she said it was about Claudia's email with the photos. We need to figure out what happened when she met Merv."

"If it *is* the same painting, then how did it get from her uncle's house to Merv Peters office? That would be pretty upsetting. And how did Blondell get that second photo? Was that what upset her? When Eugene gets back from Lyon, I'm going to ask him if he has any ideas."

Chapter Sixty-Eight

CAROLINE THOUGHT SHE'D START TO lose it if the trip lasted much longer. Brussels-Amsterdam-Dubai-Bangkok. Finally, she checked into her hotel, and collapsed fully dressed on the queen-sized bed. After the stress of the past few weeks, she slept for fourteen hours and woke up feeling groggy, her head hollow and aching. She had already picked out the bank where she would open her account, and in the afternoon met with a friendly young man to do the paperwork. A wistful thought: *Patrick could have/should have gotten a similar job—helping customers to open accounts didn't seem to be very difficult.*

Back at the hotel, she logged into her account at Dobrin Bank to make the first transfer. A chill ran up her spine, the muscles in her throat tightened, her heart beating as if she'd just run up a flight of stairs. Her breath returned; her eyes had not been deceiving her, the account had been closed. Despite the air conditioning, the palms of her hands were damp, her armpits moist. *Fucking Patrick.*

\#   \#   \#

Fontainebleau

More leaves had fallen into the front yard, and Patrick went outside to rake them up. Doing simple manual tasks calmed him; *maybe I should look for work as a gardener. It certainly beats making sushi or housebreaking.* He put the pile of leaves into a large grey bin liner and went back into the house—there was no point in overdoing it.

His old cell phone sat on the kitchen table. He turned it on, saw that the battery was low, and plugged it in to recharge. He heard a "ping," there were three missed calls from a number he did not recognize. But he was pretty sure he knew who the caller was, and why they were trying to reach him.

Véronique was at her apartment in Paris. They had now been living together for a few months, and he was glad to have some time by himself. The house was so quiet, only the whir of the refrigerator and the sound of the wind rattling the windows marred the silence. He'd probably get into a shouting match with his mother, and Véronique had no need to know what he had done.

That night, sleep eluded Patrick, as he ran over scenarios for the conversation he would have with his mother. It was two a.m. when he went outside to smoke a cigarette, returning inside just in time to answer the phone.

"Patrick, what the fuck have you done?"

"Hi, Mom, great to talk to you too."

"Don't give me that crap," she shrieked. "What have you done with the money?"

"Calm down, you should thank me, I've put it in a safe place where no one can touch it. Don't you see, I'm protecting you from Sandra and her pals." He could hear her breathing. Perhaps she was thinking about what he said.

"Patrick," her voice low, rising to a crescendo. "Which language do I have to speak to tell you that I NEED MONEY."

"Yes, I know," and he told her what they were going to do.

Chapter Sixty-Nine

Paris

SINCE THE FUNERAL EARLIER IN the month, Merv had been waiting to hear from Jacques or hoping that, like a malevolent fly, he'd circle into La Belle Fermière one morning. But Jacques was busy elsewhere, the portly lawyer far from his thoughts.

Merv went up to his secret garden, as he did almost every morning before leaving for work. There was an empty space where the Picasso had hung. With the unpleasant American woman dead, he was glad that *Woman in Red* now graced the wall of his office. His spirits rose until he gazed at the Bernard Buffet. He had purchased it to replace another work by the same artist that had been stolen. Jacques had said that the previous owner was a trust; in other words, he had no idea who the painting's real owner had been. The muscles around his mouth and eyes contracted to produce a frown as Merv closed the door to his gallery and set the alarm.

He felt too depressed to make his usual morning visit to La Belle Fermière and walked directly to his office. His secretary brought in the morning's post and placed it on his desk— he liked to open the mail himself. There was the usual correspondence from fellow lawyers, banks, and insurance companies, and a few checks that he put to one side. At the bottom of the pile, there was an envelope marked "personal and confidential." He opened it absentmindedly, still thinking about the Buffet and its stark, black outlines. On a plain white sheet of paper, he read:

While Merv was in his office, making all his money
The king was in his castle, thinking how it was funny
That the painters were doing pictures
That were to become fixtures
On Merv's walls
And in many other halls.
While Merv was in his office, working on a deal.
The king sent his agents far and wide to steal.
And afterward to sell
To those who knew it well
But turned a blind eye
Instead of taking the time to verify

The crude rhyme could have been written by a child, but its message was chillingly clear. Who could have sent it? And why? He looked at the envelope. The address was printed in capital letters, the postmark the Rue du Louvre post office here in Paris. His first impulse was to find Jacques and show him the message. But then he thought about Nicolas Pagès: Merv had been haunted by the idea that Jacques had had something to do with Nicolas' death. Of course, he had no proof, and the letter was probably nothing more than a nasty prank. Still, he felt it might be better to keep it to himself.

Chapter Seventy

Au Plaisir des Sens, Lyon

JACQUES WAS SEATED AT A long table, surrounded by members of the Brezikstan government and private investors from the former USSR republic. Of course, the "private" investors all had links to the government, an overlapping of interests that he specialized in managing. Jacques had a long-standing relationship with Brezikstan, rich in uranium, and ruled by the same family for over twenty years. He advised them on marketing uranium to France, guided them through complex investment structures. He even occasionally obtained and sold them a painting that had struck their fancy.

He prepared to relish the lunch that represented the culmination of his most recent efforts when two men were seated nearby. They made no noise, but turned his head in their direction.

He saw Bruno first, then Eugene Spector's profile. He removed his glasses, polished the lenses, and replaced them. Now, Bruno was getting up, coming over to him.

"Hello, Jacques. Long time, no see. How have you been?"

Jacques stood up. "Excuse me for a moment, please." He put his hand on Bruno's elbow, guiding him away from the table.

"I'm glad to see you. This is so strange. A body washed up from the river, the police said it was you. I don't understand—what happened?"

"It's a long story. I see you're with your friends from Brezikstan. Can we talk after you're done with lunch? We've got a lot to catch up on, don't we?"

Jacques looked over at Eugene. "Who's your friend, don't I know him?"

"Yeah, you might. He's an American guy, helping me to sort things out. Anyhow, see you after lunch, okay?" And with that, Bruno walked back to his table.

"Please excuse me, that was an old acquaintance," Jacques said as he regained his seat.

"No problem," said the Brezikstan Finance minister. "For a moment I thought it was that man who worked for you, what was his name?"

"Bruno, but no, it's not him, although I admit there is a resemblance."

#   #   #

The meal started with a slice of pan-fried foie gras, followed by scallops in garlic sauce. But Jacques had no appetite. Like a child, he played with his food, cutting it in pieces and spreading it around the plate. With one part of his mind, he continued a pleasant, superficial conversation with the members of the Brezikstan delegation; with the other part he calculated how he would handle Bruno. Where had Bruno gone? Why had he disappeared? And what was he doing with Jacques' nemesis, Eugene Spector? It couldn't be good. He caught quick glimpses of Bruno and Eugene; they were smiling, engrossed in a discussion. Jacques looked forward to the end of the meal with both curiosity and apprehension.

"Did you recognize anyone at his table," asked Eugene.

"Yeah, they're from the government of Brezikstan. I think the guy with the yellow tie is the finance minister."

"You didn't mention Brezikstan when we talked about Jacques' activities."

"Guess I forgot." Bruno smiled. "He does a lot of work for them, consults on their uranium contracts with the French government."

"I see. I guess Jacques must do other work for them."

"Yeah, he puts together investment deals, sometimes cleans dirty money, whatever. Why are you so interested?"

"I'm not, really. Just curious, I guess. Remember to be vague about what happened in the château; say you don't remember, which is still partly true. Don't ask about the missing painting. See if Jacques brings it up, though I doubt that he will. And Bruno, my friend, just keep your eye on the prize as we say. You want to get the money he owes you and go your own way, right?"

#   #   #

The meal was finished, and Jacques' luncheon partners were anxious to return to Paris for an evening of entertainment. Bruno and Eugene approached as the men departed. Jacques, too, looked as if he was ready to leave.

"I'm afraid I can't spend much time with you," Jacques protested. "I'm expected back in Paris later today. Why don't you call me, and we'll arrange a time to talk?"

"I did call you, Jacques, and you hung up on me. So I'd rather that we talk now if you don't mind."

Eugene was surprised at how articulate Bruno could be. Perhaps it was because he'd entered Jacques' orbit.

"I'm sorry, but I thought your call was a hoax. Tell me what happened."

"Well, to make a long story short, I was in the château, and I blacked out. I must have fallen into the river, and the next thing I knew, I was here in Lyon. For a while, I couldn't remember very much. But now my memory has started to return in bits and pieces. "

Jacques' eyes were two black orbs in his pale face. "That is a rather short story, my friend. How do you suppose you found yourself in the river? You're lucky that you got out alive. I can tell you that the police fished a body out of the river and decided it was yours. The man was cremated, and I have the ashes in a box in my office. It's all so bizarre. But my friend, if you're looking to get your job back, I don't think that will be possible. Things have changed since you've been gone."

"I understand, Jacques. But there's the little question of the money that you owe me. I don't remember the exact amount, but I do remember that I kept the records for you."

Jacques' dark eyes had lightened up, now that he saw where the discussion was headed. "Ah. Yes, of course. Why don't you come up to the château, and we can settle our accounts. But tell me, I'm curious: aside from bookkeeping, what else do you remember?"

"Like I said, just bits and pieces. But I'd rather that we meet in Paris if that's okay with you."

"Very well, Bruno. Shall we say next week? Call me, and I'll let you know the time and place." He paused. For the first time, looked at Eugene Spector, "And what is your interest in all of this, Eugene?"

"Oh, it's another long story, but let's say that I happened by chance to run into Bruno, and it turns out that we have a mutual friend."

Jacques was about to reply when his BlackBerry started to vibrate. "Yes," he answered, listening to the caller. Then he ended the call with, "Yes, that's fine." Then to Eugene and Bruno: "I'm sorry, but I need to leave you gentlemen. Let's keep in touch." And with that he exited the dining room.

The drive back to Château d'Hélène took only two hours, but it was enough time for Jacques to make his arrangements.

\#   \#   \#

In the taxi on their way back from the restaurant, Bruno looked at Eugene: "He's going to pay me and then have me killed, I know how he works."

"Then you'd best be careful, right? I'm going out of town for a few days, but call me if you need help." One thing satisfied Eugene: now Bruno knew what it was like when the shoe was on the other foot.

Chapter Seventy-One

Paris

THE WEATHER TURNED COLDER, AND Bruno had gone to De Fursac near the Place des Jacobins to buy some new clothes. Today he wore a tweed jacket, a white shirt open at the collar, impeccably tailored jeans, and low boots. He had lost weight since the beginning of the year, and he felt that he was returning to the body he had lost many years ago. He walked slowly past the cars parked outside the restaurant, to see if they were already there. But then he realized that there would be plenty of time for them to take up their positions later.

The revolving door, the muted light, the décor, it was all so familiar. Jacques was already seated, a glass of yellow-orange liquid in his hand; *it must be his bloody mango juice.* They made small talk: about the weather—it was cooling down; about Mila, killed in an automobile accident—he was sorry to hear that—until the waiter came to take their orders.

Jacques perused the wine list. "What do you feel like drinking?"

"Badoit would be fine," said Bruno.

Jacques raised his eyebrows, "I'm sorry, you're not having anything to drink?"

"Just water, thanks. It's the strangest thing, I've lost my taste for alcohol ever since my accident. Don't even like the smell."

Bruno reflected that Jacques looked disappointed; it was always easier to take care of someone if he'd had a few drinks.

"Here." Jacques placed a cream-colored envelope with the *Artixia* logo on the table. Bruno removed the single sheet of paper.

He smiled, "Yeah, that looks about right. I've got to trust you. There's still a lot that I can't recall." Jacques was a little cheat, of course. Bruno saw right away that Jacques had left out the commission on two silver chalices. But that was okay; it was better to let Jacques think he couldn't remember everything.

"Best restaurant in Paris," said Bruno, between mouthfuls of *crème de céleri aux truffles,* followed by filet of sole with Jerusalem artichokes. They skipped dessert, and it was only when the table had been cleared, and espresso served, that Jacques removed an envelope from his briefcase and handed it to Bruno.

"Here you go, my friend. I think this settles our accounts."

"Thanks, Jacques. Hope you don't mind if I run off now. I've got a train to catch."

Jacques nodded; he was already on the phone. Behind him, Bruno walked casually through the restaurant until he reached the kitchen. He pushed the swinging doors. A huge man, a network of thin purple lines extending outward from a bulbous red nose, was delivering an expletive-laced tirade to a cowering apprentice chef. In that way, he maintained the tradition of ritual bullying that gave him such pleasure. It was mid-afternoon, and he needed a drink, something that his former drinking pal could sympathize with.

"Pierrot, my man," Bruno called out, bringing a sudden stop to the stream of vulgarity. The giant's face broke into a smile as he approached Bruno and put his arms around him.

"Bruno, I heard you were dead! Good to see you're alive and well!"

"Don't believe all those nasty rumors." Holding Pierrot close, he whispered, "Can you let me out the back?

"Always up to something shady, aren't we?" chuckled Pierre-Henri as he led Bruno to the employees' entrance.

"Fuck you." Bruno grinned. "I'll be in touch."

#   #   #

Jean-Charles was polishing the Mercedes' spotless exterior as Jacques approached.

"Did you see anything?" he asked as Jean-Charles held the door open for him.

"No, sir, I didn't. But I had to move the car a few minutes ago, so maybe I missed something."

Two men sat in a black Citroen that was double-parked in front of the restaurant. Jacques walked over to it and knocked on the window. The driver shook his head, started the engine, and pulled away.

Jacques scowled. Bruno had given them the slip. He'd probably ducked out of the back of the restaurant—he should have warned the killers about that. It dawned on Jacques that the circumstances had changed. The old Bruno had had the drunkard's insouciance, even when sober. They had made a good team, Bruno knew almost as much about his business as Jacques did, and he had never betrayed his trust. At least not that he knew of. There was something different about Bruno now. Not only was he as sober as the leader of an AA meeting, but there was a different toughness about him as well. His story about blacking out and turning up in Lyon—it was unbelievable. As for his amnesia, Jacques didn't believe a word of it. What had really happened? And what was Bruno doing with that troublesome American? He wished that they hadn't seen him meeting with the delegation from Brezikstan—he was sure that Bruno recognized the finance minister. What might he have told the American? It was another royal fuck-up.

He had no choice. Bruno had to go, and this time permanently.

Chapter Seventy-Two

Lyon

THE EARLY EVENING DARKNESS HAD settled on the city, snuffing out hope the way a gust of wind blows out a candle. Things had not gotten any better for Sandra since the fruitless trip to Brussels. The atmosphere at work was heavy, distrustful. Everyone was prepared to believe that she had been in on the theft, even if there was no proof. She poured herself another glass of Côtes du Rhône and stared aimlessly at the brochures and supermarket coupons that littered the dining room table—she hadn't had the energy to throw them away.

The door to the apartment opened. It was Bruno.

"You're back," she said, somewhere between a question and a statement.

"Yes," he mumbled, and went into his room, closed the door. He counted the money Jacques had given him at lunch, divided it into two unequal piles. He took two rubber bands out of a box on the little desk and bound the money into two rolls that he put in his pockets.

He walked over to Sandra, "So, how are you feeling?"

She sighed. "The same. better not to talk about it. Oh, by the way, the doctor you saw last June, he called, wanted to know how you were doing. He asked if you'd like to come in to see him. You do remember him, don't you?"

"Yes, I remember him. I remember many things now. If you want, I'll call him, see when I can stop by." He put his hand in his pocket, and withdrew the smaller roll. "Here," he said. "This is for you. It should cover all the money you've laid out for me. And why don't you buy yourself a dress, go get your hair done, maybe you'll feel a little better? Or not so bad." He handed her the roll of bills.

"Oh, Bruno." Sandra's eyes filled with tears. "You didn't have to do this."

"It's okay. A guy owed me some money, and I want you to have part of it."

She sniffled, pulled her arm across her nose, and wiped the tears from her cheeks. "That bitch Caroline, I just can't stop thinking about what she did."

Bruno took one of her hands, it was the first time he had touched his sister: "I promise you, I'll find her and get your money. Just be patient."

She tried to smile, but the tears flowed again. Bruno went back to his bedroom to pack his suitcase. Later that evening, Bruno told Sandra that he'd be leaving Lyon in a few days and would let her know once he was settled.

Chapter Seventy-Three

THOMAS SMITH TOOK A CHANCE that the concierge wouldn't notice him and stood in the shadow of the *porte-cochère* across the street from *Artixia's* office. He remembered that Jacques had kept him waiting when they met in the apartment on Rue Lalo, and he decided that wouldn't happen again. They were to meet at 11 a.m., and at 11:10, when he saw no movement, he wondered if Jacques was indeed coming from his office. He was about ready to give up and run to the café when he saw Jacques emerge and head out in the direction of the café. A tall man—he'd seen him on Rue Lalo—walked a few paces behind Jacques.

Thomas Smith followed both figures. When he arrived at Le Vigny, he pretended that he didn't see Henri leaning against the counter. He scanned the room and saw Jacques standing in front of a row of empty tables, already set for lunch.

"Mr. Mornnais," he called out. "Sorry to be late. I hope I haven't kept you waiting." Jacques scowled and slid onto the banquette, leaving Thomas the seat with his back to the room.

"What is it that you want?"

"At first, I thought that the theft of Tony Perryman's Mondrian was a one-off, but from what I've been able to put together, there's a clear pattern."

"That's interesting. I don't see a pattern, other than just a series of coincidences. And as I told you earlier, you have no proof that the painting you think you saw on some yacht belonged to Mr. Perryman. This is all falsehoods and idle conjecture, *slander* really. And if that's it, you'll have to excuse me." Jacques started to slide off the banquette.

"No, Mr. Mornnais, that's not quite it. I think the people who were robbed would be interested by my conjectures, don't you agree? Especially when they see that they're not an isolated case. I think there's someone dishonest in your organization, someone who's been tipping off the thieves. What I propose is that you hire me as a consultant, to keep an eye on things, see that it doesn't happen again. And then I'll forget about contacting the victims."

A waiter came up to them; he asked if they were planning on eating lunch, otherwise he'd need the table.

"We'll be leaving," said Jacques. A pensive look came over his face. "A consultant, eh? You're a bright young man. Perhaps that's not a bad idea. Can you give me twenty-four hours to think it over, make the necessary arrangements? We'll have to discuss your fee and things like that."

Thomas Smith nodded, and the two men stood up. "I'll call you tomorrow afternoon, then," said Jacques.

Thomas walked out of the café; he'd need to be careful that the tall man was not following him. There was another man at the bar, shorter than Henri, with a stocky, muscular build. Jacques nodded to him as he walked out of the café and to his car, which was waiting at the curbside.

#   #   #

It's not that Thomas Smith didn't pay attention. But when he didn't see what he was looking for—the tall man from Rue Lalo—he didn't notice the short, stocky man who was shadowing him. The stocky man's name was Stéphane, and he was one of those faceless men who you passed on the street without ever seeing them.

Thomas took the metro to the Etoile station, and then hopped on the number 31 bus. He got off at Pont Cardinet and returned to his hotel on Rue Boursault. The sky was leaden, a cold, damp wind blew, pushing bits of paper and leaves into piles in the gutter.

He went out to a bakery, bought himself a sandwich and a bottle of water, and took his purchases back to his hotel room. He sat by the window, eating his sandwich and watching the trains departing from and arriving at Gare Saint-Lazare. He felt suddenly tired, the morning's tension draining from his body. A short nap was in order. When he woke up, he made a phone call; there was no answer, but instead of hanging up he left a message: "Hi Dad, it's Tom. I think I found the Mondrian that was stolen from the house. And I discovered that it's part of a larger art theft ring. I'm returning to New York tomorrow. I'll call you when I get in." He looked out the window again; the sun was already low in the sky, black clouds had rolled in, and soon it would be nightfall. He wanted to visit the Square des Batignolles one more time. He didn't know when he'd be back here again.

Stéphane had been walking up and down Rue Boursault, trying to stay warm and keeping an eye pealed on the hotel. If the man didn't come out, he thought of calling Henri to ask his advice. But just at that moment, Thomas Smith exited the hotel. Stephane followed him to Square des Batignolles, and trailed behind him as Thomas ambled through the park. It was 5 p.m., the sky had turned a darker shade of gray. Closing time was less than an hour away. The park was deserted: mothers and housekeepers with children in tow had already headed home. Thomas sat on a bench by the pond, watching the ducks swimming back and forth. He felt at peace and excited at the same time. His father would be proud of him, and Jacques Mornnais would be held accountable. Thomas Smith hardly noticed the man who sat down nearby. The man was reading a newspaper, and at the back of his mind Thomas Smith thought it odd that he was reading a newspaper in the dwindling light. As the thought developed, he felt a searing pain in his side, then another pain in his chest. It was his last thought.

Thomas Smith slipped into a reclining position on the bench, a thin stream of blood beginning to drip to the ground. Stéphane looked around. The park was empty, and he quickly went through the man's pockets until he found his room card and walked away. A few minutes later, as the guardian was making her rounds, she came across Thomas Smith's lifeless body.

Stéphane returned to the hotel, asked if he could book a room for the night. The desk clerk considered his small backpack, asked Stéphane to pay for the night in advance, and gave him his room card. Upstairs, he walked along the corridor, the threadbare carpet barely blocking out the noise of his footsteps. He started to try each of the rooms, first listening for voices, then slipping Thomas Smith's room card into the locks of the unoccupied rooms. On the fourth try, he got lucky.

Inside, he found a laptop computer and a folder with an airplane ticket. Stéphane slowly opened the door. The corridor was empty, and he picked up the computer and the folder and carried them down the hallway to his room. He crammed them into his backpack and waited until midnight. Downstairs, he checked that the front door was unlocked and that no one was manning the front desk. He returned to his room, put on his backpack, and left the hotel.

#   #   #

Trubenne

Alex had done a search on Google for '*Hotel Bour*' and three names turned up: Le Bourg Tibourg. Hotel La Bourdonnais. Hotel Boursault. The first two were upscale hotels, and although she doubted that Thomas Smith was staying there, she tried them anyway. She came up emptyhanded and tried the third hotel on her list. *This is my last chance to find him, please be there.*

"Thomas Smith? No, there is no one by that name staying here." Alex made a stab in the dark: "Is there another guest named Thomas?"

A moment's hesitation before the desk clerk replied, "I'm sorry, Madame, but that information is confidential."

#   #   #

On a cold day that smelled of showers and rotting leaves, Stéphane descended the steps that led from the quay to the edge of the river Seine. He stood at the water's edge, and seeing no one nearby, he bent and slid the computer into the river. At the office on Rue de Prony, Jacques had taken the airplane ticket out of the folder and studied it; he scowled and shook his head, then he smiled as he dropped a lighted match on the ticket in the sink. Nothing remained of Thomas Smith's ill-begotten project, or so he thought.

Chapter Seventy-Four

November 2010
Lyon

ON ALL SAINTS DAY THE weather turned cold and gray, with a thin, bone-chilling drizzle. Eugene looked out the window giving onto Quai de Saône, the river mirroring the overcast sky. The only sign of life was an open florist shop. A few people, willing to brave the depressing weather, were buying potted chrysanthemums to take to the cemetery.

Mid-morning Travis and Julie emerged from their bedroom. Eugene, engaged in the hypnotic exercise of surfing the net, looked up and smiled. "Making the most of All Saints Day, I see." Travis grinned, sat on the sofa opposite Eugene, cradling a hot mug of coffee.

"I think I've imposed on your privacy for too long," said Eugene. "Thanks for putting up with me, I'll be leaving tomorrow."

"It's been our pleasure. So you're finished with your business in Lyon?"

"About as finished as it can be, I guess."

Travis' looked out over the rim of his mug, eyebrows raised like two half-moons, "Oh really."

"Yeah. It looks like our little bird, Caroline, got away. Probably living the life out in the East. Thanks for your help, anyway."

"And the dead art dealer?"

"Nicolas Pagès? You said to consider the file closed, so I did."

"Mm. I shouldn't be telling you this, but I will. Jacques Mornnais is untouchable, there's someone high up in the French government protecting him, probably because he seems to control the uranium deals with Brezikstan. So forget about the forgeries and the thefts, forget about the dead art dealer. Go to Trubenne and leave well enough alone."

"Those sound like wise words," said Eugene, and he went to pack his bags.

#   #   #

Trubenne

The Mistral blew sheets of rain against the neoclassical façade of the Nîmes train station. Inside, it was cold and drafty, and Alex tightened the scarf around her neck and hurried to meet Eugene's train. Her hair was plastered to her head by the rain, but Eugene saw only clear blue eyes and rosy cheeks. They embraced, standing under the cavernous ceiling until the chill sent them out to the car.

"I missed you," he whispered.

"Me too," she replied. Forgotten was her frustration at how long he'd been away, forgotten was his resentment at her declining to come to meet him in Lyon.

#   #   #

Later that night, Alex snuggled up to Eugene; Richard insisted on turning down the heat at night, and the old stone walls held in the chill night air.

"I realized that it's just about a year since you and your sister came to rent my house in Washington. It's hard to believe how much has happened over the past twelve months."

"Yes," he murmured, "but I hope you're not going to go over all that again."

Alex gave no sign that she'd heard what he was trying to say: *please Alex, no more questions.* Instead, she continued: "But there's something else. Actually, a few things. They all have to do with the week I spent working for Jacques."

Eugene had started to feel drowsy, that lovely zone between sleep and wakefulness where all the barriers are down. He came back with a start. "Tell me about it. All of it."

"First of all, I think Jacques suspects something. He sent a man around— probably Henri—to check on Nathalie Martin, and the man learned that Nathalie is short with dark hair, so definitely not me."

"How do you know that?"

"Because Nathalie called to tell me that a neighbor called her and told her. By the way, she was not pleased."

"Well, Jacques may know that you're *not* Nathalie, but that doesn't mean he knows who you are."

"I know, but it gives me the creeps to think that he's looking for me. You probably think it sounds silly, but I was worried about running into him when you asked me to come to Lyon. And there's more. While I was working for Jacques, I met a man named Thomas Smith. I don't know what his business with Jacques was, but he left an envelope for Jacques, and I managed to take a picture of the contents. It's just one sheet of paper, and it looks like this Mr. Smith thinks there's a connection between collectors featured in *Artixia* and thefts of artwork from their homes." She smiled and ran her finger along his jaw. "And I thought that could be of interest, you know, give you some leverage when you approach Jacques. That's what you're looking for, right?"

Eugene was wide awake now. "Could be. Nice work, my friend, very nice work."

"One more thing."

"Oh, you're on a roll."

"I have a hunch that Thomas Smith is staying at a hotel on Rue Boursault in the seventeenth, but under another name, and I thought it might be worth a trip to Paris to try to see him. What do you think?"

"What do I think? You're a remarkable woman, do you know that?" The golden flecks danced in his eyes as he kissed the hollow of her neck.

"I don't feel very remarkable. If you must know, I'm just trying to keep my head above water." It was a statement in search of a question—*why do you say that?*—but none was forthcoming.

"Well, I think you're mistaken."

A sigh and a smile. "Maybe," she said.

"Let's talk about all this tomorrow morning." Eugene took a deep breath, drew Alex closer to him and fell asleep. Alex remained awake for some time, thinking about Jacques Mornnais.

Chapter Seventy-Five

"ARE YOU DONE WITH YOUR affairs in Lyon, then?" Richard asked as they ate breakfast.

"Oh, very much so. I'm looking forward to life in the countryside. It seems like there's plenty of work to be done here," said Eugene.

"It never ends," sighed Alex.

"Maybe Eugene can help us decide where to hang some of the paintings. I'm not sure that I want all those Vesla de Trubenne ancestors looking down at me," laughed Charlotte.

"Speaking of paintings," said Alex, "Marie-Agnès told me the most incredible story. It has to do with Blondell. Mag felt that Blondell was distraught when she called to invite her over for dinner, and we have always wondered why."

"And?" asked Charlotte.

Alex recounted the story of her meeting with Merv Peters, Mag's discovery of the Murakami agenda with the photocopies, and the email from Claudia.

When she finished, Charlotte asked, "What are you going to do now?"

"I was thinking about paying another visit to Mr. Merv Peters."

"But what will you tell him, Alex? We don't know if Blondell's uncle ever even owned the painting in the photograph. And where was the second photo taken, the one with the painting hanging on a wall?" asked Eugene.

"We can make some assumptions, though," said Alex. "Like I'm going to assume that when Blondell opened Claudia's email, she recognized the painting. According to her agenda, she met Merv Peters three times in the week preceding her death. So, I'm going to assume that it had something to do with the painting. It could be that Merv gave her the second photo, or maybe she took it herself. I'll bet he was trying to sell the Picasso to Blondell, and that she suspected that it was her uncle's missing tableau."

"That's a nice story, but unsupported by the facts. We don't even know when Merv Peters acquired the Picasso, or even if it *is* a Picasso." Eugene stopped to think, "but look, I believe I can help you there. We located Nicolas Pagès' files, and if Merv bought the Picasso through him, then there ought to be a record. I'll have to make a trip to Fontainebleau, but why not, if that will put your mind to rest."

#   #   #

Later in the day, Eugene called Patrick. "How's your mother?"

"Oh, she's fine, thanks."

"I was wondering if I could stop by, I'd like to check something in Véronique's father's files. It won't take long."

"Um…" There was hesitation in Patrick's voice. Was the boy really going to say no? But, after a pause, he said, "Okay, so when would you like to come?"

"How about tomorrow, does that work for you?"

#   #   #

Eugene left Trubenne early the following morning and arrived in Fontainebleau in the late afternoon. Patrick came to the door. He was glad that Véronique was in Paris—it just made things easier. He and Eugene walked up the street to Asia Garden, where Sum and Corinne were preparing for the evening clients. "Do you mind if we take a quick look at the files in the basement?"

In a few minutes, Eugene had found the file for the sale to Mervin Peters of "Woman in Red." He checked through the records for Jacques Mornnais and discovered that Nicolas had obtained the painting from Jacques. "I'll just take these," he said to Patrick. It was cold and damp in the basement, and Patrick was eager to return to the warmth of the restaurant. "Sure, whatever you want. Let's get out of here, I'm cold."

"Let me invite you to dinner," Eugene said to Patrick. He felt he owed that to Sum and Corinne, and he knew that Patrick wouldn't turn down a free meal. "Can you put me up for tonight?" he asked Patrick over dinner.

"No problem."

Eugene was long gone when Patrick awoke. He sensed that Patrick felt ill at ease in his presence, and he hoped that they would not be seeing each other again.

#   #   #

Eugene arrived back at Trubenne the following afternoon, and he was now in the warm, brightly lit kitchen. He filled two mugs with coffee for himself and Alex. They read through the two thin folders—blue for Merv Peters, green for Jacques Mornnais—that lay open on the table.

Given the scant amount of information, it had not taken very long. Eugene Googled Dr. Whittaker, Blondell's uncle; he'd already done that earlier in the year, but he wanted to check the man's obituary. According to the file, Merv Peters had paid eighty thousand euros for Pablo Picasso's "Woman in Red," around a year before Dr. Whittaker's death.

"At that price, it has to be a fake," said Eugene.

"Coming from Jacques Mornnais, I would definitely say so. And did you see the provenance, "Estate of Pavel Korsikov?" Don't make me laugh! How could Merv have fallen for this scam?"

"Ah, Alex, self-delusion overrides rational thinking all the time. Merv probably felt superior, getting an unheard-of good deal on a Picasso. I guess he ignored the saying *if it's too good to be true, then it probably is.*"

"But Blondell didn't know that Merv's painting was a fake. And I'll bet she was convinced that Merv had bought her uncle's painting, although she probably didn't know that Merv had purchased the painting a year before her uncle's death."

"Are you saying that her uncle's painting was genuine and that Merv's is a fake, but that Blondell didn't know that?"

"That's one version of what happened."

"So, who has the original?"

"I don't know. Maybe there *is* no original."

Alex got up to pour herself another cup of coffee. "Refill?" she asked.

"No thanks, I'm good. The fact is, we'll never know the truth for sure. So it looks like you've come to the end of the road with our friend Merv Peters."

"Not so fast, I need to talk to Mag."

Chapter Seventy-Six

ON HIS WAY TO THE doctor's office, Bruno stopped by Chez Michel to say goodbye, tell him that he was moving on. The doctor kept him for over an hour, questioning him about how his memory started to return, the stimulus provided by meeting the two women and the American man. Bruno told him that while he was happy to know who he was, there were many memories that he'd just as soon be rid of. "But I'm not complaining, I can live with it. I just hope that I do."

The door closed behind him. He paused, reviewing his conversation with the doctor. What had he said: *I'm happy to know who I am.* That was true, but it was only part of the story. He sensed that some chapters were still missing, but what were they? *Unknown unknowns.*

Lost in thought, his glance fell on the courtyard at the base of the stairway. He saw two men with closely shaved heads, the one tall and lanky, the other shorter, built more thickly, having a whispered discussion. He recognized the pair: Henri and Stéphane. They were smarter than Samuel and Cosimo, it looked like Jacques was sparing no expense to get rid of him.

There was a recess on each floor next to the elevator. On the other side of the elevator, there was the entrance to an apartment. Bruno stepped back into the recess next to his doctor's office and waited. He heard a pair of footsteps coming up the stairway. So that's how they were planning to do it: one man to attack him and a second below to make sure that he didn't escape. *We'll see about that.*

As he heard the uncertain footsteps, Bruno guessed that his attackers didn't know which floor he had gone to. He heard Stéphane's heavy breathing as the shorter of the two men stopped to catch his breath at each level before continuing. Stéphane was taking his time, and his taller companion must have been getting impatient. Bruno heard Henri call out to his friend, "Have you found him?" as he started to follow Stéphane up the stairway.

"Shut the fuck up," Stéphane hissed.

Stéphane had reached the fourth-floor landing, winded by the climb. As he approached the recess, Bruno jumped out, slammed a fist into his head, and another into his stomach. Doubled over in pain, Stéphane staggered backward; Bruno grabbed him under the armpits and pushed him down the stairway, his head bouncing on the stone steps. Stéphane rolled into Henri, who had reached the third-floor landing.

Bruno started down the stairway. He remembered smelling fresh paint on his way up the stairs, and on the third floor he saw a large can of paint outside one of the apartments. He picked it up, it felt heavy—it could be half full. Henri, bent over his inert partner, looked up as Bruno ran down the stairs. Was the man reaching for his gun, or a knife? Bruno hurled the can of paint. It grazed Henri's head, stunning him for a few seconds as Bruno ran past. When he reached the first floor, he grabbed the railing and dropped to the courtyard, he'd done that so many times as a child.

Bruno had a choice. He could continue running—Henri would never catch him— or he could finish the job. He descended the stairs, but instead of exiting the *traboule*, he stepped into the enclosure where the mailboxes were lined up. In one corner of the room, there was a pile of rubble, the remains of a bathroom renovation.

He knew what Jacques would have told the men, *no fuck*-ups; there was no way that they'd dare to come back with bad news. He grabbed a length of pipe and waited.

Footsteps on the stairway leading to the lower level of the *traboule*. It was an old woman. He turned to face the cubbyholes, pretending to check for mail. She shuffled in, opened her box, looked at the letters in her hand, and felt Bruno's eyes on her. He hadn't moved, but he frightened her, and she hurried out of the room.

Another set of footsteps—this time, they were for him. For a moment, the room turned black. Bruno squeezed his eyes shut. When he opened them, the black veil had lifted. Henri moved past the mailboxes, but he never reached the stairs that led to the alleyway. An arm circled his neck; with his free arm, Bruno brought the pipe down on his head. Henri staggered forward, and, robot-like, Bruno continued to beat his head, as the black veil rose and fell. Henri fell to the ground, his face and head soaked in blood. *Hey Jacques, it looks like your men fucked up big time.*

Bruno stepped over the man, walked down the stairs, left the *traboule*, and went home to pick up his bags.

Chapter Seventy-Seven

"ARE YOU SURE YOU WOULDN'T like me to come with you?" asked Eugene. They were at the station in Nîmes, waiting for the Paris-bound train to pull in.

Alex smiled. "No, I'm fine. You've already been a great help, but I need to finish this on my own."

Three hours later, Alex arrived at Gare de Lyon. The train ride had been nerve-wracking; she could not stop herself from imagining Jacques walking down the aisle. Now, carried along by the movement of the crowds, she half-expected to see his head bobbing alongside. *Not likely*—she tried to calm herself—*but what about Henri?*

Her appointment with Merv would take place in an hour. He hadn't been too enthusiastic about seeing her. "What is it about?" he'd asked.

"The Whittakers were wondering if you could help them with something, I'll tell you about it when we meet."

"Please have a seat," said the receptionist. "He's running late."

"Oh, not to worry." Alex smiled. As though Merv keeping her cooling her heels would change anything.

Eventually, Merv came out to greet her. "So nice to see you again, Madame Vesla de Trubenne." He'd asked around since Alex's last visit, learned that they were indeed a very old, aristocratic family. Now, behind his desk, he assumed his *wise, but I don't have a lot of time* demeanor.

Alex saw that the Picasso was now hanging on the wall beside his desk. "You must be very busy, so I'll be brief." Smiling, she spread the two photocopies of "Woman in Red" on his desk—they were the ones Blondell had shown Merv at their last meeting. "Have a look at these."

Merv's face turned a shade of red that matched the painting. "What is this supposed to mean?" He was half-standing, leaning across the desk.

Alex continued to smile. "Blondell's family believe that you unwittingly purchased a painting that was stolen from their home, and they asked me to make you aware of the situation."

Merv recalled the last time he saw Blondell; she had more or less accused him of stealing her uncle's painting. But when he had heard nothing further from the family, he thought that she'd not had time to mention it.

"I'm sorry, but when Madame Royston came to see me, she made that ridiculous assertion, and I assured her that this painting"—he pointed to the wall—"had an impeccable provenance."

"Actually, we've looked into that. It appears that your painting purports to be from the estate of a Russian oligarch, who in turn purchased it from an anonymous buyer in Singapore." Alex was enjoying herself. "That's hardly an impeccable provenance."

"What do you mean, you've looked into it?" Merv had raised his voice, the all too familiar pain in his abdomen had returned. "I mean, that's confidential information."

"There isn't much you can't find on the internet, the dark web, and all of that. It's too bad that the man who researched your provenance is no longer with us—Nicolas Pagès was his name, I believe."

Merv had grown calmer. "Look, Madame—I wonder if you're really from the Vesla de Trubenne family—what is it that you want?"

Alex ignored his remark. "It seems to me that you have a clear choice: provide adequate proof of your bona fide ownership or return the painting to its rightful owner." She rose. "I do not want to take any more of your valuable time. I'll call you in a week, and you can let me know your decision. Then the family can take whatever action they deem appropriate."

#   #   #

Merv left his office early. There was no point in sticking around; he couldn't concentrate. That bitch Blondell Royston. So she had had time to talk about the painting. Should he call Jacques? What would he do, prepare some bullshit provenance? He knew what Blondell's family would do. They'd get some aggressive French lawyer who'd drag his name through the mud, whether or not they succeeded in proving that the painting was not lawfully his. He was out of options.

#   #   #

Alex looked at her watch; she had plenty of time before catching the train. *I'll surprise Eugene and show him that I'm the most remarkable woman he's ever known.* Her taxi dropped her in front of the Hotel Boursault. *With a little luck, Thomas Smith will be in his room.* But Thomas Smith was not in his room. "In fact," said the young woman at the front desk, "we have no guest named Thomas Smith".

"Are you sure?" asked Alex. "He's an old friend, and I'm quite sure he said he was staying here."

The regular day desk clerk was out sick, and the young woman filling in for him took an immediate dislike to the tall blonde woman with piercing blue eyes. "Yes, I'm sure," she said.

"Well… perhaps you have another Thomas staying here, do you think you could check?"

"No, I cannot. I'm sorry. Now if you'll excuse me…."

#   #   #

In the train back to Nîmes, Alex settled into her seat and ticked off the boxes in her mind.

Her search for Thomas Smith had come to a dead end. Was she disappointed that she had not found him, or that Eugene would not think her the most remarkable of women? And why did it matter so much anyway?

Her fear of running into Jacques Mornnais had subsided —*you've got to stop letting your mind run amok with wild conjectures*. And the meeting with Merv Peters had gone as well as she could expect. The next move was up to him and she felt that she'd done her best. *I deserve a glass of wine.* She made her way to the bar car. She sat on a stool in front of the window, watching as night descended on the countryside. Someone had left a newspaper on the counter; she unfolded it and idly turned the pages, until a news item sent an icy spike up her spine:

American tourist murdered in Parc des Batignolles. Thomas Perryman, son of the well-known trader Tony Perryman, was found shot to death in Parc des Batignolles two days ago. The police are investigating and the family has requested privacy at this difficult time.

Next to the article was a photo of Thomas Perryman. *Shit.* It was Thomas Smith.

Epilogue

BEFORE THEY HAD EVEN COMPLETED their restaurant management course, Marie-Agnès and Tomas had started plans to open a small restaurant. She wanted to call it "Chez Blondie." While Tomas would have preferred another name, he agreed, for what counted was not the name but the quality of their cuisine. The walls were off white, the table linens and china cream-colored, the dining room light and airy. But it looked a bit boring. Mag called Alex: did she still have the phone number of the Chinese painters who had worked for Jacques Mornnais? What did Alex think about her idea to ask them to paint a mural on one of the restaurant's walls?

Alex gave Marie-Agnès Li's phone number. A mural would be a welcome change from the usual Lyonnais restaurant décor that consisted of farm animals, hunting scenes, and kitsch posters.

As Mag chattered on about the proposed mural, Alex's thoughts focused on the small work by Daubigny, *Storm Over the Sea*, which was among the paintings waiting to be hung. She had given Eugene the copy and kept the original. At the time, it had seemed like the prudent course of action, but that was then. Now it would be unfortunate if he stumbled across the painting. She would have to explain that she hadn't trusted him at the time. So for the time being, she'd stash the Daubigny in a storage room behind some accumulated junk, just as Ella had done earlier in the year.

\#   \#   \#

Patrick had found a job at an internet bank's call center in Paris. He was not untouched by the irony of working in the same sector as his mother, but his plans did not include embezzlement. Véronique had kept her flat in Paris, and Patrick stayed there. Sometimes she joined him; otherwise, he commuted to Fontainebleau for the weekends. *Métro, boulot, dodo*—for the time being, he had joined the rat race.

Max Martolla. Merv Peters. At odd moments, their names floated through Patrick's mind. The rich were all the same, doing precisely as they pleased, to hell with everyone else. What right had the slick lawyer to go snooping around, paying for him to break into Véronique's house? It was provenance that he wanted? Well, it hadn't been difficult to find him and provide him with the fucking provenance of his paintings, although perhaps not in the form he'd expected.

\#   \#   \#

Caroline, too, had found a job, in an English-language bookstore in Phuket. Customers came into the shop, not only to buy a book but also to chat, pass the time of day. She regretted all those dull years spent staring at a computer screen in the silence of the back office. The inertia created by job security had kept her tethered to her desk like a ship tied up at the quay. As agreed, Patrick transferred money to her account every month. She found the situation amusing, and when the time was right, she'd straighten things out. She might be a thief on the run, but for now, she was enjoying a newfound sense of freedom.

\#   \#   \#

Véronique had started to sell off some of the furniture and *objets d'art* in the gallery. She made appointments to see the auctioneers at Hôtel Drouot, many of whom had known her father. They expressed their sympathy for her loss, but she had a hard time matching their words to the look in their eyes. After Eugene's visit, she couldn't deny the obvious: her father had frequently been dishonest, and it seemed that everybody knew. But when had it started, he hadn't always been that way, she was sure. She remembered the somber period of her life: drugs and petty theft. Each time her father had managed to get her off the hook, a friend had helped him, he said. She was sure now that the friend was Jacques Mornnais. And she wondered what price Jacques had exacted for his help.

#   #   #

Allen George, one of the two principals at Virginia Colonial Auctioneers, was playing a few rounds of golf with David Steiner, the attorney who handled their affairs. "It's really bizarre," said Allen. "The old lady just showed up at our offices last week with the same painting we sold for her husband a couple of years ago. He was pissed when we told him it was a fake, but we got a good price for it anyway. When we asked her how she came to have the painting, she said that it came in the mail."

David Steiner was lining up his shot. "Is she all there? You don't want to be selling stolen goods."

"No, I mean, yes. Ms. Whittaker came with her daughter, who explained that there was a note with the painting. It came from a man who had been her niece's lawyer in Paris. Blondell Jamieson, she married John Royston, he passed away, and a few years later, she died as well—a freak mugging. Which is a shame. Anyhow, in the note, the lawyer said that Blondell had always admired the painting. And he wanted to donate it to the family in her memory. Nice guy, right?"

#   #   #

Michel de Clermont d'Auvergne bent down to pick up the mail that the concierge had slipped under his door. There were the usual bills, an advertisement from an optician and a plain white envelope, unstamped and addressed to him. He went into the kitchen to make another cup of espresso; when it was ready he took the coffee and the mail into his office.

A few weeks ago, Jacques Mornnais had called: could Michel get him a copy of a passenger manifest?

"I'll see what I can do, but no promises. You know that normally the airlines don't share that information."

"Of course, my friend."

Michel welcomed the opportunity to do Jacques a favor; it was better to have the man in his debt than the other way around. He had called his contact at the airline, and before he even opened it, he guessed what the envelope would contain. He slipped the document out and perused the list of the passengers: who was the mystery woman that Jacques had met? He stopped when he reached Jacques' name and saw, right below to it, *Alexia Thornhill.*

Earlier in the year he'd received a phone call from Richard Vesla de Trubenne, an old friend of his father's. A young woman—a friend of Richard's niece Alexia—had taken some compromising photos at Jacques Mornnais' château. What should they do with the photos, Richard had asked him. *Send them to me,* he'd replied. He'd deleted the photos and thought that was the end of the incident.

"He's a nasty piece of work," he'd told Richard, *"Tell your niece to stay away from the man."* Had Alexia Thornhill followed his advice? Was she the person Jacques was looking for? And why?

Michel's father was a close friend of Richard Vesla de Trubenne; he owed it to Richard to protect his niece from a parvenu like Jacques Mornnais. When they could, people of Michel's class needed to stick together. He'd forego the opportunity to do Jacques a favor and there would be no need to trouble Richard. As with the photos, he just wanted to make the situation disappear: "Jacques, my friend, I'm so sorry, but no luck with your passenger manifest. It seems that the government has tightened the regulations. Terrorism and all that."

#   #   #

Tony Perryman waited for a week after his son's funeral and called Jacques.

"I'm sorry for your loss."

Tony thanked him but didn't add what a disappointment his son had been to him and his wife. Wasting his life away studying art history when he could have made a brilliant career in law or business. And what kind of a wild goose chase had he been on in France? Perhaps Mornnais could help get to the bottom of this.

"My son called me the night before he died and left a message that he'd found my stolen Mondrian and had discovered a ring of art thieves. I'd be surprised if Tom found anything of the sort—unfortunately that kind of initiative was hardly like him—but perhaps you could sniff around, see if you hear of anything."

"Of course, Tony. It will be my pleasure. I'll let you know if anything turns up. And again, I'm so sorry for your loss."

#   #   #

Eugene was organizing his workroom, a nook under the stairway that led to the Rapunzel tower. As he lined up his tools, he thought again about the photograph that Alex had taken. It was a good start, but short on the information necessary to support Thomas Perryman's claims. He'd ask the Bureau to do some research before he confronted Jacques Mornnais. They owed him that much. He turned his attention to sorting through a box of ancient nails; they might come in handy when repairing an old piece of furniture.

#   #   #

Alex put on her rubber boots and went for a walk in the vineyard—she needed time to think. The vines were bare, the mud had solidified into hard ruts, clouds scudded across the colorless sky, the desolate scene reflecting her mood.

In her mind's eye Alex saw herself meeting Thomas Perryman in Café

Vigny. Then she remembered Henri standing at the bar: had he seen the two of them talking? What had he told Jacques? If it was true that Jacques was behind the thefts in Thomas' summary, she was certain that Jacques had had him killed. Another image: she was on the phone with Nathalie Martin, learning that someone had come looking for a tall blonde. That meant that Jacques was on her trail. He didn't know her name yet, but what if that changed? It would not be difficult to find her here at Trubenne; an isolated château in a hamlet named after her family. As fear gripped her midsection, the thought that had haunted her arose once again: was it wise to stay at Trubenne?

Over lunch the next afternoon, Charlotte told Richard that she needed to take some time off. She'd spent years—happily, she added—at Trubenne, but she was not looking forward to the damp and cold of another winter. "I'm not getting any younger," she told him, "and I want to spend a few months by the sea."

Richard smiled. "I think that's a wonderful idea. And where were you thinking of going?"

"Marseilles," Charlotte said. "I'm going to Marseilles."

"If you don't mind," said Alex, "I think I'll join you."

THE END

CASTLE BRIDGE MEDIA RECOMMENDS...

If you liked this book, you might also enjoy reading the following titles from Castle Bridge Media available on Amazon or by order at your favorite book store:

Animal Charmer
By Rain Nox

Austinites
By In Churl Yo

Bloodsucker City
By Jim Towns

THE CASTLE OF HORROR ANTHOLOGY SERIES
Volume 1
Volume 2: Holiday Horrors
Volume 3: Scary Summer Stories
Volume 4: Women Running From Houses
Volume 5: Thinly Veiled: The 70s
Volume 6: Femme Fatales*
Volume 7: Love Gone Wrong
Volume 8: Thinly Veiled: The 80s
Volume 9: Young Adult
Volume 10: Thinly Veiled: Saturday Mournings
Edited By Jason Henderson and In Churl Yo
*Edited By P.J. Hoover

Castle of Horror Podcast Book of Great Horror: Our Favorites, Top Tens and Bizarre Pleasures
Edited By Jason Henderson

Dream State
By Martin Ott

Dominic
By Lee Guzman

FRENCH DECEPTION
A Forgery in Paris
By Janice Nagourney
A Forgery in Lyon
By Janice Nagourney

FuturePast Sci-Fi Anthology
Edited by In Churl Yo

GLAZIER'S GAP
Ghosts of the Forbidden
By Leanna Renee Hieber

The Hermes Protocol
By Chris M. Arnone

Isonation
By In Churl Yo

Junk Film: Why Bad Movies Matter
By Katharine Coldiron

MID-LIFE CRISIS THRILLERS
18 Miles From Town
By Jason Henderson
Lost Angel
By Sam Knight

Nightwalkers: Gothic Horror Movies
By Bruce Lanier Wright

THE PATH
The Blue-Spangled Blue
By David Bowles
The Deepest Green
By David Bowles

SURF MYSTIC
Night of the Book Man
By Peyton Douglas
Dark of the Curl
By Peyton Douglas

Yesterday's Tomorrows: The Golden Age of Science Fiction Movies
By Bruce Lanier Wright

Please remember to leave us your reviews on Amazon and Goodreads!

THANK YOU FOR SUPPORTING INDEPENDENT PUBLISHERS AND AUTHORS!

castlebridgemedia.com